"Acharya, I had a marvelous dream."

"I was here, in the forest. And all the trees turned bright gold. It was dazzling, wonderful—"

"Oh, my poor boy, I'm sorry to hear that." Rajaswami's face fell. "Not a happy dream. To see trees turn to gold—a bad omen. It foretells death."

Tamar's good spirits chilled. "Mine. A fitting dream."

"Not necessarily," Rajaswami hastened to assure him. "Yours—perhaps. Or, indeed, mine. Or someone else altogether. Put it from your thoughts. The dream is done; you can't change it."

They ate quickly and in silence, neither one with appetite, then set off, walking their horses through the denser stretches of forest. Recalling Jaya's description of Mahapura, Tamar planned to bear east to the Sabla River and follow it to its headwaters. The sun was high as the forest thinned a little and a hard-packed trail opened. Tamar halted in midstride.

A man had stepped into the path. His face was scarred and weather-beaten. He wore hunting garments much like Tamar's, with a stained rag knotted around his head. Tamar quickly motioned for Rajaswami to back away.

The hunter had drawn a heavy bow to full stretch. Notched and ready on the string, a barbed arrow pointed at Tamar's throat.

★"At every turn, there is adventure, magic, and often treachery, but most of all the quest for honor. . . . Alexander offers a tale that is thoughtful without being leaden and moral without being moralistic. Alexander's legion of fans will respond to the moments of high adventure as well as the many twists and turns, internal and external, that will make them think."

—*Booklist*, starred review

BOOKS BY LLOYD ALEXANDER

The Prydain Chronicles
The Book of Three
The Black Cauldron
The Castle of Llyr
Taran Wanderer
The High King
The Foundling

The Westmark Trilogy
Westmark
The Kestrel
The Beggar Queen

The Vesper Holly Adventures
The Illyrian Adventure
The El Dorado Adventure
The Drackenberg Adventure
The Jedera Adventure
The Philadelphia Adventure

The
IRON RING

Lloyd Alexander

PUFFIN BOOKS

PUFFIN BOOKS

Published by the Penguin Group

Penguin Putnam Books for Young Readers,

345 Hudson Street, New York, New York 10014, U.S.A.

Penguin Books Ltd, 27 Wrights Lane, London W8 5TZ, England

Penguin Books Australia Ltd, Ringwood, Victoria, Australia

Penguin Books Canada Ltd, 10 Alcorn Avenue, Toronto, Ontario, Canada M4V 3B2

Penguin Books (N.Z.) Ltd, 182-190 Wairau Road, Auckland 10, New Zealand

Penguin Books Ltd, Registered Offices: Harmondsworth, Middlesex, England

First published in the United States of America by Dutton Children's Books,
a division of Penguin Books USA Inc., 1997
Published by Puffin Books,
a member of Penguin Putnam Books for Young Readers, 1999

THE LIBRARY OF CONGRESS HAS CATALOGED THE DUTTON EDITION AS FOLLOWS:

Alexander, Lloyd.

The iron ring / by Lloyd Alexander.—1st ed.

p. cm.

Summary: Driven by his sense of "dharma," or honor, young King Tamar sets off on a
perilous journey, with a significance greater than he can imagine, during which
he meets talking animals, villainous and noble kings, and the love of his life.

ISBN 0-525-45597-3

[1. Fantasy.] I. Title.

PZ7.A3774Ir 1997 [Fic]—dc21 96-29730 CIP AC

Puffin Books ISBN 0-14-130348-4

Printed in the United States of America

For promise-keepers
and true dreamers

Author's Note

The dazzling mythology of ancient India has always delighted and fascinated me—but, at first, in bits and pieces. Only later in life, when I ventured to explore it more deeply, did I realize, as many other writers have realized, that this marvelous literature is a treasure trove of fairy tales, folktales, animal fables, and teaching-stories. India's great national epics, the *Mahabharata* and the *Ramayana*, are profound, powerful masterpieces that rival the *Iliad* and the Arthurian legend.

Admittedly, this mythology may seem alien, strange, even forbiddingly complex. As in any encounter with a different culture, what appears difficult or incomprehensible quickly grows familiar. The farther we journey through its rich landscape, the more we understand that what lies beneath the brilliant, exotic surface is, in essence, a world we clearly recognize. The warrior's code of honor, for example, is nearly identical with the knightly code of chivalry. Earthshaking clashes between good and evil, courageous heroines and gallant heroes, steadfast love, daring rescues, loss and recovery—these are elements in our universal heritage of story.

Dharma, the driving force in this present tale, is equally familiar. It encompasses ideals of goodness, conscience, doing what is compassionate and right. These qualities and values lie at the heart of all the world's great literature.

The following pages are not intended as a picture of India some thousands of years ago. While the story evokes the atmosphere, themes, and concerns threading through Indian literature, it is a work of imagination, its author's response to a deeply moving experience, a loving homage to its source. I hope it offers a kind of feast of many flavors: high adventure, poetic romance, moments of wild comedy and dark tragedy, anguish at promises broken, joy at promises kept. I hope especially that readers may find more similarities than differences between cultures, and, between human hearts, no boundaries at all.

Drexel Hill,   LLOYD ALEXANDER
Pennsylvania

Contents

Contents

List of Characters and Places

Adi-Kavi (*ah*dee-*kah*vee): journeyer with unusual powers, first met while living in an anthill

Akka (*ah*-kah): adventurous young monkey with a taste for flying

Arvati (ahr-*vah*-tee): mild, gentle elephant, ill-treated in captivity

Ashwara (ahsh-*wahr*-ah): lion-eyed fugitive king of Rana-pura

Bala (*bah*-lah): shrewd, calculating king of Muktara

Chandragar (*chahn*-dra-gahr): kingdom ruled by King Rudra

Danda-Vana (*dahn*da-*vah*nah): ancient, mysterious forest with impassable thornbushes

Darshan (*dahr*-shan): trusted commander of Tamar's army

Garuda (gah-*roo*-dah): eagle fallen on hard times, constantly protesting and complaining, yelling "Shmaa!"

Gayatri (gah-*yah*-tree): Tamar's beloved white mare

Griva (*gree*-vah): a rough, unwelcome intruder

Hashkat (*hash*-kat): king of the monkeys; practical joker punished by a powerful *rishi*

Jagati (jah-*gah*-tee): dapple-gray horse of Rajaswami

Jamba-Van (*jahm*-bah *van*): philosophical bear; calms his quick temper by smashing crockery

Jaya (*jah*-yah): sinister, mysterious king who challenges Tamar to a fateful game

Kana (*kah*-nah): arrogant nobleman, nephew of Nahusha

Kirin (*kee*-rin): devoted younger brother of Ashwara

Kumeru and Sumeru (*koo*-meh-roo, *soo*-meh-roo): twin peaks, the highest in the Snow Mountains

Kurma (*koor*-mah): river, near Mirri's village

Mahapura (*mah*-hah-*poor*-ah): Jaya's stronghold

Mirri (*mee*-ree): beautiful, brave cow-tender who first meets Tamar in the middle of a river

Muktara (mook-*tah*-rah): realm of King Bala

Nahusha (nah-*hoo*-sha): villainous traitor, cruel and murderous cousin of the noble Ashwara

Nanda (*nahn*-dah): village chief, foster father of Mirri

Rajaswami (*rah*-ja-*swah*-mee): Tamar's old teacher, unfailingly cheerful, who always urges him to look on the bright side

Rana (*rah*-nah): river and valley west of Ranapura

Ranapura (*rah*-nah-*poor*-ah): Ashwara's kingdom and fortified city

Rasha (*rah*-shah): one of Ashwara's treacherous troop captains

Rudra (*roo*-drah): king of Chandragar; staunch ally of Ashwara

Sabla (*sah*-blah): river with headwaters in the Snow Mountains

Sala (*sah*-lah): cruel elephant master

Shesha (*sheh*-shah): prince of the Serpent Realm, wears a brilliant sapphire on his head; wrestles Tamar

Shila Rani (*shee*-lah *rah*-nee): queen of the Serpent Realm

Skanda (*skahn*-dah): Ashwara's adoring youngest brother

Snow Mountains: high range north of Ranapura

Soma-Nandi (*so*-mah *nahn*-dee): tiger trapped while seeking her lost mate

Sunda (*soon*-dah): Soma-Nandi's lost mate

Sundari (soon-*dah*-ree): Tamar's small kingdom

Surabi (soo-*rah*-bee): Mirri's favorite white cow, named after mythical cow who could grant all wishes

Takshaka (tahk-*shah*-kah): the Naga Raja, ancient king of the Serpent Realm, who offers Tamar a choice of jewels

Tamar (*tah*-mahr): noble-hearted young king of Sundari, honor-bound to keep a dreadful promise

Vati (*vah*-tee): little girl from Mirri's village who sings song explaining the Choosing festival

Yashoda (yah-*show*-dah): wife of village chief Nanda; foster mother of Mirri

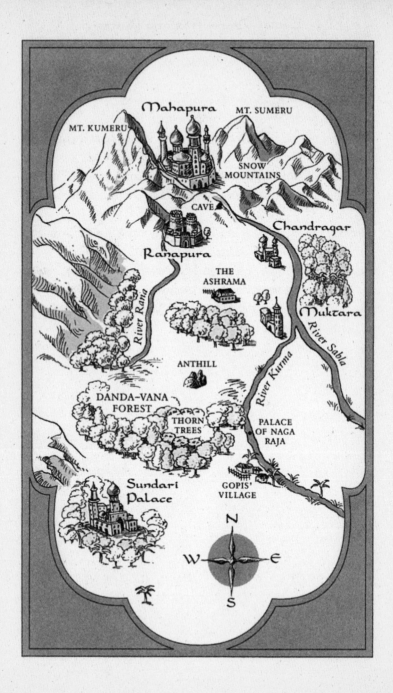

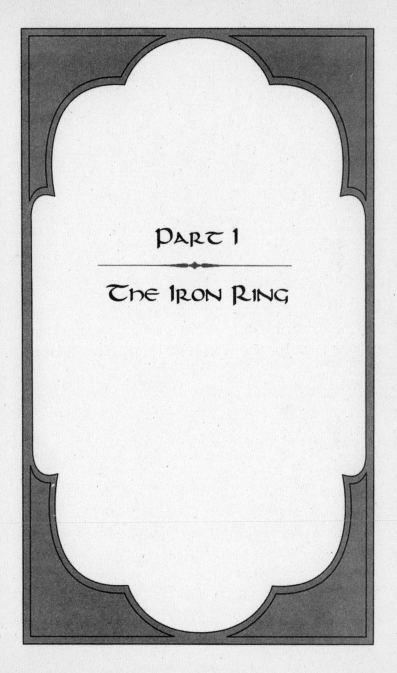

Part 1

The Iron Ring

1. A Friendly Game of Aksha

Elephants were in Sundari Palace courtyard, half a dozen or more, torchlight flickering on tusks ornamented with gold bands and ropes of pearls; horses with jeweled saddles; chariots flying flags and banners; and a dark figure striding through the gates. Servants ran to wake the young king, Tamar, already up and watching from his balcony. Curious, naturally. Not altogether pleased. No more than anyone would be, jolted out of a sound sleep by unexpected elephants.

Lamps were being lit throughout the palace when Rajaswami bustled in, beard sleep-tangled, robe kilted askew. Usually, Tamar's old tutor serenely smiled on all around him like a benevolent baby. At the moment, he twittered.

"Dress quickly, my boy. I'm told someone calling himself King Jaya has arrived. Most remarkable! I've never seen the like—clearly, a great monarch. A veritable maharajah. A little too much display and ostentation," Rajaswami added, "but overdoing things is in the nature of maharajahs."

"Revered teacher," Tamar said, "remarkable it may be —but does anyone know who he is? What he wants? And whatever he wants, why does he want it from me?"

"I haven't the slightest idea. We may assume he comes in peace. Neither he nor his retainers bear arms, not a weapon to be seen. He seeks hospitality. By custom, you must grant it."

"Which I do. Have refreshment and lodging ordered for him and his people," Tamar told a servant, "and see his animals well tended."

"One thing more," said Rajaswami. "He demands an audience."

"I'd have liked it better if he'd said 'requests.' Even so, I must receive him. Honor requires it."

"There's yet another thing," said Rajaswami. "He insists on seeing you immediately."

"Demands? Insists? Immediately? Maharajah or not, he could still show common courtesy. Well, to the devil with him. He can wait. Morning will do. He'll have time to mend his manners."

"Tut, tut, my boy. You're entitled to be prickly on occasion. That's quite as it should be. You're a king, after all. But never answer discourtesy with discourtesy. Surely, I've taught you better than that."

Rajaswami had indeed been his instructor from earliest childhood. Tamar's army commander, Darshan, had trained him in the skills of a noble warrior, a *kshatriya*. But it was Rajaswami who had taught him reading and writing; schooled him in proper behavior; and, above all, taught him the principles of dharma—the code of honor, conscience, the obligation to do what was right and royally virtuous. Tamar, sitting at Rajaswami's feet, had always listened eagerly and lovingly to the kindly old sage's teachings and would have rather given up his life than lose his honor or break his dharma.

"Always look on the bright side," Rajaswami added.

"Being gracious to the ungracious is all the more to your credit. Besides, nobility does have its obligations:

> *A king must ever be polite,*
> *Even in the middle of the night.*

"I may run short of patience, but you'll never run short of verses," Tamar said. He laughed fondly. "This king obviously hasn't enjoyed the benefit of a Rajaswami. So be it. I'll receive him now and have done with it."

So, he beckoned for the servants to replace his night linen with formal robes and bind up his hair. When one offered him the royal sword, Tamar shook his head.

"Since this maharajah carries no weapons, neither will I. Come, let's be polite hosts to an impolite guest."

By the time they reached the durbar hall, the great audience chamber, all the courtiers had gathered at the canopied throne. Darshan, shrewd old warrior, suspicious of unknown newcomers, stood alert and none too happy; nor were the ministers of state overjoyed to be summoned from their beds.

Tamar turned to the unexpected guest waiting alone in the middle of the hall: a big, dark-bearded man, head and shoulders taller than Tamar; a hard-muscled frame under soft, silken robes. Around his neck, jewels hung from gold chains; bracelets gleamed on his wrists and forearms. His heavy-lidded eyes seemed to have looked at the world and found it insufficiently amusing.

"Be welcome." Tamar pressed his palms together. "I hope your patience has not been too sorely tried. We are not used to such grand—and urgent—visitations."

"I should think not. Forgive this intrusion," Jaya replied, as if it made no difference to him whether he was forgiven or not. "I am on a long journey. My people and animals are weary. Night fell upon us; I required food and shelter for them.

"I gather your kingdom is small," Jaya went on. "Not unpleasant, from what little I have seen. Sundari? I am not familiar with it."

"Nor I with yours."

"Mahapura. It lies to the north, in the valley between Mount Kumeru and Mount Sumeru, where the Sabla River takes its source. Tucked away in your charming, quiet little realm, it would surprise me had you heard of mine."

"I hope my charming, quiet little realm, as you call it, offers hospitality fitting your needs." Tamar gestured toward a side table set with as many dishes as the palace cooks could prepare at short notice. Inviting Darshan and Rajaswami to join them, Tamar himself served portions to his guest, who only picked at the food. When Darshan tried to draw him out, asking details about Mahapura, the nature of its fortifications and warriors, Jaya shrugged.

"My mountains are defenses better than any I could devise. I need no army and thus am happily spared dealing with inquisitive officers." While Darshan bristled, Jaya glanced at Tamar.

"And you, Majesty, tell me: Is your kingdom a happy one?"

"I hope it is. I wish it could be more so."

Jaya gave a dry laugh. "A little misery is not such a bad thing."

"A curious idea." Tamar frowned. "You'll permit me to disagree."

"What I mean is this," Jaya said. "There are many kings more powerful than you. Like wild dogs on the hunt, they scent ways of adding to their dominions. A thriving, prosperous—and small—realm makes a tempting morsel to gulp down."

"We have not been troubled by these wild dogs," Tamar said, "nor do we expect to be."

"Nevertheless," Jaya replied, "it is always wiser not to draw too much attention upon yourself. Is there not the old tale of a hawk and a sparrow?"

"There is, indeed," put in Rajaswami. "I shall most willingly recite it."

Jaya sighed and looked up at the ceiling as Rajaswami began:

> *A lordly hawk once told a sparrow,*
> *"Dear bird, your nest is far too narrow,*
> *With barely room to hatch your eggs,*
> *To spread your wings or stretch your legs.*
> *You need a home that's far more ample.*
> *Larger chambers, for example."*
>
> *"How true," the smaller bird replied.*
> *And so, with diligence and pride,*
> *She added terraces and bowers,*
> *Balconies all decked with flowers.*
>
> *The hawk observed with envious eye:*
> *"Fit for a king to occupy,*
> *This better suits a bird like me."*
> *He drove her out and said, "You see,*
> *Instead of tearing you apart,*
> *I spared you. I've a tender heart."*

"Instructive little verses," said Rajaswami. "If you would care to hear others—"

"King of Mahapura," Tamar broke in, "do you suggest that I am a sparrow?"

"Put it that I do not see you as a hawk," Jaya answered. "Enough of these matters. Small talk between kings grows rapidly tiresome: military affairs and money, money and military affairs. Such conversation is limited and soon exhausted. May you and I sit privately at our ease?"

"If you wish." As Tamar rose from the table, Darshan plucked at his sleeve.

"Majesty, let me stand at your side," he murmured. "This king troubles me."

"He troubles me as well," Tamar said in passing, "though not for long. Why should he linger and delay his journey? Under my own roof, what danger can there be?"

He led King Jaya to a chamber adjoining the hall. After his guest had settled himself on a couch, Tamar spoke plainly:

"King of Mahapura, what business have you with me, so urgent it could not have waited a few hours?"

"My urgent business at this moment," Jaya said, leaning back amid the cushions, "is to rest in comfort, perhaps with some small distraction to lighten a tedious day."

"Do you wish music? Let me summon my performers to play for us."

"In Mahapura, I keep my own musicians. None rival them in sweetness of sound. They have, regrettably, spoiled my taste for anything less."

"Naturally, they would. Singers, then? Dancers? Not comparable to yours, no doubt, but they may offer modest entertainment."

Jaya stifled a yawn. Tamar, his patience rubbing a little ragged, went on:

"Acrobats? Jugglers? My household, as you have observed, is limited in its diversions."

Jaya glanced around the room. His eyes fell on a dice table with its ebony cup and ivory cubes. "Do you play *aksha?*"

"Only to pass an idle moment. It is more a child's pastime; the game turns neither on strength nor skill, only luck."

"Exactly. That is why it pleases me. A king's commands are obeyed to the letter, his orders carried out to the last jot and tittle. It is amusing and refreshing, from time to time, for a king—whose word is law—to subject himself to the vagaries of the dice and bow to a law greater than any of his own: the law of chance. Will you play a while? A friendly little game?"

"If you like." Tamar brought the table and set it between them. Jaya nodded, with the first flicker of interest that Tamar had seen from him.

"As your guest," Jaya said, "it is I who set the stakes and first roll the dice. Agreed?"

"Of course. That is the rule."

"The wager. What shall it be?" Jaya toyed with his beard. "Something of no consequence, a mere token for the sake of the game."

From his neck, Jaya took one of the chains, which he dropped offhandedly on the table. "For you, King of Sundari, to match."

Tamar stiffened. The links were heavy, of solid gold, worth more than enough to keep all his household fed and clothed for many months. What made him catch his breath was not the chain alone. Twice the size of a dove's egg, the diamond flashing at the end was a fortune in itself.

"Does this inconvenience you?" Jaya glimpsed the look on Tamar's face. "We are kings, not children playing for sweetmeats. Once laid down, the wager cannot be changed. But, in our harmless amusement, the rules may bend a little. I gladly withdraw it for something less, better fitting your circumstances."

"No. It stands." Tamar's chin went up. "We play by the rules, as they are. I have no single jewel like this, but I will have all my finest gems brought. You shall choose as many as needed to equal its value."

"Leave them in your treasury. We shall settle once the game is over. You have pledged them. Your word is sufficient."

Jaya dropped the cubes into the ebony cup, rattled them a moment, and rolled them out. He raised an eyebrow. "A number difficult to surpass. The odds favor me, it would seem. But who knows the subtle ways of chance? You, now, King of Sundari."

Tamar, in his turn, shook the cup and cast the dice onto the board.

2. The Iron Ring

K ing of Sundari"—Jaya half smiled—"I spoke of the vagaries of the dice. Here you see proof. The odds were in my favor, yet fortune stood at your side. You have won."

"Yes." Tamar breathed again. He stared at the diamond. Jaya scooped up the dice and once more dropped them into the cup.

"A small loss," he said, "but I shall try to regain it."

"No need." Tamar pushed the diamond and chain across the board. His hands shook, as if he had just been pulled back from the edge of a cliff. "Enough. I have no desire to play again. A friendly game—friends do not keep each other's possessions. Take back your wager. I shall find you some better distraction, if it pleases you."

"It does not please me. You dishonor me by scorning what you rightfully won."

"Call it a gift. Call it whatever you choose. I play no more."

"That is not for you to say," Jaya returned. "By rule, it is I who declare the game over. No. I set the stakes again. Double what they were."

Tamar's face tightened. What Jaya proposed would have put most of Sundari's treasure at risk. Tamar shook his head. "A king serves his people as well as himself, and answers to

them for his actions. For me, it would be reckless steward-
ship."

"Will you be reckless with your honor? You agreed to
the rules of *aksha,* did you not? Obey them."

"Lower the stakes, then, as you first offered to do."

"At first, yes. You did not accept. I no longer offer."
Jaya leaned over the table. "The game continues; we will
play it out. A childish pastime? Also a question of dharma.
We are both bound by dharma, King of Sundari.

"I do not break dharma," Jaya went on. "But you, if
you choose to break yours by refusing, so be it. End the
game—and shame yourself."

Tamar's blood rose. "Take up the dice."

Jaya rattled the cup and casually spilled out its contents.
"How interesting. Once more, the odds favor me. Once
more, will fortune favor you?"

The dice danced on the board as Tamar threw in turn.
Jaya's smile was thin as a thread.

"You have won again, King of Sundari. Now, to me.
At triple the stakes."

Without awaiting a reply, Jaya cast the dice. When
Tamar played in turn, his head spun like the ivory cubes.
He dimly grasped that his score was higher than his
opponent's.

"Truly, you are fortune's darling," Jaya said. "We play
on. Triple what I have lost."

How long even a maharajah might continue so rashly,
Tamar could not guess. Winning the next turn yet again,
Tamar gave up trying to calculate what he had gained. King
though he was, he had never imagined such wealth within
his reach. His thoughts raced over all the plans he had, until

now, only dreamed: waterways from the outlying hills to the public squares, parks and gardens throughout the city, wide streets, shining new buildings, houses for even the poorest of his subjects. He seized the dice cup eagerly, threw—and won again. He was giddy, flushed with wild joy and soaked in cold sweat.

The king of Mahapura yawned. "The game grows boring. One final throw for each of us. But, to play for meaningless trinkets—surely there are more exciting wagers. Something to add a touch of spice, a little stimulation."

"Wager what you please," Tamar said impatiently. The game had caught him up and held him in its arms like a lover, whispering in his ear.

"Honor binds you to accept it."

"As I do. Lay down the stakes."

"Life against life."

Tamar's head went back as if he had been struck. He was suddenly cold. "I do not understand."

"Very simple." Jaya folded his arms and looked impassively at Tamar. "Win, my life is yours to do with as you please. Lose, your life is forfeit to me."

"I cannot—"

"Can. And must." With a lazy movement, Jaya scattered the dice over the board. He pursed his lips. "Fortune still favors you. My score is small, easily surpassed."

Tamar's fingers had gone numb, scarcely able to hold the cup. The dice seemed to leap out by their own will.

"King of Sundari," Jaya said, "you have lost."

For long moments, Tamar did not speak. Then, in a voice he barely recognized as his own, he murmured, "This is folly. Madness."

"No. It is honor," Jaya said. "And you, so proud of keeping it, learn what it truly is. Have you ever tested it? I think not."

"I lost a wager. I still keep my honor."

"Then obey dharma." Jaya rose, taller than he had first appeared. "Hear me; understand me well. I leave you now; I have other matters to deal with. But, from this moment, you are at my command. You will go to my palace in Mahapura and there make good on your debt. Vow to do so without fail."

Tamar stood and looked squarely at Jaya. "You have my word as king and *kshatriya*."

"I accept it." Jaya nodded. He gripped Tamar's wrist in one hand with such strength that Tamar clenched his teeth to keep from crying out; and, with the other, set a ring of black iron on his finger.

"The emblem of your pledge," Jaya said. "Your life is my property."

"So, King of Mahapura," Tamar flung back, "what will you do with it?"

"How dare you question me?" Jaya answered in a voice of cold stones grinding against each other. "Do I explain myself to a dog if I choose to kill him?" He dropped Tamar's wrist and turned away.

"I am not your dog!" Tamar lunged after him. Jaya was already through the doorway. Tamar would have followed, but a roar like breaking surf filled his ears. His legs gave way; he stumbled and fell to the floor. The ring felt as if it had been bound tight around his heart.

"I am not your dog!" he shouted again. And again. Until he drowned in the echoes.

3. Questions in the Palace

He woke sprawled on the carpet. The gaming table had been knocked over, dice and cup scattered. The iron ring circled his finger. Shuddering, he turned his face away. Then Rajaswami was there, and Darshan. Counselors and attendants crowded behind them. He could not understand why all were in night-robes.

"Are you ill, my boy?" Rajaswami knelt beside him. "Why aren't you in your bedchamber? Whatever happened? We heard you shouting. You roused the whole palace."

"Jaya. The king of Mahapura." Tamar sat up. "Where has he gone?"

Darshan put a hand on Tamar's shoulder. "What king, lad? No one's been here."

"He was. He came with horses, chariots, elephants. I saw them. You yourself warned me against him." Tamar turned to Rajaswami. "And you—you recited verses. The hawk and the sparrow."

"Recited? Dear boy, I haven't left my bed all night. Ah, of course. You've had a dream. Not a pleasant one, I should guess."

"And this?" Tamar thrust out his hand. "Look at it. Touch it. King Jaya put it on my finger." He blurted out all that had happened during the night. "We gambled," he said finally. "At the end, I wagered my life against his. I lost.

I gave my word of honor; I swore to surrender myself at Mahapura. And so I must."

"Surely you must not," Darshan said bluntly. "You dreamed. A dream binds you to nothing. No strange king has been in the palace. That is fact. How the ring comes to be on your finger, I cannot say. For the rest, put it from your thoughts. I tell you plainly and simply: It did not happen."

Darshan had spoken with so much certainty that Tamar almost believed him, and longed to believe him. He shook his head. "It happened," he murmured, "exactly as I said. I wish it had not. But it did. The debt is to be paid. Have I any other honorable choice?"

He turned to Rajaswami who, so far, had stayed silent and thoughtful. "*Acharya,* dear teacher," Tamar said, addressing the old man as he had done when a child, "guide me in this. What should I do?"

"A question not easily answered," Rajaswami replied. "Word given, word kept. Yes, that is dharma. But it does not apply to a vow made in a dream. The more difficult problem: Was it indeed a dream? How can you, or I, be certain we are not dreaming this very moment? Are you merely part of my dream? Am I merely part of yours? Was your game of *aksha* real, and what seems here-and-now is illusion?"

"How, then, can I know?" Tamar asked, in an anguished voice. "Tell me, *acharya.* My life depends on it."

"Alas, there is no way that you can be certain." Rajaswami sighed heavily. "This is beyond my guidance."

Tamar bowed his head. For some while, he said nothing. When at last he spoke, his voice was low and questioning:

"Perhaps there is some simple explanation for the ring.

As for the king of Mahapura, none of you saw him, his retainers, or his animals. I believe you. There is no sign he was ever here. And so it may well have been only a dream.

"Yes, I doubt that it happened—and yet, at the same time, I believe that it did. There is a way, and one way only, to be sure: I go to Mahapura."

"No!" Darshan burst out. "There's more in this than your own honor. You owe a debt? What do you owe to your kingdom? Your people?"

"Can I be a worthy king unless I'm first an honorable man?"

"Can you be a worthy king if you're dead? Throw your life away? If you think that's honorable—then, lad, you know nothing of the world and its ways.

"Do not do this," Darshan pressed. "No realm could hope for a finer king. Lad, when you first came to the throne, some of your own counselors spoke against you; you were too young; they doubted you could rule wisely. But I and your *acharya* knew your heart; we were sure of your worth. Your people love you. Do not abandon them for the sake of a foolish dream. All your hopes and plans for Sundari—will you leave them in the hands of self-serving courtiers?"

"I leave Sundari in the best of hands," Tamar said. "Yours."

"Not mine," Darshan returned. "I'm no courtier. I'm a soldier."

"Then obey your king," Tamar said. "I start for Mahapura now. To linger would only grieve me all the more."

"Are you sure that is what you wish to do?" said Rajaswami. "To undertake such a journey when you are filled with doubts and uncertainties?"

Tamar smiled at him. "I'll have to take my doubts and uncertainties with me."

"At least go in strength," Darshan urged. "Lead your army there. Make a show of force. The king of Mahapura —if such there be—will not dare to harm you."

"Will an army follow an uncertain leader on what may be a pointless quest?" replied Tamar. "A dream? Or not? I ask no one else to follow it."

"Not alone," said Rajaswami. "I shall go with you."

Tamar shook his head. "No. Dear *acharya*, I can't let you. Leave your studies and meditations for a long journey? The hardships will be more than you can bear."

"I shall bear them nevertheless," Rajaswami said. "I must. I swore to your parents I would be always at your side. Dear boy, I was there when you were born. I shall be there when you die, if it comes to that. It is my dharma."

"I can't order you to break it." Tamar smiled and embraced the old teacher. "Nor do I wish to."

They set off later that morning. Tamar had agreed that Darshan and a cavalry troop would escort them to the outlying Danda-Vana forest. Astride Gayatri, his beloved white mare, Tamar had exchanged royal silks for hunter's buckskins, his only weapons a sword and hunting knife, a bow and quiver of arrows. Rajaswami, in his usual white robe and scarf, perched uncomfortably on the dapple-gray Jagati.

Throughout the city, word had spread of the king's departure and the fate likely in store for him. Tamar could barely bring himself to look into the eyes of the townspeople crowding the streets. Some wept; some called out, begging him to stay; some watched in silent grief. He feared he might weaken and gladly turn back.

At the forest fringe, Darshan again pleaded to ride with Tamar; and again, Tamar refused.

"Stay as I ordered. If I live, I promise to return. If not, Rajaswami will bring you word. Until then, old friend, care for my people as I would do."

"I have laid your sandals on your throne," Darshan replied. "They will stay there as token that you are still king of Sundari and, to me, will always be."

Darshan and his warriors turned their mounts and rode from the forest. Tamar watched until they were out of sight. His heart was heavier than ever it had been. The light was fading. He tethered the horses and spread blankets from the saddle packs.

"I'm sorry, *acharya,*" he said. "This is the best hospitality we can expect."

"For the moment, perhaps," Rajaswami said cheerfully, all the while rubbing his stiff legs. "We may find shelter in the occasional hermitage. Forests have always been a refuge for sages who prefer to shun the world's distractions. They dwell in their cottages and *ashrama*s and pursue their contemplations. I suspect they enjoy a visitation now and again, a welcome relief from their rigorous mental exertions."

"For your sake, I hope so," Tamar said. "Rough living and cold comfort—I don't have an easy mind about your well-being."

"I shall manage, never fear," said Rajaswami. "You, my boy, are trained to endure hardship. You are a *kshatriya,* born to the caste of warriors, highest and noblest—except, of course, for the *brahmana,* my own caste; whereas we *brah-*

*mana*s are devoted to matters of the spirit—high thinking, not earthly physicalities. But I shall accommodate myself, even to this fearsome place."

"Why fearsome? One forest is like another."

"Not this. It was old when much of the world was young. It was full-grown even in the Golden Age, those ancient days when gods and goddesses walked the earth, as the tales tell, and forest creatures could speak with human-kind.

"It's only for you, dear boy, that I'm here now. I've read of too many strange happenings; I'd prefer to leave this forest to itself. Furthermore, if a creature addressed me—why, I should hardly know what to answer."

With that, Rajaswami curled up on the grass. Tamar sat awhile. Darshan's words still troubled him. He was doing what honor demanded; but was it honor only for himself, not his kingdom? He had chosen duty to his warrior's code over duty to his people. A misjudgment? A false step on the path of what Rajaswami called "karma"—actions good or bad, all combining to shape a destiny, each deed sending ripples, like a stone dropped into a pond. Had his fate already encircled him in an iron ring of its own? No answer came, and he was too wearied to seek further.

To his surprise, next morning he woke lighthearted. *"Acharya,* I had a marvelous dream. I was here, in the forest. And all the trees turned bright gold. It was dazzling, wonderful—"

"Oh, my poor boy, I'm sorry to hear that." Rajaswami's face fell. "Not a happy dream. To see trees turn to gold—a bad omen. It foretells death."

Tamar's good spirits chilled. "Mine. A fitting dream."

"Not necessarily," Rajaswami hastened to assure him.

"Yours—perhaps. Or, indeed, mine. Or someone else altogether. Put it from your thoughts. The dream is done; you can't change it."

They ate quickly and in silence, neither one with appetite, then set off, walking their horses through the denser stretches of forest. Recalling Jaya's description of Mahapura, Tamar planned to bear east to the Sabla River and follow it to its headwaters. The sun was high as the forest thinned a little and a hard-packed trail opened. Tamar halted in midstride.

A man had stepped into the path. His face was scarred and weather-beaten. He wore hunting garments much like Tamar's, with a stained rag knotted around his head. Tamar quickly motioned for Rajaswami to back away.

The hunter had drawn a heavy bow to full stretch. Notched and ready on the string, a barbed arrow pointed at Tamar's throat.

4. Questions in the Forest

Loosen your bow." Tamar spread his empty hands. "You have no quarrel with us."

"For me to say." The hunter's eyes narrowed. "I have a quarrel with all who come to poach in my forest."

"Yours?" Tamar said lightly. He glanced around. "Do you claim all this as your realm? A mighty kingdom."

"My hunting grounds. Will you dispute it?"

"Where you hunt is no interest to me," Tamar said. "We are not here to steal your game. We only pass through. We have other business."

"If you could direct us to a nearby *ashrama*," put in Rajaswami, "we would be greatly obliged. I find the lack of even rudimentary means of cleanliness unsettling, which you"—Rajaswami cast a disapproving eye on the hunter's grimy face and tangled, greasy hair—"apparently do not."

The hunter squinted. "What kind of old loon is this?"

"My good fellow, I am a *brahmana*." Rajaswami drew himself up in dignity. "As you should realize from my costume. My person is inviolate, not to be threatened with insults and arrows."

"Well, *brahmana*, you ask directions. I'll give them. I direct you to turn around and go back where you came from. You keep your life. I keep your horses. A fair exchange."

While the hunter's glare was on Rajaswami, Tamar un-shouldered his bow. In one swift motion, he snatched an arrow from the quiver and had it notched and aimed at the man.

"What you keep," said Tamar, "is your distance."

"Clever. Well done." The hunter gave a barking laugh. "Where did you learn that trick? Now, the question is: Can you loose your shaft faster than I can loose mine? Or have you the stomach to do so?"

"Find out for yourself."

The hunter stood awhile, holding his aim. He shrugged and lowered his bow. "I have no time for games of bravado. Go where you please. Wait!" he called, as Tamar stepped ahead. "Who are you?"

"Not your concern."

"Call it my curiosity. I let you live. You owe me an answer."

"I let you live. We are even. I owe you nothing."

"Tell me this, at least: What do you judge to be most valuable?"

"What is that to you?"

"Very little. Tell me, even so."

"An easy question, an easy answer," said Tamar. "Honor."

"What is the most dangerous battle?"

"With a stronger, better-armed enemy."

"And the best end to a battle?"

"When the enemy is defeated," Tamar said. "What else could it be?"

"Those are warrior's answers," the hunter said. "You are no poacher of rabbits."

"As I told you."

"One thing more. For amusement. To see if you can hit a mark as easily as you drew your bow." The hunter unstrung his own bow and threw it to the ground. "No fear. See, I am disarmed.

"Look there." The hunter pointed at a gnarled tree, almost out of bowshot down the path. "Do you see the knot in the trunk? Can you hit it?"

"Like you," replied Tamar, "I have no time for games."

"Or is the game too difficult? Would a closer target suit you better?"

"You chose it," Tamar said. "It will serve."

He drew the bowstring full and loosed the arrow. The shaft hissed through the air, straight to the tree and the center of the knot. The arrow strike had roused a hulking, ungainly bird, which flapped up from the branches, beat its ragged wings, and sped off in a lopsided flight, squawking indignantly.

"I left room for your own arrow." Tamar stepped back a pace. The hunter, along with his bow, had vanished. The forest was silent except for the fading screeches of the bird.

"Gone so fast?" Tamar looked around. "Where?"

"I didn't notice," said Rajaswami. "I was watching your arrow. Obviously, he slunk away ashamed, as well he ought to be."

Puzzled, Tamar whistled for the horses. With Rajaswami trotting at his heels, he strode toward the tree, but stopped short. From close at hand rose shrieks and howls, and desperate shouts for help. On the instant, beckoning to Rajaswami, he set off through the brush, scrambling over tangles of roots, plunging into the high grass and foliage lining a riverbank. At first, he thought he saw a man, half in half out of the water, clutching at the ground.

It was a monkey, nearly the size of Tamar himself, with arms longer than his own. A huge serpent had wrapped its coils around the creature, who yelled and squealed, struggling to keep from being dragged into the current.

"For mercy! Save me!" the monkey burst out, seeing Tamar. "Set me free of this overgrown worm. He'll drown me—if he doesn't first squeeze me to death."

"Hold on." Tamar sprang to the side of the monkey, whose face puckered and whose eyes rolled as his grip weakened. "I'll get you loose."

"You have my undying gratitude," the monkey gasped. "Undying, that is, if you'll be quicker about it."

Tamar sought to unwind the enormous reptile; but its coils were as big around as his waist and, for all his strength, he could not budge them. He drew his sword.

"That's good. Cut him to pieces," urged the monkey. "Chop him in two. Or three or four. The more the better. Only mind you don't slice my tail."

As Tamar raised his sword and was about to swing it down, the serpent lifted its head and hissed a warning:

"Stay your hand. You do ill to take my life. You have no right to interfere. It is a matter between this sneaking simian and myself."

"No longer," Tamar replied. "He begged me for help; I said I would give it, and so I must. Now it is a matter between you and me."

"You spoke too quickly," said the serpent, "in ignorance of my grievance against him."

Rajaswami, meantime, had clambered down the bank. "He has a point," he murmured to Tamar. "You've put yourself in a difficult situation without knowing the facts."

"I do no more than execute simple justice," the serpent said.

"A simple lie!" bawled the monkey. "Pay no attention. I'm the innocent victim of this armless, legless, hairless slug. He's a snake; he's likely to tell you anything. Ignore him. Chop away. I didn't do any harm."

Tamar looked from one to the other. "I'll judge the truth of that. As for you," he added to the serpent, "set him loose. He's in my charge while I hear your accusations."

"So be it." The great snake uncoiled. The monkey scrambled out of the water and flung himself to the bank, muttering insults and stretching the cramps from his arms and legs.

"I am Shesha, prince of the Naga-loka, the Serpent Realm," the snake began, raising himself partly upright. His scales glistened in rainbow colors; his tongue darted in and out like forked lightning. He spread his wide hood and Tamar saw that he bore on his head a sapphire, the gem as blue as the sky and even brighter.

"The facts are clear," Shesha went on, fixing Tamar with an unblinking eye. "I wished only to take my rest in the sun, here on this riverbank. While I slept, this insolent ape—"

"I'm not an ape, you scaly piece of rope," put in the monkey. "There's a difference—"

"Not to me," replied Shesha. "You are insolent, whatever you may be, and a thief as well." He returned his gaze to Tamar. "This jabbering creature came to steal my jewel. And would have done so, had I not awakened in time."

"You'd still be snoring away," said the monkey, "if some frowsy bird hadn't flown by, screeching its head off. That's what roused you. There's the real cause of the trouble. Otherwise—"

"Otherwise, you would have snatched my gem and made off with it. Yes, the bird woke me, for which I am grateful."

"And then?" said Tamar.

"There is no more than that," replied Shesha. "Because the bird luckily disturbed my repose, I was able to catch a thief red-handed. Now, King of Sundari, judge whether I have the right to punish him."

Tamar, taken aback at hearing himself so addressed, had no time to ask how Shesha knew this, for the monkey bounced up with a gleeful cry.

"We are fellow kings! I, Hashkat, am ruler of the Bandar-loka, the Monkey Realm." He lowered his voice and spoke hastily in Tamar's ear. "Between kings, one helps the other. A matter of professional courtesy."

"A matter of justice, even between kings," replied Tamar. "I have heard Prince Shesha. Now, King Hashkat, I will hear you."

"Nothing of what this prince of wigglers has told you is true," declared Hashkat. "The bird, yes, that much is correct. But I didn't come here with malice aforethought; I happened to pass this way by accident. One of my people is missing. No one can find him."

"What does this matter to me?" The Naga prince eyed Hashkat. "It is your concern, not mine."

"Tie a knot in that forked tongue of yours," retorted Hashkat. "As I was trying to explain, I myself was looking for little Akka. My search brought me here. I had no intention of stealing this reptile's jewel. It caught my eye; I stopped to admire. What harm in that? Even had I taken the jewel, I swear on my honor—"

"A monkey's honor?" Shesha hissed scornfully. "There is no such thing."

"There certainly is," Hashkat flung back. "I follow my dharma as faithfully as anyone."

"Do monkeys have dharma?" Tamar asked Rajaswami.

"Of course," the *acharya* replied. "All creatures do. Theirs, however, may be altogether different from yours."

"That's right," agreed Hashkat. "In this case, what someone else might call stealing is, among the Bandar-loka, a matter of highest principle. We devoutly believe that if something isn't nailed down, it's free for the taking; and if it can be pried loose—it isn't nailed down.

"Apart from that," Hashkat went on, "as far as the jewel is concerned, I'd have surely given it back. Probably. Maybe. If I'd been asked politely."

"Enough!" broke in Shesha. "You have heard us both. There can be no question in your mind. Justice must be executed."

"Yes, so long as it is justice," Tamar said. "For the sake of a jewel, I see no cause to take a life, even a monkey's. Prince Shesha, I cannot allow you to do so."

"And I do not abide by your judgment," replied Shesha. "You have a sword to enforce it," the Naga prince added. "With it, you can easily kill me if you choose, whereas I have no such weapon. If you wish to dispute me, do so without your blade. Unarmed, strength against strength. This monkey's miserable life? I challenge you to wrestle me for it."

5. Naga Raja

No, no, that won't do at all." Rajaswami raised a protesting hand. "My dear Prince Shesha, you complained of being at a disadvantage. What you propose is entirely to your own advantage. The match is grossly unfair."

"There, you see how he is," put in Hashkat, who left off grooming his long and luxuriantly furry tail. "Sneaky and slippery. Of course he'd choose wrestling. With those wriggling, writhing coils, he'd have it all his way. I suggest a footrace."

"Be silent," ordered Shesha. "You have no say in this."

"And you, my boy," Rajaswami added to Tamar, "I'm not certain it would be proper for you to take the risk. After all, you have a previous engagement, so to speak."

"By the code of honor, a warrior doesn't refuse a challenge," replied Tamar.

"Perhaps I can think of some exception to that rule," said Rajaswami.

"No discussions," the Naga prince hissed. "No hairsplitting excuses."

"A fine one to talk of hair," muttered Hashkat, curling a long upper lip. "Bald from head to tail."

"These are my terms," Shesha went on, ignoring the monkey. "We wrestle in the water—"

"Really, prince, you go too far," Rajaswami interrupted. "There you are even more at home than on land."

"Let him continue," Tamar said, "and make his challenge clear."

"If, even for an instant, you bring any part of me to dry ground," said the Naga prince, "I withdraw my claim. If you fail, or if you choose to give up the contest, his life is forfeit."

"Agreed and accepted. And you, king of monkeys," Tamar said, "stay here until the match is decided."

"What?" cried Hashkat. "I sit and cool my heels, my life in the balance, while you two flop around in a river? Majesty, with all respect, suppose you lose? I'm expected to give myself into his hands—hah, what hands?—and be swallowed up or squeezed into a pulp?"

"You'll wait with Rajaswami," Tamar ordered. "I want your solemn vow as a king."

"Of course, of course." Hashkat grumbled, "I know all about kings' solemn vows."

"See that you keep yours." Tamar stripped off his buckskins and shed his sandals while Hashkat hunkered down on the bank.

The Naga prince had already slithered into the river, leaving barely a ripple in his wake. Tamar plunged after him. No sooner was he in the water than he realized his mistake. He had misjudged the swiftness of the current, and had to fight against it even before grappling with Shesha.

He shook his dripping hair from his eyes. At first, he saw nothing of the serpent. When he did glimpse Shesha's head surfacing for a moment, he understood that he had made yet another miscalculation. The Naga prince intended staying in the middle of the river, making it all the more difficult for Tamar to force him to either shore.

Strong swimmer though he was, by the time he reached the spot where he had seen Shesha, Tamar's muscles ached with the strain of battling the current. The Naga prince had vanished. Treading water, Tamar cast around for Shesha.

Suddenly the river churned into foam. Shesha's tail lashed around Tamar's waist. Next instant, he was being dragged toward the river bottom. The Naga prince, Tamar realized, had chosen to fight not *in* the water but under it.

Before Shesha could throw another coil around him, Tamar squeezed free and shot to the surface, filling his lungs with air as the serpent turned and attacked. His best hope, he calculated, was to swim for shore, staying always a little out of reach, luring the Naga prince into the shallows.

Kicking his legs, sweeping his arms, Tamar struck out for the green line of the riverbank. Shesha writhed ahead of him, swung around to block his way, then lunged to seize him. Tamar flung himself aside as water roiled around him, and once more made for the river's edge. Shesha, however, gripped him by a leg and plunged downward.

Mud and gravel from the river bottom swirled in a yellow-brown cloud. Tamar, blinded, could not tell whether he was grasping Shesha's head or tail, but threw himself astride the scaly body and clung as to a bucking horse. The Naga prince heaved up and down, thrashing first one way then another, to dislodge his rider.

Their struggle brought them to the surface, but Tamar had only a moment of breath before Shesha dove again, straight to the riverbed; and there rolled over, slithering through weeds and water plants, across jagged rocks, seeking to scrape Tamar loose. Here, Shesha made his own mis-calculation. The serpent lunged through a tangle of dead branches that clawed Tamar away, but left the Naga prince trapped amid the limbs as if caught in a net.

Tamar floated free. He glimpsed Shesha flailing vainly in the mesh of branches. The Naga prince halted a moment, swung his head around, and stared coldly. Tamar hesitated; he had only to swim upward into air and sunlight, leaving Shesha below in a death trap. The serpent was watching him without a sign of surrender or plea for help, only the flat, steady gaze.

A few strokes brought Tamar to the imprisoning branches. Holding what breath he had left, he threw all his strength against the underwater thicket, while Shesha heaved and strained until the limbs gave way. Tamar kicked clear of them and headed for the surface.

The Naga prince seized him. For all his outraged strug-gles, his fury at betrayal instead of gratitude, Tamar could not escape. Shesha bore him farther along the riverbed. Lungs ready to burst, Tamar found himself dragged into a black tunnel.

The passageway curved downward, turned up sharply first one way then another. Tamar could breathe again. The water had fallen away. Shesha wriggled onto the wide shelf of what seemed the mouth of a cavern. Still gripping Tamar, the serpent slid through the arching entrance and unwound his coils. Panting, Tamar stumbled to his feet and turned, angry and questioning, on Shesha.

"You have broken off our contest, Prince Shesha. Do you dare claim to have won?"

"Our combat is unfinished," Shesha declared, "but, since you saved my life, I fight no more against you. As there is no clear victor, I leave it to my father to say in his wisdom where justice lies."

Shesha motioned with his head. At the far end of the cavern, two huge serpents lay on thrones of carved crystal. Both wore crowns encrusted with jewels. The chamber itself blazed with gems set into the walls and heaped high in every corner.

Tamar stared at the dazzling stones. "Where have you brought me?"

"To the heart of the Naga-loka," replied Shesha. "This is the palace of my father and mother."

The elder serpent stretched up and spread his hood. His ancient scales were thick, heavy as armor, gleaming and twinkling as he swayed erect. His tongue flickered in and out while his voice came as a long, sighing whisper.

"Approach, King of Sundari. I am Takshaka, the Naga Raja; and, here, my revered wife, Shila Rani."

"How do you know me?" Tamar stepped closer to the thrones. On either side, he saw other serpents, the Naga courtiers and attendants, coiled and looking at him in silent curiosity.

"You have been observed many times," Takshaka replied. "The domain of the Naga-loka reaches through all waterways, through all rivers and lakes. We see you here and there in Sundari when you take your ease at a woodland pool or ramble along a stream."

"The doings of a small king of a small kingdom should hardly interest the Naga folk," Tamar said.

"The deeds of kings are always of interest," said Takshaka, "to others, if not to themselves. The actions of the powerful have bearing on all around them."

"This is true," Shila Rani said. "Listen."

One day, beside a brook,
A half-grown boy
Played in the grass
And laughed with joy
To see a Naga
Hatching from its shell.

The lad was strong and fearless
And could well
Have crushed the feeble snake
Beneath his heel
Without a second thought
Or need to feel
Remorse or grief. But, no,
He turned aside

And let the Naga live
That might have died.

"The new-hatched Naga was Prince Shesha," explained Shila Rani, "and you were that half-grown boy."

"If I left him unharmed, I'm glad," replied Tamar, "but I remember nothing of that day."

"We remember," said Takshaka. "We Naga are an ancient folk. We have seen much. Little happens in your human realm that escapes our notice. And we forget nothing."

"Even so," said Shila, "we are puzzled to find you in our kingdom."

"I begin a long journey," Tamar said. "Allow me to continue it."

"Not yet," said Shesha. "We wrestled over the life of Hashkat, the one who calls himself king of the Bandar-loka," he added to Takshaka, "and now ask you to judge us."

"Why concern yourself with foolish monkey folk?" asked the Naga Raja.

"I am concerned when anyone dares to steal what is mine," said Shesha, beginning his account of what happened at the riverside. When he had finished, Tamar offered his own.

"All that Prince Shesha tells is true," he concluded. "Whether Hashkat would have stolen the gem or given it back, I do not know. I cannot guess his intentions. In any case, the gem was not stolen. Prince Shesha has it still, and has lost nothing. Should Hashkat be punished for what he might have intended, but did not do? Perhaps, perhaps not. Either way, it should not cost him his life. I say no more than that."

"Prince Shesha acted correctly," the Naga Raja declared. "He was gravely offended. It was his right—indeed, his dharma required it. Correct—yes, but only up to a point. The punishment would have gone beyond that point."

The Naga Raja turned to Shesha. "You allowed your wrath to overwhelm you. That was an offense against reason. You would have used power against the powerless. That, my son, was an offense against compassion. In the light of those considerations, hear my judgment: The monkey's life is to be spared."

"I am reprimanded." Shesha bowed his head. "You have spoken in your wisdom. Let it be as you have decided."

"And you, King of Sundari," put in Shila Rani, "we are curious to know what led you to this encounter. A journey, you said? What is the nature of it?"

"A dream," Tamar said, after describing his night in the

palace. "Sometimes I think it is nothing more. Yet, when I see the ring on my finger I must believe it happened, then only doubt and wonder again.

"Can you help me?" he went on. "Your domain reaches far and wide. Do you know of King Jaya? Of Mahapura? That would assure me there is such a person, at least."

"Only vague rumors, nothing more," answered Takshaka. "I am saddened I cannot ease your heart."

"I, too," Tamar said. "Now let me join my *acharya* and Hashkat. The monkey will be glad to hear your judgment."

"You have my leave," the Naga Raja said. "Prince Shesha will guide you through the passageways. First, as token of our goodwill, choose gems from any that you see here."

"Thank you," replied Tamar, "but your goodwill needs no token. Where I go, I have no need of jewels."

"Will you dishonor us by refusing an offered gift?" said Shila Rani. "Take as many as you please, King of Sundari."

Takshaka likewise insisted. So obliged, Tamar went to the heaps of precious stones, scanning one after the other. Among them glittered diamonds bigger even than Jaya's. Any one of them would have made his kingdom rich, if he broke off his journey and brought this treasure back to Sundari. He wondered if it was his karma to do so, and if this was the purpose of his dream. Ruefully, he shook his head. His eye fell on the smallest of the gems: a ruby that fit easily into the palm of his hand as he bent and picked it up.

"I choose this one," he said, "though your generosity is greater than any of your jewels."

The Naga courtiers whispered among themselves. Takshaka nodded approval.

"You have chosen modestly, without greed," the Naga

Raja said. "I commend you. Your choice is more interesting than you know. We call it 'Fire Flower.' See the lotus carved on it. This is the most curious of our treasures. One of my people found it by chance in a lake bed and bore it to me. How or why it came to be there is a mystery."

"And may always be," added Shila. "Now it is yours."

As Tamar pressed his palms together in the gesture of *namaste,* to thank and honor the Nagas, Prince Shesha declared:

"I will take you back to the river. Tell the monkey he is fortunate that my father was more lenient than I."

Tamar followed Shesha from the cavern and took firm hold of his tail as they slid through the tunnels. Once gaining the shallows, Shesha twisted away, leaving Tamar to find his footing amid the pebbles and flat stones of the riverbed.

The Naga prince vanished. Tamar stood, pulling off the strands of weeds clinging to his face. Before he could wipe the water from his eyes and clamber ashore, laughter burst from the riverbank.

6. A Beautiful Gopi

Some dozen dark-skinned and bold-eyed girls knelt by the shallows where they had been doing their laundry. By the time Tamar, taken by the sight, realized he had left his buckskins with Rajaswami, the girls burst into greater fits of laughter. Stepping back into deeper water, he slipped and went floundering head over heels, making them laugh all the more. He came up choking; and, even for a king, found it as difficult to keep his dignity as it was to keep his footing. He wondered if he was blushing royally.

The girls, meantime, giggled among themselves. Some frankly stared; others made a show of covering their faces with the ends of their saris, or whispered behind their hands, all of them finding his predicament marvelously entertaining.

In better circumstances, Tamar would not have objected to the attentions of winsome young women; by now, however, he had had his fill of being soaked and chilled, let alone being giggled at, and he called out to them to throw him one of the garments they had been scrubbing.

This set off a new chorus of laughter as the maidens waved pieces of laundry at him, urging him to come ashore and fetch them for himself.

"Never fear, we won't harm you," cried a girl. "We're only bashful *gopis*—cow-tenders, village milkmaids. You see how shy we are."

One of the *gopi*s at last had mercy on him. She picked up a length of cloth and waded knee-deep into the current. Some of her companions egged her on; others teased her as much as they had Tamar.

"Look at Mirri, the shameless creature," clucked one. "How does she dare? A stranger! Who knows what sort he is?"

"A handsome sort," replied her neighbor. "You're only vexed you didn't think of it first."

Instead of wrapping himself in the linen that the *gopi* named Mirri held out to him, Tamar only gaped like a smitten idiot. Of darker complexion than her companions, her skin glowed richly; her shining black hair fell to her waist. The ruby was clutched safely in his hand, but his heart was leaping every which way like a fish on a line. Paying no attention to the *gopi*s whooping merrily along the shore, his gaze never leaving Mirri, who stood with the current swirling around her, he began:

> *A stranger, lost, from riverbed I rise*
> *To lose myself once more in lotus eyes*
> *And dark-hued grace no king has ever seen.*
> *What realm is this, so blest with such a queen?*

To which Mirri lightly answered:

> *A queen am I, with all I could desire.*
> *My palace is the pasture and the byre.*
> *My royal robe, a cowgirl's rough attire.*

Tamar went on:

> *If made of flowers, as the poets tell,*
> *How do love's arrows fly so well?*

Swift to my breast they go and there strike deep
A heart no longer mine, a gopi's now to keep.

Mirri, with the trace of a smile, replied:

Fresh in their colorful array,
Flowers that blossom in a day
May by evening fade away.

On lotus, dew soon turns to frost.
Gopis discover, at their cost,
A heart can be too quickly lost.

With that, Mirri turned and waded to the riverbank. Tamar hastily wrapped the length of cloth about his waist and tucked away the ruby. As he climbed ashore, the *gopis* surrounded him, chattering questions and casting appraising glances, until Mirri at last had to shoo them off.

"Thank you for these elegant garments." Tamar grinned and pressed his palms together. "I never knew that *gopis* had this custom of welcoming strangers."

"Perhaps because we see so few of them." The girl's black eyes looked steadily at Tamar. She stood as tall as Tamar himself, with a slender neck and narrow shoulders. From her bearing, Tamar judged that she had considerable authority among her companions. "Let alone strangers who claim to lose their hearts while up to their ears in a river," Mirri added. "I could also ask if it's the custom, wherever you're from, to try to turn the head of a humble village cowgirl?"

"If that's what you please to call yourself," replied Tamar. "I've seen princesses less royal."

"If you say so," Mirri answered. "No doubt you've seen more princesses than I have."

"Did you come for the Choosing?" piped up one of the smaller girls.

"Hush, Vati," Mirri said to her. "If he did, you'll find out soon enough. Let him first tell us who he is."

However, when Tamar gave his name, Mirri shrugged. "I don't know any more of you than I did before. A name says nothing of the one who carries it. I think there may even be a king called Tamar, in the realm of Sundari."

"There used to be," Tamar said. "No longer. And your village? To what kingdom does it belong?"

"To none," Mirri said proudly. "Ours is a free village, and so it has always been. We grow enough to feed ourselves, we tend our cattle, we don't steal our neighbors' herds or land, and our doings are of no interest to anyone but ourselves."

"The Choosing! The Choosing!" The girl called Vati interrupted, poking at Tamar. "Is that why you're here?"

"Small *gopi,*" Tamar said, "if I knew what it was, I could answer you better."

"Everybody knows," Vati insisted. "The song tells it."

> *Village lads and cowherds vie,*
> *Striving to catch a* gopi's *eye.*

> Gopis *raise melodious voices*
> *And declare their loving choices.*

> *A wreath of flowers is the token*
> *Of a pledge that's never broken.*

Handsome youth and maiden fair
Join to make a happy pair.

Feasts are set, musicians play
To mark this joyful wedding day.

"It's our betrothal festival," Mirri explained. "When the girls turn the age to wed, our young men show off their strength and skill—running, wrestling, shooting arrows, and all such. Each girl chooses the one who best pleases her and sets a wreath of flowers 'round his neck."

"And you," Tamar said to Mirri, "of course, you have your eye on some strapping village lad, and your mind already made up."

"No. I'll take no part in it."

"Why not? You'll break the heart of some adoring, hopeful cowherd."

"Because I care to make no choice."

"I've never seen such a festival. I'd like to be on hand for the happy occasion."

Mirri looked away and did not answer. Tamar went on:

"First, I need to find my companion. We were separated, I don't know what's become of him, and he knows nothing of what's become of me."

During this, he had been anxiously glancing up and down the riverbank. As best he could reckon, the current had borne him downstream. He would have to retrace his steps to where he had left Rajaswami and Hashkat. He shuddered at the thought of the *acharya* on his own in the wilds with only a monkey—and a feckless one, at that.

When he asked Mirri if he might borrow some better

clothing and a pair of sandals, she nodded, tight-lipped, and gestured toward the nearby village.

With the *gopis* trailing behind, chattering among themselves, he followed Mirri to a cluster of flat-roofed, openfronted buildings. A handful of youngsters was sweeping and sprinkling the market square to keep down the dust; banners had already been hoisted on long poles, with garlands slung between. Beyond lay cattle pens and fenced pastures of sweet grass.

Mirri led him across the veranda of the largest house and into a cool, shaded common room. The thickset man who came to greet them, his bronze skin darkened still more by sun and wind, was Nanda, the village chief. He had, as Mirri explained, adopted her when her parents died. His wife, Yashoda, a gray-haired, vigorous woman in a neatly wrapped sari, hurried to offer a tray of fruit, then spoke apart with Mirri.

As Tamar sat on a bench at the wooden table, the two women disappeared, while Nanda eased into a place beside him and eyed the unexpected guest with curiosity. Unwilling to break hospitality by too closely questioning Tamar's business, Nanda took the countryman's way of sniffing around the edges of the subject. Tamar, however, told only of encountering the maidens on his way to the Sabla.

"Well, you're on the right path," Nanda said, "though you've a good long ways to go. This river here is the Kurma. Just you follow it upstream. You'll find where it branches from the Sabla.

"As for our village girls, pay no heed to their antics. Before the Choosing, they all go light-headed."

"Not all," replied Tamar. "There's one who tells me she won't take part."

"Mirri. Yes." Nanda sighed. "It's time for her to wed, and expected of her. And there's not a lad who wouldn't be overjoyed if she chose him. Even if I put my foot down and insisted—eh, she'd still do as she pleases. We love her as dearly as if she'd been born to us, but she's willful, with a mind of her own. Always was. A real marvel with our animals, though. The cows even give better when she's the one to milk them, as if they know what she wants and are happy to oblige.

"No, I'll not force her to marry. Even when she was tiny, there were times when she seemed to be waiting, looking for something no one else could see. So, best leave her to decide matters for herself.

"You, now." He cocked an eye at Tamar. "You're a high-caste sort of fellow, plain as day to see, and a good many cuts above us folk here. You'd not be much interested in our doings, would you?"

Before Tamar could answer, Yashoda came with sandals, tunic, and cowherd's leggings. Tamar went to a corner of the room and put on the coarse garments. Through the open back door, he caught sight of Mirri by the pasture fence, where a white cow nuzzled her hand. He stepped outside and went to her.

She started as he drew closer, then said, "You're better dressed than you were, but no one would mistake you for a cowherd. I thought you'd go looking for your friend."

"I will. I wanted to thank you. I hope I didn't interrupt your conversation."

"With Surabi? I've named her after the magical cow in the old tales, the one who could grant any wish."

"So you were wishing? What for?"

"If I could wish"—Mirri hesitated, then turned her eyes full on Tamar—"I might wish you'd never come here."

Tamar bridled. "I hadn't planned on it. What does it matter to you, in any case?"

"Because you've set my life topsy-turvy. I was happily going about my business—until you came. I hadn't expected someone popping out of a river. My heart was my own, before that. As I wanted it to be."

"And now?"

"I don't know. It's all changed. I don't know what to do about you. I don't even know who you are."

"I told you all that was needed."

"You told me nothing." She seized his hand as Tamar reached out to her. "What are these?" She touched the thin white scars deeply bitten into his wrist. "The marks of a bowstring. Warrior's marks?"

"And if they are?" He broke off. Yashoda was calling him. Mirri turned away. Tamar hurried into the house. From the veranda Yashoda beckoned urgently, saying that some-one had come asking for him.

There was great excitement in the square. Nanda and a crowd of villagers had gathered to admire the pair of fine horses and to murmur over the splendid quality of the sword, bow, and quiver tied to Gayatri's saddle pack.

"Rajaswami!" Tamar pressed through the circle of on-lookers to embrace the old *acharya*.

"Ah, here you are, safe and sound." Rajaswami's face lit up at the sight of Tamar. "Excellent. And what a pleasant little spot for a rest. My bunions need some consolation after scrambling along that riverbank."

"How did you find me?" Tamar, much relieved, drew

him apart. "Where's Hashkat? His life is spared. He'll be glad to know."

"I'm sure he would be, if he'd waited to find out. But, you see, he ran off—"

"Broke his word? Wretch! He promised, he swore—"

"Don't think too harshly of him," said Rajaswami. "A monkey's dharma no doubt encourages that sort of behavior. Otherwise, he was most helpful. He went up and down the river, watching for you. When he saw you come out, he ran back to tell me. So, here I am. And you, my boy, where did you get those clothes? They have a distinct odor of cow."

Yashoda, meantime, had come to welcome this second visitor. Tamar signaled Rajaswami to say nothing of their quest. Yashoda, in any case, asked no explanation and invited the grateful *acharya* to wash and tidy himself. She ordered some of the village youngsters to fetch buckets of water; and, in a quiet corner behind the house, Rajaswami scrubbed away the dust and grime while Tamar replaced the cowherd's garments with his own buckskins.

As the *acharya* wrung water from his beard and soaked his tender toes, Tamar quickly told him of Shesha, Naga Raja, and the gift of the ruby; and finally, of the *gopis* and his meeting with Mirri.

"Ah—yes, one thing more," Tamar admitted after some hesitation. "You see, what's happened—*acharya,* I'm in love with her."

Instead of showing surprise or disapproval, Rajaswami only smiled cheerfully and shook his head. "Oh, my boy, I doubt that very much. You may believe so at the moment —you're a young man, after all. But, no. Let me point this out:

What seems to be love beyond any question
Is usually a case of simple indigestion.

"I'm quite sure she's a perfectly splendid young lady,"
Rajaswami went on, "but I needn't remind you there's a
question of caste. Plainly put, you're of the nobility,
whereas, dear boy, she's a *shudra,* the lowest caste of all—
except, of course, for the *chandala*s, so low they count as
nothing whatever.

"That in itself presents a serious difficulty," he warned.
"Even apart from the difference in caste, you're hardly in
proper circumstances for affairs of the heart. But, cheer up.
By tomorrow, when we're on our way again, it will all be
forgotten."

"No, it won't—" Tamar began.

Yashoda was calling them for the evening meal. Rajaswami eagerly took a place at table beside Nanda. Tamar,
without appetite, barely touched the food that Mirri silently
brought. The girl, in fact, never spoke or looked at him, but
stayed with Yashoda, talking in whispers.

Only after all had eaten, and Yashoda was laying down
mats for the visitors to sleep on the veranda, did Mirri step
forward. She stood a moment, gave Tamar a quick glance,
then turned to Nanda.

"I've changed my mind," she said, as if in challenge.
"Tomorrow, I'll take part in the Choosing."

7. Thorns

Rajaswami had been too well fed to be very much awake. Tamar was too happy to sleep at all. Sitting cross-legged on the dark veranda while the *acharya* drowsed, he kept up a long, one-sided conversation, going over every word he and Mirri had exchanged as if he were admiring precious jewels.

"She'll be at the Choosing," he said, for the third or fourth time. "You know what that means."

Rajaswami opened one eye. "It means, as you've already told me, she'll choose her future husband. As will the other village girls. It should be an enjoyable rustic festival. We might spare a few moments to observe it from a distance."

"What distance? *Acharya,* she's going to choose me; I'm sure she will."

"Or is that what you want to believe?" Rajaswami, yawning, sat up. "I've only been half asleep, so I heard half of what you told me the first time, and the other half the second time. And didn't you say she wished you hadn't come here? That you'd upset everything?

"Besides, dear boy, you can't take part. You? No, no, out of the question."

"Why not? These games—running, wrestling, archery —how can I lose? Against cowherds? I'm a warrior, with better skill than any—"

"That's precisely why you must stay out of it. You, a trained warrior, a king, set yourself against village lads? Absolutely improper! By the warrior's code, you may never challenge a lesser opponent. To do otherwise would be dishonor past mending.

"As for marriage between high caste and low," continued Rajaswami, "that could possibly be overlooked in a special case. But, my boy, the young lady may well choose some village youth merely to keep her life from being turned upside down by an unknown wanderer. And your own life? It is yours no longer. You pledged it to King Jaya—if he exists. You have no business giving your heart to anyone, let alone accepting Mirri's, even if she offers it."

"*Acharya,* do you tell me I have no right to love?"

"Ah, my boy, at your age grand passions come and go. There's always another. It may sting and smart at the moment, and you have my sympathy; but, keep looking on the bright side.

"Apart from that," Rajaswami added, "you have all your journey ahead of you. The promise you made—"

"But if it was only a dream? *Acharya,* what do you expect of me?"

"The proper question is: What do you expect of yourself? Will you break your dharma? My heart aches for you, whatever you decide; but it's altogether up to you."

Tamar stood and leaned over the veranda railing. The little square was empty in the moonlight. By morning, he well imagined, it would be alive with eager suitors, *gopi*s and their wreaths of flowers, Mirri among them. He clenched his hand so tightly that the iron ring bit into the flesh of his palm.

"Come, *acharya*," he said at last, in a flat voice. "I'll fetch the horses."

"Now?" Rajaswami frowned. "Leave in the middle of the night, without a word of thanks for hospitality? A farewell to the young lady?"

"Don't ask me to do more than I can bear. Get your things ready."

Gayatri whickered fondly as Tamar patted her neck and swung astride. With Rajaswami trotting behind him, they rode silently across the square and toward the river. Only once did Tamar allow himself to look back. By then, the village was lost to sight.

———◆◆———

"Majesty!"

Tamar reined up. In the pink traces of dawn, he glimpsed a long-tailed, slope-shouldered figure scuttling from the bushes. As Tamar dismounted, Hashkat, in a bowlegged, lurching gait, came to a halt in front of him.

"Forgive me." Hashkat wrinkled his brow and pressed his palms together. "It's not my fault."

"Forgive you for what?" Tamar eyed the monkey severely. "For being dishonorable? For breaking your word to me? For running off when I told you to wait? Or whatever else? You've been pardoned by the Naga Raja himself. Why ask forgiveness?"

"Well, I don't. Not really, not for any of that," Hashkat replied, with no sign of being any way ashamed of himself. "Considering the possibility of being gobbled up and digested by some ill-tempered reptile, I did what any decent, right-thinking monkey would have done: left the premises

immediately. Among us Bandar-loka, one of the highest virtues is: Don't get eaten."

"I rather suspected that was the case," said Rajaswami.
"My boy, you can't blame him for adhering to his principles."

"I only ask forgiveness for not joining you sooner," said
Hashkat. "I gather you won the wrestling match and I simply wanted to thank you. I may be a monkey, but I'm not
an ingrate. I saw you go into the village. I didn't dare follow.
I'm too well known. I couldn't risk it."

"Of course not. An upcountry little village of cowherds
and farmers is surely a dangerous place."

"For me it is," said Hashkat. "Oh, I used to venture in
from time to time, lurking about here and there. Once,
when the *gopis* were bathing in the river"—at this, Hashkat
gave a toothy grin, wagged his head, and chuckled gleefully—"I crept up and stole away their clothes. They came
after me like a swarm of hornets, but I was too quick for
them. They spent the day plucking their saris off tree limbs.
I can't say that endeared me to them.

"Naturally," he went on, "I'd sometimes pop into one
house or another and make off with a nice lump of butter
or some tasty victuals."

"You're a thief on top of everything else?" Tamar exclaimed. "A shameless robber?"

"Of course. Completely shameless," agreed Hashkat.
"You have to understand. That's what we monkeys do. Our
business, so to speak, is—monkey business. What else? But
now, in any case, I won't set foot in the village. One night,
you see, I was a bit thirsty and sneaked into a cowshed. One
of the *gopis* caught me milking her cow.

" 'Milk do you want?' she cried. 'Milk you'll have!' So she poured it all over my head. And swore if I ever came back she'd tie so many knots in my tail I'd never unravel them.

"That was warning enough." Hashkat protectively curled his tail around him. "She'd have done it, for sure. A handsome, buxom *gopi,* but a tiger when she's roused. 'I'm king of the monkeys,' I tell her. 'Then here's your crown,' says she, and bangs the bucket down on my head—it took me half an hour to pull it off. No, I won't risk crossing that one's path again.

"So, I waited until you left the village. But, indeed, I'm in your debt. You wrestled that overweening angleworm for my sake. You saved my life—a small matter to a king like you, but of intense personal interest to me. Another essential rule in a monkey's dharma: Stay alive."

Rajaswami, meantime, had been clearing his throat and making hungry noises. Tamar, without much interest, lit a cook fire and laid out a meal from the saddle packs. Food being the furthest thing from Tamar's mind, Hashkat helpfully downed his benefactor's portion, smacking his lips, sucking his long fingers, and scooping up any leftovers.

"Now," said Hashkat, leaning back on his haunches, "I've told you I'm searching for little Akka—a promising young fellow, I hope he's come to no harm—dare I ask what brings you from Sundari?"

"I should think His Majesty's purposes are no concern of yours," said Rajaswami.

"Of course, they aren't," said Hashkat. "But that's another rule among the Bandar-loka: If it's none of your business, be sure to stick your nose in it."

Tamar's heart still weighed so heavily that he was glad

to unburden it even to a monkey, and he explained the circumstances that had set him on his journey.

"You obey a stern dharma," Hashkat remarked, when Tamar finished. "Very noble, honorable, commendable, and all that. I admire and revere you for it, but—well, it's just not my style."

"You follow your own rules," said Tamar. "A monkey would hardly understand a warrior's code of honor."

"Oh, but I do," protested Hashkat. "I used to have one. I was born into the warrior caste—"

"What?" exclaimed Tamar. "What are you telling us? A monkey—and a *kshatriya?* Impossible!"

"Majesty, it's true," Hashkat insisted. "You see, I wasn't always a monkey. I was born a human being of noble family in the kingdom of Muktara. I confess I never took to being a warrior, to the disappointment of my parents. They chided me for being idle and frivolous, which I certainly was. When my classmates were diligently studying matters of dharma, or exercising with weapons, I preferred swimming in the river or climbing trees in the forest.

"When I was grown, they expected me to go off shooting arrows and chucking spears every time the king squabbled with his neighbors. The more I thought about that, the more I wondered: Why should I do harm to total strangers? And, for that matter, why should total strangers do harm to me? So I quit the warrior trade and took to the road, free as the breeze, living by my wits. Ignoble cowardice, according to the code of honor; to me, plain common sense."

"That tells us nothing about your being a monkey," said Tamar.

"I'm coming to it," said Hashkat. "Yes, well, I was walking along the road one afternoon and there's a *brahmana* sound asleep under a tree. This old geezer had the longest beard I'd ever seen. I couldn't resist. I took the end of his beard and tied it around his ankles. Then I tickled his nose with a blade of grass until he woke, scrambled up the tree as fast as I could, and sat on a limb to watch the fun.

"Oh, you should have seen him stumbling, tripping over his feet, getting himself knotted worse than ever. I laughed so hard I nearly fell out of the tree. When he finally untangled his beard, he shook his fist at me, calling me a disrespectful, impudent ne'er-do-well.

" 'Make sport of a *brahmana?*' he cries, his eyes like a pair of hot coals. 'Come down immediately, you wretch, and accept the punishment you deserve.'

" 'I don't think so,' I say, safe on my perch. 'If you mean to punish me, you'll have to catch me first.'

" 'Insolent rogue,' the old coot says, pointing a skinny finger at me, 'you'll get your comeuppance no matter how high you climb. Hear me well:

> *Monkey see, monkey do.*
> *Monkey's just the same as you.*
> *Do like a monkey, be a monkey too.'*

"Next thing I know," said Hashkat, "I'm a monkey, tail and all. The *brahmana* vanished, I don't know how or where. I was too busy wondering what had happened to me. Plainly and simply, I've been a monkey ever since."

"He transformed you? Then and there? Unbelievable!" Tamar turned to Rajaswami. "Can this be so? Can such a thing happen?"

"Oh, yes," Rajaswami said. "There have been many similar cases. I've read about them in the old lore. But this can be done only by a great sage, a most mighty *rishi* who studied long, hard years to gain the secret of such power. The one who transformed Hashkat was no ordinary *brahmana.*"

"A terrible punishment." Tamar put a hand on Hashkat's hairy shoulder. "I'm sorry for what happened to you."

"No need," said Hashkat. "Once I got used to being a monkey, I was grateful to that *rishi*. It's a relaxing life, without much to do except look for mischief. Easier than when I was expected to behave like a warrior. Besides, since I was bigger and stronger than your average monkey, in no time at all the Bandar-loka chose me as their king—which made things even pleasanter."

"You never miss being a human?" asked Tamar.

"A little bit from time to time," said Hashkat, happily scratching himself. "A monkey's life has its limitations, but a monkey's dharma suits me very well. What it comes down to is: If it tastes good, eat it; if it feels good, do it. I recommend your trying it. Why go on a journey when you expect to be killed at the end of it? No sensible monkey would consider such a thing.

"I'll tell you what I'll gladly do," Hashkat went on. "The realm of the Bandar-loka is large. Actually, it's anywhere and everywhere we happen to be. Stay with me and I'll share my kingship with you. For one thing, you saved my life, so I'm obliged to you; for another, you're a real king and know more about that business than I do. We'll divide the responsibilities—there aren't many. Nobody can really govern monkeys. Who would want to?"

"That's a generous offer." Tamar smiled and shook his head. "But I mean to keep on with my journey."

"Your dharma must pinch you something awful,"

replied Hashkat. "You'd find a little elbow room a lot more comfortable. As I said, I admire you, but I don't envy you. In any case, let me do you a service by warning you: Don't follow the river, not at this point. You'll come up against a heavy thorn forest just ahead. You can't get past. Turn off, circle around. Then you double back to the Kurma."

"Turn aside only because of thorns?" Tamar said. "I have an advantage." He pointed at his sword. "I'll cut a passage through them."

"A warrior's way of doing," said Hashkat. "Straight ahead, hacking and hewing. I should have expected that of you. Well then, let me come along and save myself some time."

To this, Tamar willingly agreed; and they set off, leading the horses, with Hashkat scuttling ahead. As the monkey king had warned, a tall curtain of tangled vines soon rose in front of them, stretching in both directions as far as Tamar could see. There were, at least, fewer thorns than he expected.

He hesitated, wondering if there were some better way past the barrier. But since he had already declared his decision, he drew his sword and took a powerful swing at the prickly obstacle. The blade bit deeply into the vines. However, when he tried to pull it loose and launch another stroke, the sword would not come free. He gripped the hilt in both hands and, for better leverage, set a foot against the vines. For all his strength, the sword still would not budge. Nor would his foot.

With a cry of annoyance and impatience, he tried to struggle free. Hoping by sheer force to part the thorny curtain, he grasped the vines, only to find his hands caught as tightly as his foot. Now alarmed as well as vexed, he heaved himself back and forth, thrashing up and down, side to side, which made his predicament all the worse.

The vines had captured him.

8. A Miserable Bird

At first, he believed the thorns had trapped him; but Tamar quickly understood otherwise. What held him fast was a sticky juice, a thick resin oozing from the vines. Hashkat scurried to help. Before Tamar could warn him, the monkey was firmly glued and in an even worse plight. His long tail was caught, and his struggles only succeeded in turning him head over heels, dangling upside down.

Rajaswami trotted up. "Good heavens, whatever are you doing?"

"Keep back," Tamar called over his shoulder. "Or you'll be stuck along with us." The sap from the vines was hardening and he saw it was urgent to break free; yet each movement embedded him deeper.

"*Acharya*, listen to me carefully," Tamar ordered. "We'll need the horses to haul us loose. Fetch ropes from the saddle packs."

"Step lively, too," put in Hashkat, flailing back and forth. "Do you think I enjoy hanging here like a bat?"

"Hashkat first," Tamar said, when Rajaswami hobbled back with the coils of rope. "You'll need to make a harness for him; then hitch the line to Gayatri."

The more the *acharya* attempted to heed Tamar's directions, the more he fumbled vainly with the cords, and almost tangled himself into them. At last, despairing, he threw up his hands.

"Forgive me, I can't do it," he moaned. "There has to be a better way. Let me contemplate. Something will come to mind." He plumped himself down on the ground, crossed his legs, and folded his arms. "An idea's bound to seize me."

"I'll seize you, if I ever get loose!" yelled Hashkat.

"Acharya, there's no time." Tamar renewed his struggling. The sap had begun to glaze and turn nearly solid.

"There's a sight," declared a familiar voice. "One sound asleep, the other—"

"I'm not asleep," Rajaswami broke in. "I'm contemplating."

Tamar twisted his head around to stare into the shining black eyes of Mirri. Her long hair had been bound up and she wore the jacket and leggings of a cowherd.

"The other stuck in brambles," she went on, "and still another—"

"It's the *gopi!"* squealed Hashkat. "The one who crowned me with a bucket."

"And—what, the king of the monkeys again?" Mirri set her hands on her hips and cocked an eye at Hashkat. "Well, Your Monkeyship, you've got yourself in a new pickle."

"How did you find us?" Tamar broke in. "What are you doing here?"

"Nanda told me you were heading north along the river," Mirri said, all the while taking stock of Tamar's situation. "You were easy to follow."

With no need for instruction, Mirri looped the rope around Tamar's waist and under his arms, tying the knots deftly and securely, then did the same for Hashkat. Hitching up the horses, she urged them to start pulling. Tamar felt his harness tighten, biting into his chest and almost cutting off his breath. The sap refused to give up its grip; until, at last, one of Tamar's feet came free, then the other. His hands suddenly tore loose and he tumbled to the ground. Hashkat rolled onto the grass beside him. Mirri undid the ropes and lashed them around the hilt of Tamar's sword, and the horses hauled it clear as well. Tamar's hands smarted where shreds of skin had been ripped away. Hashkat had fared worse. Patches of his fur clung to the vines, and a good length of his tail was stripped raw.

"What I don't understand," said Mirri, while Tamar sheathed his sword and Hashkat ruefully eyed the damage to his tail, "is how you got in such a mess to begin with. You should have seen right away you couldn't get through."

"We have to get through." Tamar glared at the brambles as if they were an enemy who had bested him. "I said I would."

"That's how he is," put in Hashkat. "With him, it's a point of honor."

"Honor's one thing, stubbornness is another," returned Mirri.

"Tut, tut," Hashkat snapped, "that's no way to speak to the king of Sundari."

"The what of what?" Mirri rounded on Tamar. "King? You lied to me at the river—"

"I didn't lie," Tamar protested. "I'm not the king of Sundari. I gave it up. I turned the kingdom over to my army commander."

"You're splitting hairs," Mirri retorted, eyes flashing.

"Leave that sort of niggling to the *brahmanas*. I guessed you were at least a warrior, and you said nothing. And what about those fine words you were spouting when you were up to your neck in water? I want to know more about this king who isn't a king."

Tamar nodded. "Yes. You have every right."

"My boy," Rajaswami interrupted, "this is hardly the moment for amatory confessions. If you don't wish to delay, you'll have to turn aside and circle around these brambles."

"You could go to the river's edge and swim past," said Mirri.

"Goodness, no," cried Rajaswami. "I can't swim. That won't do at all."

"We could pull you along by your beard," suggested Hashkat. "It looks pretty well stuck to your chin."

"Certainly not," sniffed Rajaswami. "As a *brahmana,* I insist on maintaining a measure of dignity."

"If you knew as much about country life as you do about your honor," Mirri said to Tamar, "you might have figured how to go at it." She led him to the thorny barrier. "That sticky sap—we have bushes near our village that put out something like it; not as strong, but much the same kind of resin. We collect it and use it in our lamps. It burns brighter than oil. What I'm wondering—"

"Set fire to the vines?"

"We can try. See what happens." Mirri strode to a chestnut mare grazing beside Gayatri and Jagati. "Nanda let me borrow a horse," she called back, adding, with a glance at Hashkat: "I'm not a monkey—I didn't steal it."

The girl rummaged through her saddle pack and drew out a flintstone and steel fire-striker. Warning Hashkat and

Rajaswami to keep their distance, she knelt at the roots of the vine. Tamar watched closely while she struck a spark that went dancing into the brambles.

The sticky resin hissed and flared. A yellow flame spurted, small at first, then soon rose crackling and licking at the vines, blossoming in all directions. Another moment and the fire was roaring, burning faster than Tamar could have imagined. He flung up his arms to shield his face from the sudden burst of heat.

Mirri, instead of drawing back, seized a dead branch and began thrusting at the blaze, stirring and spreading it deeper into the brambles. She struck away the charred vines and plunged into the gap, driving the fire ahead of her until she had hacked out a flaming tunnel.

"It's burned through to the other side," she called, beckoning to Tamar. "Get the *brahmana* and the monkey. Blindfold the horses, or they won't go near the fire."

"Gayatri will do whatever I ask," Tamar called back. "The others will follow her."

While Mirri continued to clear away the smoldering vines, Tamar sent Rajaswami stumbling headlong through the passage, then shoved Hashkat after him. He ran back to fetch the horses, who whinnied fearfully but nevertheless heaved their way through the dense, black smoke and showering sparks. At the same time, Tamar heard loud squawks and screeches from somewhere above. Paying no heed, he hastily led Gayatri and the other two steeds into the open air beyond the brambles.

There, Rajaswami was coughing and rubbing his eyes. Hashkat, brushing cinders from his fur, protested that he could have had his tail burnt to a crisp. Mirri, her face smudged still darker by soot, closely observed the smoldering passageway.

"Bravely done." Tamar went quickly to her. "You have the heart of a warrior."

"I hope not," Mirri said. She pointed at the brambles. "Look, the flames are dying down. Good. Otherwise, I'd have to find a way to keep them from spreading too far."

"What does it matter? You got us through it."

"Burn down a whole forest for the sake of convenience? That might be a warrior's way, but it's not mine. Strange, though. The vines are growing again."

Even as Tamar watched, new tendrils sprouted, fresh and green, beginning to entwine and fill the burned-out gap. He called over Rajaswami, who peered at the thicket, which had grown almost as dense as it had been.

"Most peculiar," murmured the *acharya,* as puzzled as Tamar. "Not at all to be expected from ordinary vegetation." He frowned uneasily. "Very odd, indeed. Even magical."

"The door's closed behind us, so to speak," said Hashkat. He glanced at his scorched tail. "That's all right. I don't intend going back. I admit the *gopi* did us a service, but I might have ended up roasted."

That same instant, before Tamar was aware what was happening, a large and lopsided bundle of ragged feathers came swooping straight at him, beating its widespread wings, buffeting him about the head and shoulders, screeching furiously.

"Shmaa! Shmaa!" squawked the bird. "Enough is enough. I'll stand for no more of your persecution and harassment. You've gone too far."

While Tamar fended off the assault, the bird kept up its cries of outrage and indignation until, suddenly, it flopped to the ground, rolled onto its back, and shut its eyes tightly.

"What is this creature?" exclaimed Tamar, still bewildered by the attack. Mirri and Rajaswami drew closer, to stare curiously at the motionless form. Hashkat squatted down and poked it with a finger.

"It looks like a cross between a buzzard and a trash heap," said the monkey, "whatever it's called."

The bird opened one red-rimmed eye. "Garuda is what it's called. Not that it matters. Who cares? It's just poor, helpless Garuda. Call him a buzzard, call him trash, whatever you please. Go ahead, you grinning idiot, aren't you going to kick me when I'm down? You might as well. You've done your worst already."

"What are you talking about?" Tamar knelt beside the disheveled bird, who rolled over and stood up on a pair of scabby legs. "We've done nothing to you."

"Nothing?" Garuda snapped his hooked beak. "Of course not. Nothing to make you lose a wink of sleep, nothing to weigh on your conscience for even an instant. No, you've only burned up my nest, destroyed my home—Well, this time I've lost patience. You've driven me past endurance."

"I'm sorry," Mirri began, reaching out a hand to calm the bird. "I didn't know you had a nest there."

"A likely story," Garuda flung back. "I should believe that? Why do you think I built it in the thorniest place I could find, and avoiding that horrible goo? To get a little peace and quiet. Don't tell me you—and he, and the *brahmana,* and the scruffy-tailed banana-gobbler didn't plan the whole thing. What's to do for sport this morning? Why, let's go burn Garuda's home to cinders.

"You aren't the only ones after me," Garuda pressed on. "Just the other day, I'm perched on a tree, minding my own business, when some malicious fool shoots an arrow at me. Missed me by a hair. I flew off as fast as I could before the numbskull tried again."

"So, he's the one who woke up the snake and got me in trouble," said Hashkat.

"I shot the arrow," Tamar said. "I was aiming at the tree; I saw no bird."

"Aha!" cried Garuda. "You're all in it together, just as I thought."

"He's quite mad," Hashkat muttered to Tamar. "Leave him. Let's be on our way."

"Oh, no, you don't!" cried Garuda. "You wrecked my home. You owe me. You owe me plenty for all the pain and misery you've caused."

"I regret to say," Rajaswami told Tamar, "accident though it was, the young lady acted for your benefit, so you must bear some responsibility. And you were the one who disturbed him in the first place. As he claims, you owe him something:

> *A king never forgets*
> *To pay his debts.*

"He's not a king anymore," Hashkat protested. "Let this moth-eaten sack of feathers build another nest. What else does he have to do with his time? Or, he can go roost with his fellow vultures."

"First, you call me a buzzard—now, a vulture!" cried Garuda, so furious that he was quacking like a duck. "You don't know who you're dealing with. I'm an eagle!"

9. Lost and Found

Eagle?" Hashkat slapped his knees and hooted with laughter. "What, did a wandering *rishi* lay a curse on you, as one did to me when I was a human?"

"So that's what happened to His Monkeyship," Mirri said apart to Tamar. "Somehow, I'm not surprised."

"Whatever you did, I'm sure you deserved to be cursed for it," snapped Garuda. "I'm an eagle now and always have been." The bird shook his wings and looked down his beak at Hashkat. "I'll have you know, in my better days—ah, ah, better days they were—I served a mighty king."

"As what?" Hashkat stuck out his tongue. "A feather duster?"

"His trusted messenger," Garuda retorted, with an air of shabby dignity. "No errand was too difficult or dangerous. One day, His Majesty sent me on a most important mission.

"A treacherous servant had stolen an extremely valuable gem and given it to a *rakshasa,* an evil demon, in exchange for the gift of eternal life. You can see how precious the jewel was, to be worth that sort of bargain. The *rakshasa* didn't keep his word."

"They never do," put in Rajaswami. "When will people realize there's simply no dealing with them?"

"Feel free to interrupt whenever you please." Garuda

glared at the *acharya*. "I'm only telling you the story of my life.

"As I was saying— Eh? Where was I?" Garuda blinked and wagged his head. "Ah. Yes. The servant came to a messy end. The *rakshasa* and the jewel vanished.

"In time, my royal master learned the *rakshasa* had hidden the gem in a mountain cavern, protected by a ring of fire. Who had strength even to reach that cavern? Or, once there, courage to risk the flames?"

Garuda paused and glanced around. "I just asked a civil question. It's too much, I suppose, to hope for a civil answer."

"You were the one," Mirri said, with an encouraging smile. "The king sent you, of course. Then what?"

"Thank you for your interest," said Garuda. "Yes, I went. Oh, my wings—they ache when I think of it. How long I flew over peaks poking up at me like daggers, through rain and hail, sleet, snowstorms—"

"All right," said Hashkat. "How long?"

Garuda rolled his eyes. "I can't remember. But, at last, I found the cavern.

"And there was the gem in the midst of a circle of flames. Not for an instant did I hesitate. I plunged through —oh, the pain, the pain!—I could smell my feathers burning, my talons shriveling, but I snatched up the gem in my beak. Hard to believe such a small ruby could be worth so much. For a moment, I wondered if it was the right one. No mistake. As I'd been told, it had a lotus flower carved on it—"

Tamar stiffened. He was about to interrupt, but Mirri put a finger to her lips. Garuda went on:

"I flew from the cavern. The fire had scorched and blackened my golden plumage, my tail feathers were little more than a charred stump. No matter. I had served my king well, proved worthy of his trust, done as he commanded."

Garuda shuddered and bowed his head. "I had nearly reached the palace when another bird flew by—an ill-favored, ungainly creature who had the gall to mock me. 'What's this?' he called. 'A plucked chicken ready for the oven?' He kept up his taunts and jeers until I could stand no more. Goaded by pride and anger, forgetting the prize I carried, I opened my beak to answer insult with insult.

"I dropped the ruby," Garuda said in a choked voice. "It fell into a mountain lake. I swooped down, dove into the icy water, again and again. Soaked and freezing, I searched until I could search no more. I had lost the gem, past finding.

"I was too ashamed to face my master. So I never went back. I hid myself deep in this forest—" Garuda broke off his account and gave way to sighs and moans.

"Poor bird," Mirri said. "No wonder he's in such a state."

"I can help him set things right," Tamar said, while Mirri stroked Garuda's ruffled feathers.

Tamar reached into his jacket. "Garuda, I have something to show you."

"What, something else to aggravate me?" Garuda snapped. "Let me be. I don't want to see it."

"I think you do." Tamar drew out the ruby and held it glittering in his palm. "Do you recognize this? Is it the one you lost?"

Garuda stared at the gem. For a moment, his beak

opened and shut silently; then he burst into furious squawks:

"Shmaa! That's it! How did you get your hands on it? Where? Stolen, I'm sure. You're keeping it for yourself, just to torment me."

"A gift I didn't ask for and didn't want," Tamar said, ignoring Garuda's reproaches. "It has followed a strange path back to you, but here it is. Carry it to your master. Your dharma will be whole again. Take it. That pays my debt to you."

"Oh, no, it doesn't," Garuda retorted.

"Miserable creature!" Hashkat burst out. "It's worth more than some frowsy nest."

"Correct," agreed Rajaswami. "A most generous settlement."

"No." Garuda snapped his beak. "What, in my condition? Look at me! I hardly know what I'm doing from one day to the next. Sometimes I even forget how to flap my wings. Shmaa! I'm not the eagle I used to be."

"For certain," muttered Hashkat.

"I'd lose the jewel again before I was halfway to Mahapura," Garuda rattled on. "Can you see me in those mountains? Me? Alone, friendless, scorned—"

"Mahapura?" Tamar broke in, shaken to hear the name. "Between the mountains Kumeru and Sumeru?"

"Where else would it be?" said Garuda.

"Who is king there?"

"As I said—or did I say?" Garuda replied. "I think of him often. Sometimes I dream about him, and see his kindly, wrinkled old face, his snow-white beard. I wish I could forget; the memory pains me too much. The king? Oh, yes. A great ruler: King Jaya."

Tamar caught his breath. He glanced at Rajaswami.

"That's not the same one I diced with. Yet, one calling himself Jaya commanded me to his palace in Mahapura." He drew closer to Garuda. "What more can you tell me of this king? I journey to see him."

"You can first explain to me what you're talking about," said Mirri. As Tamar began his account, she listened more and more intently. When he finished, she said quietly, "You told me none of this before."

"Who cares what he told or didn't tell? Who cares how or why a bunch of snakes got the ruby?" squawked Garuda. "What about it right now? You carry it for me; you're going to Mahapura anyway. That's the least you can do. You owe me that much, and a lot more besides."

"You'd trust me with it?" said Tamar.

"Of course not," Garuda snapped back. "I'll be keeping an eye on you every step of the way."

"There's a joyful prospect," said Hashkat.

When Tamar agreed to hold the gem in safekeeping, Garuda seemed grudgingly satisfied. Mirri did not. She beckoned for Tamar to follow her a little way across the clearing.

"I don't want His Monkeyship eavesdropping on us," she said, leading him to the side of a huge anthill, its peaks and pinnacles head and shoulders taller than Tamar himself. "You and I have something to settle."

"Yes, we do." Tamar sat down at the foot of the ant castle. "One thing, first: Why did you leave the Choosing?"

"Why did you?"

"It was for the best."

"You could have asked my opinion about that."

"What would you have said?"

"Had you waited," replied Mirri, "you'd have found out."

Tamar shook his head. "I had no right to stay in the village. Do you think I didn't want to? I had no right to ask or offer anything. How could I? My life isn't my own. Do you understand that now?"

"I understand you pledged your life to someone who might not even exist. Yes, I understand that very well, and it makes no sense to me."

"To me, it does," Tamar insisted. "At first I doubted. I thought it could have been a dream. Now, Garuda talks about a realm called Mahapura and a king named Jaya."

"A king nothing like the one who came to you in Sundari."

"That puzzles me," said Tamar. "I don't know what to make of it. I'm still not sure; but sure enough to keep on with my journey. If I'm right—"

"If you're right"—Mirri bit her lips and looked away— "you'll find your death waiting for you at the end of it."

"You forget I'm a warrior. We learn how to die." Tamar took Mirri's face between his hands. "I promised only my life to Jaya. Not my heart."

Before Mirri could answer, Hashkat scuttled up. "You two, come! Better not stay here."

"Let us alone, will you?" Mirri burst out. "Can't you see we're talking?"

"I'll go away." Hashkat shrugged his shoulders. "I don't think *they* will."

The monkey drew Tamar from the wall of the anthill and pointed across the clearing. From the distant fringe of trees, four riders galloped toward them. "Quick! They've seen us, but if we run for those woods—"

"Why should we do that?" asked Tamar.

"They have swords."

"So do I."

"We don't know who they are."

"Then I'll find out. Stay by Rajaswami. Mirri will go with you." Tamar stepped away from the hill and waited for the horsemen to come closer. Though Hashkat had scurried off, the girl was still there. "Go with the monkey. As I said."

"Are you king of Sundari again? A royal command?"

"They're warriors. I know how to deal with them."

"They're men. I know how to deal with them."

By now the horsemen had reined up and dismounted some paces away. One beckoned and called out:

"You, huntsman! Here. Lord Kana wants to see you."

"He sees me." Tamar folded his arms.

The man scowled and muttered something to the tallest of the riders, who was richly dressed in embroidered vest and kilt, a silk scarf draped casually over his shoulders. With long, fair hair held by a gold headband, an arrogant arch to his high-bridged nose, he was, Tamar recognized, not only a warrior but a noble of highest station.

Lord Kana, as Tamar knew he must be, stood for a moment studying him with an air of amused contempt; then, his attendants following, he took a few strides forward.

"Ashwara is in sorry state," remarked Kana, looking Tamar up and down, "if he seeks help from a common huntsman, let alone a *shudra* herd boy.

"What have you to do with him?" Kana's voice hardened. "Are you to meet him here? Is that why you signaled? We saw the smoke, as could anyone for miles around. That was not clever of you."

"We signaled no one," Tamar coldly replied. "I have never heard of this Ashwara, whoever he is or whatever state he may be in."

"He's lying," muttered one of the attendants.

"Perhaps," said Kana. "Perhaps not. These folk are too simpleminded to be good liars. Or, they might be excellent ones."

Tamar's face flushed. "I told you the truth. Now, you tell me who you are. I hear accusation in your words and I have been called a liar, which I do not accept."

"Temper your own words, huntsman." Kana's chin went up. "You speak above your caste. Respect your betters."

"I do," replied Tamar, paying no heed to Mirri nudging him to hold his tongue. "When I meet them."

"We were only burning some vines," Mirri hastily put in, as Kana's face tightened. "We have no idea what you're talking about. We're on our way north, in company with a devout *brahmana*."

Kana, turning closer attention to Mirri, clapped his hands and gave a drawling laugh. "Herd boy? No, by heaven, a *gopi*! Let's have a better look at the creature. If it were properly groomed, and rid of the cow-barn stink, even I would make room for it in my kennel."

"Your kennel is no doubt already crowded," Mirri answered, tightening her grip on Tamar's arm as he angrily tried to lunge forward. "I prefer cows to dog-fanciers, in any case."

"A quick tongue! All the better." Kana hesitated, then sighed and shook his head. "Unfortunately, I have no time for pleasure."

"Your loss," Mirri said. "Not mine."

"I seek a traitor, not a passing amusement." Kana stood for some moments studying Mirri and Tamar, then waved a hand. "These are not Ashwara's people," he told an attendant. "They interest me no longer. Come."

"Hold." Tamar flung free of Mirri's grasp. "We are not finished, you and I."

"Idiot!" Mirri whispered. "What are you doing?"

"What I must."

"Let be, you fool. Walk away."

"I have been thought a liar, accused falsely of what I know nothing." Tamar's hand went to his sword as he faced Kana. "You have spoken ill to a woman. No affront goes unanswered, and so I answer yours now. *Kshatriya,* arm yourself."

"A ferocious fellow, indeed." Kana raised his eyebrows in mock terror. "And a vexing one. Let me teach you better conduct."

Kana suddenly swung up his arm and with the back of his hand struck Tamar full in the face. "There, boy. Study that lesson."

Tamar snatched out his sword, unmindful of the blood streaming from his mouth. "Your men will stand away," he said, between clenched teeth. "You and I only. In single combat. By the warrior's code."

"You challenge me? I accept no challenge from inferiors. I do not fight them." Kana drew his blade. "I slaughter them."

10. Ashwara

Tamar flung Mirri behind him. Kana's men had drawn their blades. Tamar crouched, his glance darting from one warrior to another, his sword point flickering. "Which of you?" he cried. "Come!"

Kana himself was first to spring forward. His sword hissed in a long, slicing stroke. Tamar caught its edge on the hilt of his blade, then threw himself against the *kshatriya,* jolting him back. One of the warriors leaped past Kana to thrust at Tamar's face, while the others attacked his open flank. Tamar spun around, whirling his blade in a flashing circle.

Rajaswami clapped his hands to his head and stammered unheeded protests. Hashkat, meantime, went bounding toward the anthill. Teeth bared, he pummeled one of Kana's retainers about the head and shoulders. The warrior, more astonished than hurt by this onslaught from a monkey nearly as big as himself, swung his blade, missed widely, then kicked out to send Hashkat to the ground.

Garuda, screeching at the top of his voice, flew back and forth, beating his wings and pecking at the assailants. Kana had stepped into the fray again, but Mirri scooped up a handful of loose dirt and gravel and threw it with all her strength into his face.

Darshan had taught him well, but Tamar's opponents

were more seasoned, craftier *kshatriya*s; nor had he reckoned on them breaking the warrior's code by setting upon him all at once. His skill counted little against sheer weight of numbers, and he was growing arm-weary fending off attacks from every side. Against all honor, one of Kana's men launched a blow at Mirri. Raging, forgetting the others, Tamar leaped in front of her and furiously beat the blade aside.

Another of Kana's retainers seized the chance to spring at Tamar, but the man stiffened as though frozen in mid-stroke. Eyes staring, mouth agape, he dropped the blade and plucked at the *chakra,* the sharp-edged iron discus thrown with all force to lodge in his chest.

"Kana! Kana! Face me!" From the edge of the clearing ran the man who had flung this deadly missile. He was tall, big-framed, in deerskin vest and kilt. His tawny hair hung about his shoulders; his golden eyes blazed. Sword raised, he strode past the fallen warrior, making straight for Kana. Leaving Tamar where he stood, the remaining attendants sprang to challenge the stranger. Before Tamar could help him, the newcomer swung a deep-cutting blow at one and, in the same instant, sent the other sprawling.

Kana raced to mount his horse. The attendants, one bleeding heavily, stumbled to their own horses and galloped after him. The stranger made no attempt at pursuit and was about to turn away when Tamar approached him.

"I thank you for your help." Tamar pressed his palms together. "Who are you, to have risked your life for us? I think," he added, "you are called Ashwara."

The man's lion eyes glittered. "Yes."

"Also called a traitor."

Ashwara smiled bitterly. "When a man does a crime

against another, what better than to cry treachery? It is a balm for his conscience."

"Kana accused us of signaling you," Tamar said. "Why? It was not us but you that he was seeking."

"And found me," said Ashwara. "He knows where I am, which is more than he knew yesterday. I regret that. It makes my task more difficult.

"I too saw the smoke and wondered what caused it," Ashwara went on. "You and your friends seemed no threat to me, and I would have gone my way. When Kana and his people set upon you, in all honor I could not have let him kill you. He would have spared none of you, not even the *brahmana.*"

"We are all in your debt," Tamar said. "You did us a service, traitor or not."

"Judge what I am when you know more," Ashwara said.

"I already know you're very quick at killing people," said Mirri.

"Only my enemies," Ashwara replied. "As for that, one duty remains." He glanced at the warrior on the ground. "I took his life. I will not disgrace his death."

The tawny-haired man bent and lifted the figure as if it weighed nothing and carried it beyond the trees. Mirri watched until he disappeared into the overgrowth.

"He frightens me a little," she said in a low voice. "I don't know what to make of him. He kills a man without batting an eye, then he's tenderly concerned for his body. I have a feeling he draws trouble like a honeypot draws flies."

"He's in worse trouble now," Tamar said. "He put himself at risk because of us. If he hadn't stopped to help—"

"And if you hadn't challenged Kana—"

"Be that as it may, my dear *gopi,*" Rajaswami said.

"We must look on the bright side. We are missing no bodily parts or essential organs and have survived undamaged."

"Speak for yourself, you silly *brahmana,*" cackled Garuda. "What about me? Harassed, aggravated, put upon—"

"We're grateful to you," Tamar began. "You did your best for us."

"For you lot?" snapped the bird. "For my ruby! Suppose you'd been chopped to pieces? Where would that leave me? Suppose they'd taken the ruby from your horribly mangled cadaver? A fine fix I'd be in!"

"So would we all." Mirri turned to Tamar. "That's one thing. The other is: We shouldn't have been in a fix to begin with. If only you'd kept your mouth shut—"

"How could I? He offended you, insulted me, struck me. By the warrior's code—"

"Yes, well, my code is: Use common sense. You should have just walked away. Your warrior's honor might have got us all killed. As it is, there's one man dead."

"Two, in fact," put in Ashwara, who had come back to join them. "The second has his death wound. He will not live out the day. It is my fault. I am sorry."

"And should be," said Mirri.

"Sorry I did not slay them all," Ashwara continued, to Mirri's dismay. "Kana dishonored himself when he did not stand against me. I would have pursued him, but I have already been too long delayed. No matter. He counts little, and there will be another time.

"But now let me see closer who has turned me off my path." Ashwara folded his arms and looked around with curiosity. "A bird of some sort—"

"Eagle," said Garuda.

"—and a remarkably large monkey. A charming young

gopi disguised as a herd boy. A huntsman who fights like a warrior—"

"We already know who we are," put in Mirri, "which is more than we can say about you."

"It is no secret." Ashwara pressed his palms together and inclined his head toward Mirri. "I am the king of Rana-pura."

"Amazing!" Hashkat clapped his hands. "Yet another king!"

"Be quiet, Your Royal Monkeyship," Mirri said. "I want to know why this one's hiding in a forest."

"For much of it, I blame myself." Ashwara bent his long legs and set his back against the anthill. "For some time, there had been whispers that my kinsman, Lord Nahusha, was scheming to seize my kingdom for himself. I turned a deaf ear, refusing to believe them.

"Nahusha was of my blood, he had sworn allegiance to me," Ashwara went on. "That he would break dharma, forfeit sacred honor by treachery? Impossible. Yet, as I found out only later, he had promised lands and riches to neighboring princes if they would support his plot; he turned many high officers and ministers against me as well. At the end, he sought to slay my two brothers and myself."

"He dared even that?" Tamar said. "A *kshatriya* and your own kinsman?"

"Even that." Ashwara nodded grimly. "Nahusha, all smiles and loving concern, offered us a pleasure-cottage on his estate. He urged us to take our ease there, hunt in his park, boat on his lake, and enjoy his openhanded hospitality a little while. Unwitting, my brothers and I accepted this poisoned generosity."

Ashwara's golden eyes flashed as he continued. "Nahusha had made the house a firetrap, soaked the roof, walls, and rafters with oil and wax.

"Kana, Nahusha's nephew, willingly agreed to set it ablaze while we slept. A loyal servant warned us in time. The cottage burned to ashes, but we escaped. We went into hiding, knowing that Nahusha would murder us if we were found.

"He crowned himself king of Ranapura and occupied my city with his troops. Since then, he has ruled by terror and torture. Those who so much as murmur protest are imprisoned or slain. Of his own officers, the ones who urged even some small measure of moderation were put to a slow death. I have heard that Nahusha himself watches with pleasure as they die in agony. I have heard, as well, that he seeks to spread his rule beyond Ranapura. No kingdom may call itself truly safe."

"This is evil on top of evil," Tamar said. "No man of honor can allow it."

"Nor will I," Ashwara said. "My brothers and I rallied what troops we could. Also, we journeyed seeking help from other kings. When Nahusha learned of this, he proclaimed me a traitor." Ashwara smiled bitterly. "Having stolen my throne and tried to burn me to death, he accused me of plotting against him."

"A *kshatriya*'s sacred honor?" Mirri said under her breath. "It seems more a matter of convenience."

"Nahusha sent searchers to find and kill us," Ashwara went on. "We have eluded them. Until now. Kana has seen me. He will carry word to Nahusha. Meantime, I have my own task."

Ashwara stood and softly whistled. A black stallion

trotted from the woods and came to nuzzle his master's shoulder.

"I ride to Muktara, a few days north," Ashwara said. "I must treat with King Bala and persuade him to join forces with me. I have already spent too long following roundabout ways to keep Nahusha's warriors off my trail. I can delay no more."

"You hindered yourself by helping us," Tamar said. "No debt may go unpaid. Ask of me what you will."

"Your intention is honorable," Ashwara said, "but how shall a lone huntsman aid my cause?"

"No huntsman!" exclaimed Hashkat. "He's the king of Sundari!"

Ashwara narrowed his eyes at Tamar. "Truth? How can this be?"

Ashwara listened closely while Tamar explained his circumstances. "A strange tale and not a happy one. What to make of it?"

"I'll give you my own opinion," said a muffled voice.

The anthill's high earthen rampart stirred and cracked. From the breach, a pair of sharp, gray eyes peered out; then, a broad face, wide-browed, stubble-bearded, clotted with dirt and sand. The man broke a larger opening, thrust out his head, shook his burly shoulders, and stepped clear of the hill.

11. The Choosing

"O ne moment." The heavyset man scooped up earth and
gravel to patch the broken side of the hill. "There. It's
hardly good manners for a guest to leave someone's home
in ruins. As I was saying—"

"Guest?" Tamar, like the others, had been staring in
astonishment. "You—inside? How? Doing what?"

"A guest of the ants." The big man dusted off his thread-
bare vest and wiped his hands on the grimy cloth wrapped
around his middle. "Doing? Living with them, naturally."

"I wouldn't call it natural," put in Hashkat, as Ashwara,
having drawn his sword, slid it back into its sheath. "Trees
are for monkeys, hills for ants. You're neither. What I want
to know is why you were there in the first place."

"My name is Adi-Kavi," the man replied. "I came to
be there by happy accident. I had sat down, one morning,
to meditate—so deeply that time went by faster than I realized. When I opened my eyes, the ants had built their
castle around me. They invited me to stay, which I did.
Excellent folk, as I've learned to know them. Busy, hard-
working. Very earnest. A little too single-minded, if you ask
me. But, that's their way, and it suits them.

"The commotion outside disturbed my observations,"
Adi-Kavi went on. "I've been listening—eavesdropping,
if you like, which is something I do at every opportunity.

Finally, I had to come out and see for myself. You have to understand: I'm cursed."

"What, something like Hashkat?" said Tamar.

"No," said Adi-Kavi. "Cursed with curiosity. I was born that way. And so, I was irresistibly curious to have a look at all of you.

"Here, of course, is Mirri," continued Adi-Kavi, putting his palms together. "Just as I imagined her. Lovely face, shining eyes: and, plain to see, a *gopi* of great spirit.

"And this must be the young king of Sundari." Adi-Kavi nodded to Tamar. "A strange journey you've set out on, the strangest I've ever heard of. You've started my curiosity itching ferociously. The only way I can scratch it is to find out what happens to you in Mahapura. Allow me to join you."

"I'm turning aside from my journey for a few days," Tamar said. He faced Ashwara. "I may be able to pay a little of my debt to you. I ask to be with you when you meet King Bala.

"Let Bala know that the king of Sundari supports your cause," Tamar urged. "My commander Darshan rules in my stead; but, if I wish him to do so, he will put Sundari's army at your disposal."

"Nobly offered, gladly accepted," Ashwara answered. "Beyond doubt, it would add weight to my words; enough, perhaps, to sway Bala in my favor. If so, the tables turn, and it is I who will be in debt to you."

"My curiosity itches me again," said Adi-Kavi. "Present company excepted, but kings bargaining are like thieves trying to rob each other, and much less straightforward. Still, I can't resist knowing the outcome.

"Young Tamar here puts himself at your service," Adi-

Kavi said to Ashwara. "So do I. From time to time, I've been a *suta*—a royal crier."

"A crier?" Mirri asked Tamar. "What kind of work is that?"

"A palace attendant," Tamar said. "He's paid to declaim a king's merits, his courage, wisdom, generosity—"

"Whether he has those virtues or not," put in Adi-Kavi. "In any case, it's beneath royal dignity for a king to praise himself. So, with a *suta* to put matters in their best light, a lovely *gopi* to lend an air of charm, and a *brahmana* an air of piety, King Ashwara will at least have some sort of retinue. That's always impressive. A solitary beggar may have a grudging coin flung at him. A king with retainers looks strong and prosperous and is showered with favors. Appearance counts. The less you seem to need, the more you get."

"You speak some truth, observer of ants." Ashwara smiled wryly. "I shall decide that later. Meantime, if you wish to ride with the king of Sundari and me, I shall not refuse."

"I lived in Muktara before I was turned into a monkey," said Hashkat. "I know the lay of the land and all the shorter paths. I'll guide you there and keep an eye out for little Akka on the way."

Ashwara agreed that all would go with him, and offered Adi-Kavi the horse of the slain warrior. Hashkat, about to climb up behind Ashwara, saw Garuda already perched on Tamar's saddle.

"What are you doing there?" Hashkat called to him. "You're a bird, aren't you? Why don't you fly?"

"You're a monkey, aren't you?" Garuda retorted. "Why don't you swing from tree to tree? My wings are tired. Shmaa! You expect me to walk?"

Rajaswami, before mounting, plucked Tamar's sleeve. "I must know more about this Adi-Kavi," he whispered. "If, indeed, the ants built their hill around him while he sat meditating—my goodness, do you realize how long that must have taken? And living inside? Without food or air? This is most unusual, the sort of thing you'd only expect from a *rishi,* and a powerful one. But he looks like no *rishi* I've seen."

"Whatever he is," Tamar said, "if he can do Ashwara a service, so much the better."

"Yes, yes, of course," said Rajaswami. "Still, it would be more proper, before we meet King Bala, if he might see fit to launder his clothes."

With Hashkat directing him along one forest track after another, Ashwara pressed on with rarely a halt, despite the groans from Rajaswami. If Mirri suffered fatigue, she gave no sign; but even Tamar, long trained to the saddle, felt his joints and muscles protest the strain. Nevertheless, to lag behind would have disgraced his caste. Ashwara sat easily, head high. The shafts of sunlight through the archway of tangled branches turned his face as golden as his eyes. With his noble bearing and air of kingly command, Ashwara could as well have been leading a proud army of warriors instead of this mismatched handful. Despite Adi-Kavi's assurance, Tamar had to wonder if such a retinue would make any great impression on the king of Muktara. Even so, urging Gayatri to hold pace, he kept that question to himself.

Hashkat, not Ashwara, was the one to cry a halt. The light was rapidly fading, and the monkey declared he could no longer be certain of the pathways. They dismounted in a little grove and tethered the horses near a stream. No longer fearing pursuit, Ashwara himself gathered twigs and lit a small cook fire and shared out provisions from his saddle pack. Garuda swooped down, snapped up the morsels as if they might be snatched from him at any moment, and flapped to roost on a high branch. Ashwara touched nothing until sure the others had their fill; even then, he ate and drank sparingly.

Adi-Kavi, unwilted by the hard ride, waved aside his portion. "I had a good dinner before I joined the ants. No point overloading my stomach."

"Nothing else? In all that time?" Rajaswami, settling closer to Adi-Kavi, eyed him with growing wonder.

"Only to sample a few bits and pieces of what the ants carried in," said Adi-Kavi. "Out of politeness. Not much to my taste, I admit."

"Do you do that often?" Mirri asked.

"Live with ants? No, little *gopi*. Once is enough. One anthill is much like another. But I've swum with any number of fish. Some of my fond friends are crocodiles. I've helped a few birds build their nests, and brooded a clutch of eggs until they hatched. What a mess those broken shells are."

"I thought you were a royal crier," Tamar said.

"Used to be," said Adi-Kavi. "You see, my mother was of high *brahmana* family; my father, a *kshatriya*. I claim neither caste. The *kshatriya*s disapproved, the *brahmana*s likewise, and the other castes wanted no part of me. Astonishing how you can vex so many people all at once by simply being what you are.

"I had a glib tongue. Too glib for my own good, some said. So, what better than hire out as a *suta?* An unwise choice, given the disposition of kings. Ashwara—he's something else again. I know his reputation. I've heard it told he's the best of them, a truly noble *kshatriya,*" Adi-Kavi went on, lowering his voice and glancing in the direction of Ashwara, sitting apart, silent and deep in his own thoughts. "That must make life difficult for him.

"The others—an unpleasant lot, those I've seen. As for you," he added, "you're too young at the trade to be despicable."

Tamar laughed. "You don't mince words."

"No. I respect them—when they tell the truth. Any wonder I did badly as a *suta?* What king pays good money for plain truth? Oh, I've tried my hand at all sorts of work. But when you come down to it, I'm a journeyer. I calculate, if I journey long enough and far enough, I might find out what makes the world go 'round."

"Allow me to inquire," said Rajaswami, "how you came by your highly unusual abilities. You must have been instructed by some great *rishi.*"

"I had a better teacher," said Adi-Kavi. "Curiosity. Amazing what you can learn if you're curious enough."

"If you're neither *brahmana* nor *kshatriya,*" Rajaswami pressed, "what is your dharma?"

Adi-Kavi chuckled. "I suppose my dharma's to see the world as it is."

The *suta* was interrupted by long moans, wails, and gargling noises from Garuda on the branch. Hashkat, who had been listening to Adi-Kavi with interest, shook a fist:

"Can't you be still, you dreadful bird?"

"Shmaa! Shmaa!" retorted Garuda. "I'm singing myself to sleep. It consoles me. Do you mind?"

Hashkat put his hands over his ears. Adi-Kavi fell silent.

Though Rajaswami was eager to pursue further questions, the *suta* fixed his eyes on the fire, his thoughts elsewhere. Tamar was about to speak aside with Mirri when Ashwara beckoned to him.

"I shall stand watch the first half of the night; you, the second," Ashwara ordered, then added, "I am glad for the *suta*'s good opinion." He smiled at Tamar's surprise. "A king overhears much, most of which is usually less than agreeable."

"He wishes you well," Tamar said. "All of us do. You have justice in your cause; and honor, as well."

Ashwara did not immediately reply. When he did, he spoke in a pained voice. Shadows, darker than the night around him, drifted across his face. "This is true, I know it beyond question. For all that, none can tell how matters will turn. Whichever way, one thing is certain: At the end, bloodshed. Death for friend and foe alike. I grieve for all of them, even now."

"I, too," Tamar said. "I have never sought a man's death, and never wished it. My kingdom has always been at peace, no battle ever forced upon me. But you, how can you do otherwise? You are a king and a *kshatriya,* doubly bound by your honor and your dharma. You have no different course."

Ashwara nodded slowly. "I see none. And yet—a throne, a kingdom, what are these worth in blood? Is it honor that demands such a price? Or arrogance? Is it truly dharma that compels me? Or wrath? Can a warrior's virtue lead to evil ends? Have I misunderstood what I thought I knew?"

"Are you saying," Tamar answered, hardly believing Ashwara's words, "that a king such as you has doubts?"

"Have you none? I think you do," Ashwara replied, "but you are young and bear your doubts more lightly. In time, they grow heavier." He stopped abruptly and waved a dismissing hand. "What happens, happens as it must. Go, now. See to the horses, then sleep."

Leaving the king of Ranapura standing silent, Tamar went back to the dying fire. Only Mirri was still awake. She held out her hand and walked with him to the horse lines, where Gayatri whinnied a fond greeting.

"My question still waits for an answer," Tamar said. "Why did you leave the Choosing?"

"Need you ask?" Mirri turned her face toward his. "I listened to my heart. And yours. Why should I have stayed? There was no reason to, since I'd already chosen."

From the pile of gear and harness, she opened her pack and took out a garland of white blossoms. "Do you remember little Vati's song when you and I first met? *A wreath of flowers is the token of a pledge that's never broken.* I give you mine."

As Mirri was about to put the garland around his neck, Tamar raised a hand. He could barely speak above a whisper:

"No. Go back to your village. This is a pledge that can't be kept. My journey lies between us. Would you have me give it up? Bring you to Sundari? A king shamed by breaking his dharma? Or stay with your people, knowing I'd lost all honor?

"If I could be sure my dream was nothing more than that, I'd do it gladly. I still question it. Even Ashwara questions what he must do, but will do it nevertheless. So will I."

Mirri drew away. "And so, king of Sundari, you tell me to leave you?"

"Yes. Live out your life happily, not with one who has no life to give you. Follow your own dharma."

"My dharma tells me it's better to look for a way to live instead of a way to die. It also tells me to stay with the one I love."

She threw aside the garland, turned on her heel, and strode back to the others. Tamar stood a long time by the horse lines. When at last he went to her, she was asleep, her head resting in the crook of her arm. He touched his lips to her hair, with its fragrance of clove and cinnamon. Mirri stirred but did not wake. In the forest, the only sound was Garuda's moaning.

PART 11

IN THE FOREST

12. Bala's Durbar

Next morning, Mirri announced her decision. Once they had done what they could to help Ashwara, she would ride with Tamar to Mahapura. "And that," she declared, "settles that." With only a token show of reluctance, Tamar agreed. He was, in fact, overjoyed. Rajaswami was not.

"I'm sorry, I can't approve." The *acharya* shook his head. "Expose this young lady to who-knows-what perils? No, no, no, it's simply not the correct way of things."

"*Acharya,*" replied Tamar, "do you mean to forbid—"

"I didn't say that," Rajaswami corrected. "I said I can't approve. You and your *gopi* must do as you see fit. Though I firmly disagree—dear boy, I haven't the heart to separate you two. Did you think I would?"

"I didn't." Mirri smiled at him. "You needn't worry about me."

"But I will, even so," said Rajaswami.

The *acharya,* in any case, had other difficulties to occupy him: particularly, his bald spot. In the course of the following days, as Hashkat led the retinue closer to Muktara, the forest thinned; dusty, open stretches gave little shade. Rajaswami's scalp turned bright pink, then deep red, and finally blistered. Though he draped his scarf over his smarting pate, he found no relief.

"I wouldn't want your brain to roast," said Adi-Kavi, giving him a good-natured slap on the back. "I'll take care of this."

The *suta* disappeared into the scrub, returning with handfuls of what seemed to be prickly blades of grass. With strong fingers, he squeezed out the juice and dripped it on Rajaswami's head.

Mirri came closer to watch the procedure. "I've never seen a plant like that."

"There are plants and herbs even you country folk don't know about," said Adi-Kavi. "They can do astonishing things you couldn't begin to imagine. If you're curious, I'll tell you about them. Too bad the *brahmana* didn't think cooling thoughts, to begin with. He'd have spared himself blistering."

"Thoughts can cool?" Mirri said.

"In a certain way," Adi-Kavi said. "Do it right, you can turn yourself cold or hot, forget you're hungry or tired— and a lot more besides. There's a special way, a sort of knack. My guess is," he added, with an appraising look, "you might already have the knack without knowing it. We'll find out, when things are more settled."

"This is quite remarkable," said Rajaswami, fingering his bald spot. "The sting's gone. I'm entirely comfortable."

Garuda did not fare as well. In addition to his usual daily lamentations and nightly singing, he endlessly complained of being jolted, knocked about, given indigestible food and not enough of it in the first place.

"I have a nervous stomach," he whined, as they camped for the night. "I'm not used to being flung gobs of who-knows-what. It brings on colic and makes my pinfeathers twitch."

"By the time we reach Mahapura," Tamar assured him, "you'll be better than ever."

"I should wait so long? Shmaa! There'll be nothing left of me."

"There's too much of him already," said Hashkat, as Garuda flapped to a branch. "He's putting it on; he's a malingering sack of feathers."

"I'm not so sure." Mirri glanced up. In the fading light, Garuda had tucked his head under a hunched wing. "He isn't singing himself to sleep."

"A small mercy," said Hashkat.

Next morning, Garuda was lying on the ground, head drooping, eyes half closed. When Mirri went to him, the bird gave only a feeble squawk.

"If he were a cow," Mirri said, as Tamar and the others joined her, "I'd know what to do."

"Not as bad as it looks." Adi-Kavi carefully probed the bird's midsection and blew gently into Garuda's open beak. "He'll come around. Mash his food with a little water and make a paste of it. A pinch of gravel wouldn't hurt, either."

"Oh, no," Garuda croaked, as Tamar began following the *suta*'s advice. "How do I know you aren't trying to poison me? That would suit all of you. No more Garuda. Keep the ruby for yourselves."

"Let me deal with him," said Hashkat. "I'll make sure he gets what he needs. Count on it."

"No," snapped Garuda. "I want the *gopi* to feed me."

"You scalded chicken," Hashkat retorted, "you're lucky anybody feeds you at all."

Garuda clamped his beak shut and would let no one but

Mirri spoon the mixture down his gullet. By the time the girl finished, the bird was making happy rattling and purring noises, and casting adoring glances at her.

Though Ashwara was impatient to set off, Garuda flatly declared that he could neither fly nor cling to Tamar's saddle.

"Stuff him in one of the bags," Hashkat suggested. "Then we won't have to listen to his yammering."

Mirri found a better answer. Borrowing Rajaswami's scarf, she knotted it and hung it over her neck, with Garuda slung inside. As they set off, the bird poked out his head, looking around with smug satisfaction. After another day, when he had recovered, he flapped to the girl's shoulder and had little to do with anyone else.

Late that afternoon, when they came in sight of the city, Ashwara ordered a halt, deciding it best to seek an audience with King Bala next morning.

"I've been thinking about that," said Hashkat. "If I'm to go with you, I can't go as I am. A naked monkey doesn't set the right tone. For that matter, we could all spruce up."

"You have a point," said Adi-Kavi. "Appearance, that's what counts. Ashwara and young Tamar here have weapons enough to look like they mean business, not to be trifled with. The rest of us? Nothing to be done, I'm afraid."

"I'll see about that." Hashkat pursed his lips and made hooting and barking noises.

For some while, Tamar had been aware of small shapes scuttling along amid the foliage. Now, at Hashkat's signal, half a dozen monkeys clambered from the trees to crouch a little distance away.

"Some of your subjects, Your Monkeyship?" said Mirri. "Invite them over. I'd like to meet them."

"They don't much care to associate with humans," said

Hashkat. "All things considered, that's understandable. I'll go have a few words with them. They can help. I have something in mind. Stay right here till I get back."

The monkey king went to join his subjects. Moments later, they all faded silently into the undergrowth. Garuda raised his head as they disappeared.

"It's good-bye, monkey. That's the last we'll see of him," Garuda croaked. "Once he's off cavorting with his cronies, do you imagine he'll give a thought to any troubles of mine?"

Recalling that Hashkat had run off once before, Tamar waited with a touch of uneasiness; and, as the night wore on, standing watch to relieve Ashwara, he wondered if Garuda could be right. By the first streaks of dawn, however, Hashkat reappeared. The smaller monkeys stayed in the shadows as he triumphantly threw down the bundle on his shoulder.

"Here, *suta,* a nice mantle for you. Once you're washed and scrubbed, you'll look quite impressive." Hashkat held up a length of embroidered drapery and tossed it to Adi-Kavi. "A new sari, all fine silk, for the *gopi.* A few little things for me." He produced a warrior's studded vest and leather kilt, a somewhat rusty sword, and a crested iron helmet. "And for the *brahmana*—" Hashkat proudly unfurled a large white umbrella.

"A most useful assortment," said Rajaswami, as Mirri went to change her cowherd's garb for the sari. "Especially the umbrella. My rank entitles me to carry it, and it will certainly keep my head from blistering again." He hesitated, and his happy expression turned to one of concern. "But— how did you come by them? Not, I trust, by dishonest means."

"That depends on how you look at it," said Hashkat. "The way I look at it, since they weren't nailed down—"

"You purloined them?" Rajaswami dropped the umbrella he had been admiring as if it were about to bite him. "Good heavens, you should know I can't accept stolen property. It goes against all standards of correct behavior."

"Not so fast, to talk about purloining," said Hashkat. "For one thing, the sword and armor belong to me. I buried them in my garden the day I quit the warrior business. I sneaked back there; the monkeys helped me dig them up.

"As for the clothes and umbrella," Hashkat added, "they were provided by a rich goldsmith and his wife living in my old house. I gather the two of them moved in and took it for themselves, with never a coin in payment. I consider it a matter of collecting a little overdue rent. Since they were both asleep, it was a painless transaction."

"Ah, yes, in that case there may be a measure of justice in what you did," said Rajaswami. "I'm sure if they'd been awake they'd have been happy to settle accounts. And I assume these items weren't actually nailed down. In those circumstances, yes, it might be permissible—"

"*Brahmana,*" said Hashkat, "are you starting to think like a monkey?"

"Goodness me, I certainly hope not," said Rajaswami. "It is quite a handsome umbrella. I wouldn't want to offend you by refusing it."

◆◆◆

By daybreak, they were ready to enter Muktara. Garuda railed bitterly at being left behind to wait. Only Mirri's promise to come back without delay pacified the bird. "You'll stay on your branch," Mirri said, scratching his neck.

"You'll be a good bird, behave yourself, and act like a brave eagle." Garuda muttered a few "Waas" and "Shmaas," but finally nodded his head.

They soon came to a well-paved road along the river-bank. Suddenly, Rajaswami urged Jagati to a gallop.

"Quickly, my boy! Let us get past this dreadful place," Rajaswami called out, as Tamar rode abreast of him and asked what had alarmed him.

"It's a *shmashana.*" Rajaswami shuddered and pointed toward a stretch of barren ground by the river. Here and there rose wisps of smoke. Tamar glimpsed a few half-naked figures carrying what seemed bundles of rags.

"Don't look," Rajaswami whispered. "It's the public burning ground. They're cremating paupers' bodies."

Tamar shivered in spite of himself, but could not turn his eyes away. "I've never seen the one in Sundari."

"Of course you haven't. Nor should you see one now. Did you suppose I'd ever take you to visit such a hellish spot? Good heavens, have you forgotten what I taught you? Those men doing the burning—they're *chandala*s. It's work forbidden to higher castes. Who'd want to do it in the first place? The *chandala*s are already the lowest of the low, so it makes no difference to them.

"As I warned you long ago, I remind you now," Rajaswami added. "Don't go near them. If a *chandala*'s shadow falls on your food—dear boy, you must throw it away, it's polluted instantly. Should a *chandala* touch you, even accidentally lay so much as a finger on you, your caste is broken. Worse yet, you become a *chandala* yourself, and better off dead."

Still trembling, Rajaswami turned his umbrella to screen the sight of the burning ground and galloped ahead, never

slowing until the *shmashana* lay far behind and they were
inside Muktara.

—◆—

The little procession wended its way through the bustling
streets. Adi-Kavi, dismounted, strode ahead, shouting for the
passersby to make room. Hashkat marched beside him, clad
in his old fighting gear. The monkey had coiled his tail
under the leather kilt and set his helmet, with its jutting
visor, low on his head, shadowing most of his face. Tamar
and Ashwara rode side by side. After them, wrapped in her
silken sari, Mirri held her head as proudly as a maharani.
Rajaswami, mostly recovered from the shock of seeing the
burning ground, brought up the rear, carrying his white umbrella with befitting dignity.

Though Tamar had hoped this escort would make an
impressive showing, it was Ashwara's regal bearing that
opened the gates. For all Adi-Kavi's declaiming and Hashkat's bold posture, Ashwara's air of authority, despite his
rough garments, was enough to make the palace guards step
back and bow him into the courtyard. Servants hurried to
care for the horses; officers were summoned to lead him and
his retinue to the audience hall.

At the far end of the cool, high-ceilinged room, King
Bala was already holding his morning durbar. Courtiers and
attendants drew aside as Ashwara and Tamar approached the
powerfully built figure clad richly in robes of state. Gold
bracelets circled his muscular arms; at his side, a jeweled
sword. The warriors who stood close by the throne were
grim-faced *kshatriya*s, glittering in polished helmets and gem-
studded breastplates. Bala leaned forward to observe his
visitors; his pale eyes seemed to weigh and calculate. The

king of Muktara, Tamar understood, was a man to be reckoned with—a man much aware that he was to be reckoned
with.

Adi-Kavi had only begun his praises of Ashwara and
Tamar when Bala waved him to silence, and motioned for
the *suta* to stand away.

"*Namaste,* Lion-Eyed Ashwara." Bala stood and pressed
his palms together. "I am not surprised to see you, only
surprised that you did not come sooner."

"So I would have done, Majesty," replied Ashwara, "but
certain small inconveniences hindered me. Time presses
now, and I must speak straight out, to make clear to you—"

"There is no need." Bala settled back on his throne. "I
know why you are here. I have followed all the happenings
in Ranapura with concern. It grieves me deeply to learn
what befell you and your brothers."

"Then we understand each other," said Ashwara.
"Good. I count on your troops to help me defeat Nahusha.
Your forces are strong, well equipped. When they join those
of other kings who have pledged support—"

"Do you say 'when'?" Bala interrupted. "I say 'if.' Our
kingdoms have always been linked in friendship. For you
yourself, I have the highest personal regard and affection. I
must, however, put aside my private feelings. You ask much
of me. As king of Muktara, it is my duty to ask no less of
you. What do you offer me in exchange?"

"Majesty," Tamar broke in, "you know Nahusha has
done great evil. It is your duty to side against him. You have
the opportunity to serve justice, for the sake of your honor
as a king and a *kshatriya*. What more could you ask?"

"I hear the voice of noble innocence." Bala smiled sadly.
"Yes, King of Sundari, there is merit in allegiance to a wor-

thy cause. There is also a hard question—as you may un-
derstand when you have ruled as long as I. Justice? Honor?
Admirable virtues, of course. What are they worth in blood?
A wise king does not spend lives for nothing.

"Why, then, should I?" Bala faced Ashwara. "I have no
quarrel with you, nor with your kinsman. What difference
to me who sits on the throne at Ranapura? A kingdom is a
kingdom, whoever rules it."

With that, Bala signaled an attendant to open the door
of an alcove behind the throne. A man royally garbed strode
out and halted in front of Ashwara.

"You come later than I foresaw," said Nahusha.

13. Nahusha

You look well, cousin." Nahusha stood as tall as Ashwara; his smooth-shaven face was pale, the skin stretched tight over sharp cheekbones, his lips thin and bloodless. "The life of an outlaw skulking in the forest appears to suit you."

Ashwara's chin went up, but he did not deign to answer. Tamar, not only shocked to find Nahusha at the durbar, was taken aback, as well, to realize that this noble *kshatriya*, so splendidly robed and elegantly groomed, had sought to murder his own kinsmen and tortured to death countless others.

"It is always a pleasure to greet you," Nahusha went on. "I would not have deprived myself of this satisfaction. I was already on my way to Muktara when Kana found me. I gather you killed two of my people," he continued, as if commenting on the weather; then said, with a cold smile, "I shall have blood in exchange for that."

"Your warriors attacked us for no reason!" Tamar burst out. "They dishonored me and my companions. Ashwara was within his rights to defend us."

"Is this the king of Sundari? A realm so great, its name has never reached my ears?" replied Nahusha. "Nothing here concerns you, boy. Hold your tongue or I shall have Kana bloody your nose again."

"Do you need a servant's hand? Why not try your

own?" Tamar reached for his sword, but Mirri pulled back his arm.

Nahusha waved his long white fingers as if brushing away a gnat, and turned his eyes again on Ashwara. "And now you come like a beggar to Muktara," he said. "Where is your little wooden bowl? King Bala, in his generosity, may fling you a handful of rice and send you on your way."

"That is for him to decide," answered Ashwara. "Do you speak of begging? Why else are you here?"

"I do not beg, I negotiate," said Nahusha. "There lies the difference. His Majesty and I speak as king to king. You speak as nothing.

"These are your followers?" Nahusha let an amused glance drift over Tamar and the others. "One warrior—the ugliest, most ill-favored *kshatriya* I have ever seen. A hired crier in a red curtain. A stripling with the arrogance to call himself a king. A spindle-shanked *brahmana* with an umbrella—indeed, a terrifying weapon. Oh, cousin, it grieves me to see you fallen so low."

"I really must protest in the most vigorous terms," declared Rajaswami:

> *Respect is a brahmana's due.*
> *His wisdom merits reverence, too.*

"It would be wisdom to take yourself off to a quiet *ashrama,* and far safer than consorting with my enemies. Grow vegetables, old fool," said Nahusha, "and share your sermonizing with them."

"This fellow's very good." Adi-Kavi chuckled under his breath. "He manages to exasperate people with no effort at all. A real aristocrat."

"In one thing, Kana misled me," Nahusha continued, "and I shall take him to task for it." He inclined his head toward Mirri. "He spoke of a beautiful *gopi*. He told less than the truth."

"Lord Kana offered me room in his kennel," Mirri said. "He was too generous. Those accommodations would be more worthy of his king."

"And for you, gracious *gopi*, only the palace of a maharani would be worthy. Kana was correct when he said you had a quick tongue. And, no doubt, a temper to match. I should hope so. It pleases me to tame wild creatures. Breaking them to my will presents an exhilarating challenge; in the case of a *gopi*, a delightful one."

Mirri said nothing, but her tightening grip on Tamar's arm made him wince. Ready to fling fighting words at Nahusha, this time he forced himself to swallow them.

"This is unseemly of you, Lord Nahusha." King Bala held up a reproving hand. "Your opinions of a *gopi* are no subject for expression in my durbar. We have a grave question to settle.

"I welcomed Ashwara as I welcomed you, for I hope to find some way of reconciling you. Whatever has happened in the past, there are ties of blood between you."

"Strong ties," said Nahusha, "of bad blood."

"Still no reason to spill it needlessly," said Bala. "I ask each of you: What are you willing to do to end this quarrel?"

"I have no desire to shed blood or spend lives," Ashwara began. "That is a cruel choice; I would turn from it if I could."

"Say, rather," put in Nahusha, "that you have no stomach for it."

"True, I have neither stomach nor taste for it," replied Ashwara. "I take no pleasure in killing. It is an evil karma and puts both our souls in peril. I have thought deeply, and here is my offer.

"At first, I sought revenge," Ashwara went on, "but this was blind rage; the wrath of a man, not a king. It is against dharma. A king protects and cherishes his people. He does not lead them to destruction.

"I give up my desire for revenge. I purge my heart of it. As for you: You sit on the throne by treachery and murder, not by rightful claim. What I say to you is this: I give up my desire for revenge, but I still seek justice. So shall you, in justice, give up a throne that was never yours."

"Possession is its own justice," Nahusha said. "That you lost your throne is excellent proof you were not worthy to keep it."

"I mean to have it back," said Ashwara. "Ranapura must be free of you. But this I pledge: Leave peacefully, and I will do no harm to you or any of your followers. Depart from Ranapura. Go where you please in safety, under my protection. I will not raise a hand against you.

"Such is my offer. Refuse it and I make another pledge: I will fight you to the death. Now the choice is no longer mine, but yours."

"Your generosity overwhelms me, cousin," replied Nahusha. "A beggar promises to spare my life? A truly noble gesture. I can offer nothing to match it. Nevertheless, I make one suggestion."

Nahusha turned to Bala. "I came seeking your alliance —on terms, I must add, highly advantageous and profitable to you. Those benefits remain the same. They will be yours if you agree to my small proposal. First, I ask no support from your troops."

Bala frowned. "I do not understand. You wish nothing from me?"

"I do not wish danger for my warriors or yours," Nahusha said. "A battle, even against a beggar, has its confusions, its mishaps. Why risk lives? I request only one: Ashwara. His brothers do not trouble me; they are nothing without him.

"Ashwara is here at your mercy," Nahusha continued. "So, simple. Kill him. Oh—kill the others, too. They displease me. Except the *gopi*. I shall take her to Ranapura and allow her to enjoy my favors."

"How dare you!" Bala stiffened on his throne. "How dare you ask me to break the law of hospitality? Under my roof, under my protection? No. I will not commit such an abomination."

"Ashwara's life is mine, one way or another," said Nahusha. "I intended only to save a little time and inconvenience. Well, so be it. I shall deal with him myself.

"You, cousin," added Nahusha, "are more a laughing-stock than a threat. Do you care to see my opinion of you?"

Nahusha clapped his hands. From the alcove, a servant came to give Nahusha a long chain. At the end of it, attached by a leather collar, was a monkey.

The small creature had been decked out in mockery of a king's regalia: a silk robe, belted around the waist; at his side, a wooden sword; and, on his head, a gilt paper crown.

Hashkat clenched his fists. "Nahusha's got him," he muttered between his teeth. "It's little Akka."

"I have named him 'King Ashwara,' " Nahusha said, as

the courtiers burst into laughter. "See how he struts and capers, and rattles his little sword. All in vain. I do with him as I please. Here, you jabbering beast." Nahusha gave a sharp tug at the chain. "Down. Lick my boots."

Little Akka shrieked and tried to pull away. Glimpsing Hashkat, he flung himself around and clawed at his collar. Nahusha stepped closer to the frantic animal.

"Watch, cousin, how I discipline your namesake," Nahusha said. "With you, I shall be more severe."

Nahusha raised a hand and struck the monkey across the face. Little Akka screamed and went skidding over the flagstones.

Nahusha tossed the chain to his servant. "Take the vicious brute away. Whip him diligently until he learns who is master."

Growling, teeth bared, Hashkat snatched out his sword. Tamar seized his arm, while Mirri and Adi-Kavi shouldered the struggling monkey king aside.

Murmurs of shock rose from the courtiers, for Ashwara and Nahusha had likewise drawn their blades. Eyes locked, they crouched in fighting posture. Bala sprang to his feet.

"Sheathe your swords!" The king of Muktara's command rang with anger and indignation. "There are no weapons drawn in durbar. Shame! Shame on each of you. You disgrace yourselves and dishonor me, as well."

It was all Tamar could do to force Hashkat to put away the rusty blade; and, even then, he tried to break free of Mirri and the *suta*. "Stop it, you fool," Tamar hissed in his ear. "We can't do anything right now."

"I have seen and heard enough," declared Bala, holding his voice in tight rein. "I will abide no more outbursts and reproaches. I have come to my decision."

14. Bala's Decision

ear me well." Bala's stern glance went from Ashwara to Nahusha. "Enemies you may be; kinsmen, even so. You share blood and lineage. Therefore, the quarrel is within your family. It is improper for one outside that family to interfere in its disputes. Set your own house in order. I give my support to neither of you."

Ashwara bowed his tawny head. "If that is your thoughtful decision, so be it."

"A thoughtful decision indeed, but a costly one," said Nahusha. "I must, of course, withdraw those benefits I discussed with you. Apart from that, is it a wise decision? When families throw stones at one another, an onlooker may get his own head broken. However, you have chosen to make no choice." Nahusha shrugged. "I abide by it."

"Go from here, Ashwara. I urge you to go quickly," said Bala. "Nahusha, I remind you: My hospitality reaches beyond these palace walls. As long as he is within my borders, Ashwara remains under my protection. Make no attempt to harm or hinder him."

"Would I disrespect your royal will?" replied Nahusha. "I only hope my noble cousin and I soon meet on other grounds.

"I cherish the same hope for this ravishing *gopi*." Nahusha's eyes rested on Mirri. "May the path of her karma and mine one day cross."

"That," said Mirri, "would be a day you'd never forget."

"And you," Nahusha added to Tamar, "trot back to your vast kingdom. The world is a dangerous place for a mighty monarch like you. As you shall find out if ever you come within sword's length of me. Bark all you please, puppy. I bite."

Tamar's face burned. It took all his strength to choke back the challenge he would have flung at Nahusha. He was trembling with fury. Ashwara motioned for him and the others to follow as he strode from the hall. The crowd parted to make way. Hashkat, still agitated, kept looking back. Akka had not reappeared.

Only in the courtyard, waiting for their horses to be brought, and beyond earshot of unwanted listeners, did Tamar speak.

"We failed you," he said bitterly to Ashwara. "Our help meant nothing. How was I fool enough to think otherwise? Impressive escort? A pitiful band."

"Our *gopi* made an impression," put in Adi-Kavi. "You have to admit that much."

"So did you," Mirri said to Tamar. "The dangerous kind. You don't need an enemy like Nahusha. But—I'm proud of you. It must have rattled your warrior's code, but at least you had sense enough to keep your mouth shut. Most of the time.

"Besides," she went on, turning to Ashwara, "I don't think it was all that much of a failure. Something good came of it. Am I right?"

"You are," said Ashwara. "Yes, I was disappointed when

Bala refused me. But he also refused Nahusha. Had Bala sided with him, it would have tipped the balance against me. With the king of Muktara standing apart, I am well satisfied.

"Keep on your journey and take my friendship with you," Ashwara said to Tamar. "Should need arise, I shall find you. However," he added, "be cautious. Ranapura is well to the north of here, where the Snow Mountains begin to rise. That is the direction you should take, but it will bring you into lands that Nahusha controls. Avoid them. Turn east before you come to Ranapura's borders. They straddle the Sabla River, so you must cross and make a long circle back to the mountains. I dare not try to guide you, much as I wish to do."

"You have your own task," Tamar said. "Bala warned you to go quickly. You are under his protection here, but I think he knows Nahusha will not honor it."

Hashkat, during this, had been impatiently nudging Tamar, reminding him Akka was still a prisoner. "I have to get him free, the sooner the better. The way that villain treats him, he won't last long."

"What help can I give?" said Ashwara.

"None that I can ask," said Hashkat. "You need to look out for yourself. You can't risk tangling with Nahusha. Akka's one of my Bandar-loka. He's my responsibility; it's up to me to answer for his safety."

"O king of monkeys," said Ashwara, smiling and touching his palms together, "you are less a monkey and more a king than I supposed. *Namaste.* I revere the spirit in you.

"I can help by telling you this much," Ashwara went on. "Nahusha has surely traveled with a grand escort: chariots, horses, perhaps elephants. So, they must follow the only good road along the Sabla. Whatever plan you shape, set it

in motion there. And soon, before he passes into his own
territory."

Servants now came, leading their horses. Ashwara turned
to Tamar. "King of Sundari, what can I wish for you? That
you go well and swiftly to Mahapura, knowing what awaits
you? If I read your heart aright, there is some nobility in it.
Whether you dreamed or not: Whatever the outcome, may
it be to your honor.

"And this *gopi?*" Ashwara looked fondly at Mirri. "What
shall I wish for you? That is not for me to say, since you
may be wiser than any of us. Trust what your heart and
your dharma bid you. To you both: *Namaste.*"

Ashwara embraced all, including Rajaswami, who reminded him to keep looking on the bright side. No sooner
had he galloped from the courtyard than Hashkat rounded
ferociously on the grooms.

"Where's my horse?" he shouted, shaking his fist. "Idiots, why haven't you brought it? How dare you keep a
kshatriya waiting! What are you up to? Are you trying to
switch mounts and fob off some other? What crooked
scheme are you hatching? I'll have all your heads for that."

The confused and terrified grooms, pleading innocence,
offered to go immediately and find the missing animal.
Hashkat pushed them aside.

"Out of my way, fools! I don't trust you to recognize
my steed or even lay a finger on it. I'll go myself."

The trembling grooms, only too happy to escape with
their lives, scurried away. Hashkat stamped arrogantly into
the stables, while Mirri and Tamar exchanged puzzled
glances. He was back within moments, leading a prancing
bay mare.

"I needed a horse of my own," explained Hashkat. "So many to choose from, I picked the one who insisted on following me—after I untied her."

Rajaswami sighed. "Since she insisted, I suppose you couldn't have done otherwise. Even so, there are times when I fear for the state of your dharma."

"I fear for the state of my rear end," said Hashkat. "I didn't take time to borrow a saddle."

◆━◆

Galloping from the city, they left the road for the cover of the forest, where Mirri was impatient to change her sari for her cowherd's garments. She had scarcely done so when, shedding clouds of feathers, Garuda swooped down to land with a thud on the turf.

"What, you?" Mirri shook a finger at the bird. "I told you to stay and wait."

"You didn't say how long," whined Garuda. "Shmaa! I should sit in a tree forever? You told me to behave like a brave eagle. I did. I thought you might be in trouble and I'd better look for you. Just to make sure you didn't all decide to go off and leave me."

"We have trouble enough," Tamar said. "Be quiet. If you can. Akka's been caught. We're going to free him." He beckoned to Hashkat and Adi-Kavi. "Ashwara warned us to act quickly. We'll do it as soon as we see Nahusha's escort turn onto the road.

"Hashkat and I have swords," he went on. "*Suta,* can you draw a bow?"

"As well as any, better than some," said Adi-Kavi. "If you're thinking of my fighting anybody—no. By rule, it's strictly forbidden to *suta*s, as it is to *brahmana*s. Were I allowed to put an arrow into someone, it would be Nahusha. But I can't. I'm sorry."

"I understand. I respect your rule," Tamar said. "I'll make do. So, counting two warriors—"

"Which all adds up to one warrior and a monkey," Mirri put in. "You'll attack Nahusha's whole train? I can tell you how far you'll get."

"Do you think I'm that foolish? We'll attack them piecemeal, strike quickly, fall back, strike again. If I must, I'll challenge Nahusha to single combat. He knows I'm a king, so he can't refuse. That's the code."

"I'm sure he'll observe it," Mirri tartly replied.

"Be careful. They're here," interrupted Hashkat, who had been peering through the foliage at the roadside. Tamar hurried to see for himself. Ashwara had been right. The retinue was splendid: half a dozen horse-drawn chariots, each holding a driver and an armored warrior, Nahusha himself in the lead with his banner-bearer; an elephant, covered with embroidered draperies, its mahout perched on its back, carrying a sharp, hooked goad; the pack animals bringing up the rear.

"Let them go by," Mirri said. "Give them a good long head start. We'll have more time to work out something. They'll have to camp at nightfall. By then, we'll know better what we're dealing with."

"By then, we can do nothing," Tamar said impatiently. "The rules of war forbid a night battle. An unbreakable law—"

"Who said 'battle'?" Mirri countered. "We're not battling. We're quietly rescuing one of His Monkeyship's subjects."

"Quietly?" Tamar said. "That's more like 'cowardly.' "

"All the better," said Hashkat. "Not a *kshatriya*'s way, but it suits a monkey. The *gopi*'s right. Sneaky and stealthy."

"Akka's one of your folk. You decide," Tamar said. "First, we have to find out where he is. How?"

"Easily," Mirri said. She turned to Garuda, hunched on the ground beside her. "Fly over Nahusha's escort. They won't pay attention to a bird. You'll see what they've done with Akka and come right back."

"Me do what?" Garuda burst out. "Waa! My nerves won't stand it. I don't have the wings—look, I'm shedding, I'm molting."

"You're an eagle." Mirri smoothed his feathers. "I know you can do it."

"Can't. Won't." Garuda made gargling noises and snapped his beak shut. After a moment, he turned a red-rimmed eye on Mirri and bobbed his head. "All right. But you'll owe me for this, all of you. Shmaa! You'll owe me plenty."

———◆———

The sky was barely lightening when they left their horses by the roadside, with Rajaswami on watch. Much of the night they had waited, sleeping fitfully. Garuda, for all his wails of complaint, had done better than promised. Akka, the bird reported, was with the baggage and pack animals, cramped in a light wicker cage; Garuda had also been able to tell where the chariots had been drawn up, where the horses had been tethered, and how the tents had been arranged.

"What a fine eagle," Mirri had told him, while Garuda preened himself and clucked proudly, all the while turning adoring glances toward the girl. "You knew you could do it."

Now, as they approached the encampment on foot, stepping carefully through the dry weeds, Tamar admitted to himself that Mirri's cautious plan had been best. The warriors' tents had been pitched near the riverbank, with Nahusha's high silken pavilion in their midst. Nahusha, confident, had not troubled to post sentries. The cooks, first to rise, had not yet wakened; the night fires had burned to ashes.

Tamar stationed Adi-Kavi a little way behind them while he and Hashkat moved soundlessly toward the wagons. Mirri followed, keeping an eye on the tents and the servants stretched asleep on the ground, ready to give warning at any sign of Nahusha's people stirring.

Tamar put one hand on Hashkat's arm and, with the other, pointed to a wagon. On top of a pile of bundles sat the cage. Hashkat grinned and bobbed his head; then, as Tamar stood alert, scuttled to the wagon and swung over the side. The small figure curled within the cage whimpered. Hashkat made soft, chirping noises of reassurance. The dawn sky was brightening with bands of pink and gold. Tamar gestured for him to make haste. Hashkat picked up the cage and started to clamber down.

They had not reckoned with the elephant. Sensing strangers, the big animal flapped her ears, raised her trunk, and trumpeted in alarm.

Tamar snatched out his sword. Clutching the cage, Hashkat raced past him. The elephant, meantime, had uprooted the stake that secured her leg rope, and charged blindly through the camp, trampling whatever stood in her way. Bewildered warriors stumbled and scattered out of her path.

Mirri headed for the road, pulling Tamar along with her. Adi-Kavi urgently beckoned for them to follow him. Rajaswami frantically waved his umbrella.

Hashkat, with his burden, had nearly reached the waiting horses. Leaping over a hillock, he misstepped, his foot caught in a tangle of weeds. The monkey king tumbled head over heels and sprawled on the ground. The cage went spinning from his hand.

15. Little Akka

Little Akka squealed and flung his arms around his head as the cage rolled beyond Hashkat's grasp, bouncing down the slope back toward the wagons.

Tamar sprang past Hashkat, lurching to his feet, and ran to seize the wicker cage. He halted. Some of the warriors, blades drawn, were rapidly bearing down on him. Mirri turned back to join him, Adi-Kavi close behind.

That same instant, squawking and beating his wings, down swooped Garuda, feathers flying, beady eyes alight. The bird locked his talons around the bars and soared skyward, bearing the cage and its screeching contents high into the clouds and out of sight.

"He'll find us." Tamar jumped astride Gayatri. Mirri, already mounted, plunged into the forest. Hashkat and Adi-Kavi followed, with Rajaswami, brandishing his umbrella, galloping after them.

When at last they halted, well away from Nahusha's camp, Hashkat flung off his warrior's gear and clambered into the treetops. Rajaswami collapsed on the ground, murmuring "Oh, my goodness! Oh, my goodness!" while Tamar ran to the edge of the clearing, listening for any sounds of pursuit.

"Nahusha has enough to keep him busy," Adi-Kavi said. "He won't worry about a monkey."

"But I will," said Hashkat, who had climbed down without catching a glimpse of Garuda. "Akka's worse off than ever. Poor little fellow, he's in the clutches of a lunatic bird, and who knows what that maniac mophead's likely to do? Drop him in the river? That's how he lost the ruby."

While Mirri tried to calm the agitated monkey, Tamar began to calculate how long they dared to wait. He was about to raise that question when Adi-Kavi, peering upward, called out and waved his arms.

Moments later, Garuda plummeted into the clearing, letting go of the cage as he flopped heavily on his belly and skidded to a stop.

"There's my brave eagle!" Mirri cried, as Hashkat ran to break open the locked door. Adi-Kavi and Tamar hurried to help him snap the wicker bars.

Garuda, ignoring even Mirri, had begun a pigeon-toed sort of triumphal dance, treading around and around in a circle, beating his wings, fanning out his ragged tail feathers, gargling, chuckling, practically crowing like a rooster.

"I'm the one who got him!" Garuda warbled. "All you incompetent dimwits fumbling about! Shmaa! What a pack of idiots! And who saved him? Oh, no, don't bother to take time to thank me. But I'll tell you this: You owe me more than ever—all of you—especially that grinning, gibbering baboon."

"We do owe you," Mirri said, while Garuda kept on with his prancing. "That was a great deed."

"Yes," declared Garuda, sniffing haughtily, "it certainly was."

Hashkat, meantime, had reached inside the cage to lift out Akka and hold the young monkey in his arms. Akka's mouth opened and shut wordlessly. He no longer wore the

mock-royal costume; the weals and bruises from the whipping Nahusha had ordered showed on his hunched back and
spindly legs; and his curling tail, nearly as long as himself,
had lost patches of hair.

"Terrible, terrible!" clucked Rajaswami, coming to peer
anxiously at the rescued prisoner. "Poor chap! Locked up,
tormented—and, on top of it all, swept into the sky."

"That was the best part; it made up for everything else,"
Akka chattered, regaining breath and voice. "I want to do
that again! Where's the bird? Next time, I'll go higher."

"My goodness, I hope not," said Rajaswami. "Let me
remind you—and this applies to small monkeys as well as
large persons:

> *A piece of advice that is always sound:*
> *If you have no wings, keep near the ground.*

"You just be glad you're in one piece," Hashkat said
with some severity, now assured that Akka was largely undamaged. "I've been looking all over for you. What happened? How did you get in such a mess?"

"I didn't do anything," protested Akka, unwinding
himself from Hashkat's embrace and hopping to the ground.
"Well, all I did was—I only slipped into a village one night,
to have a look 'round. And here's a pile of nuts at one of
the doorsills. They might as well have been begging me,
'Please take us, don't let us sit here all by ourselves.' So, I
grabbed as many as I could."

"Naturally," said Hashkat, "as any right-thinking monkey would have done."

"But then, as soon I did, a noose goes tight around my wrist. A trap!"

"Tricky! Sneaky!" Hashkat burst out. "Present company excepted, but that's humans for you. You never know what crookery they're up to."

"That's been more or less my own observation," Adi-Kavi said. "Even so, young fellow, a clever little monkey like you should easily have got out of a trap."

"I didn't have a chance," Akka said. "Those villagers were quicker than I thought. They tied me up in a sack, enough to stifle me. They kept me awhile; then a trader came passing through and they sold me to him.

"Next thing I know," Akka went on, "I'm in Nahusha's palace. He bought me, you see, for his amusement. I wasn't the only one caged up. He's got a whole collection—birds, beasts—even a tiger."

"That's what he meant," said Mirri, "when he talked about taming wild creatures."

"How he tames them—you don't want to know." Akka shuddered. "They don't last long. He's always in the market for new ones. From what the parrots told me, he doesn't treat his people any better. They hate him, but there's not much they can do. They say Ashwara's coming back some-day to save them. Nahusha laughs at that; it doesn't bother him."

"Why so?" Tamar asked. "Does he have that strong an army? How many warriors? War chariots?"

Akka shrugged. "I don't know. He kept me in the pal-ace; I never saw any of that. One thing: He's got a plan of some sort. I overheard him talking with his officers."

"No details? Anything that might help Ashwara?"

"I only know what the parrots told me."

"It seems to me," said Mirri, "Nahusha doesn't have all that many troops. Why would he want help from Bala? He's up to something, and it sounds like trouble for Ashwara."

"I'm afraid you're right, and nothing we can do about it." Tamar turned to Hashkat. "And you? Now that you've found Akka?"

"By and large, I'd just as soon stay clear of humans. We should say farewell and I'll go back to my Bandar-loka—" Hashkat's brow puckered. He chewed at his lips a moment, then quickly went on. "No. It's not in my heart to leave you or even the *gopi,* though she did crown me with a bucket."

Hashkat put his palms together. "Let me go with you. I owe you my life; I haven't forgotten. Besides, you never know when a monkey might be useful."

"Ashwara said you were more a king than he supposed," Tamar answered. "I'd say: Better than a king, a friend. Yes, be at my side when my journey ends."

"I'll be there, as well," Adi-Kavi said. "As I told you, I'm curious to know what happens to you in Mahapura. You may turn out to be a fool, a dreamer, or both. In any case, I've taken a liking to you."

"Be welcome, then—" Tamar broke off and motioned all to keep silent. Beyond the edge of the clearing, faint sounds grew louder. He glanced at Mirri. "Nahusha's warriors?"

The horses had begun whinnying and stamping. Raja-swami defensively gripped his umbrella. Akka had already scrambled up a tree, with Garuda flapping after.

The vines and overgrowth ripped apart. Still dragging the stake roped to her leg, the elephant burst into the clear-

ing. Seeing Tamar draw his sword, she trumpeted a shrill
scream. Eyes rolling, ears standing out from the gray dome
of her head, she lunged with speed surprising for her bulk.
The blade spun from Tamar's hand as she lashed her trunk
around his waist and swung him into the air.

16. Elephant Hunters

 amar twisted back and forth, struggling to get free
of the trunk coiled around him. Mirri started forward. Adi-Kavi stepped ahead of her, arms outstretched.
Seeing what she took to be a new attacker, the elephant
flung Tamar to the ground and, bellowing, swung her head
toward the *suta* and made ready to charge.

Before she could launch herself against him, Adi-Kavi
strode deliberately to the distraught animal. Tamar shouted
a warning. Paying no heed, the *suta* laid his hands on the
creature's trunk, all the while murmuring sounds that Tamar
could not understand. The elephant reared up on her massive legs. Tamar ran to pick up his blade.

"Stay away!" the *suta* called over his shoulder. "Don't
come near her. Drop the sword."

The tone of command in Adi-Kavi's voice made Tamar,
still alarmed, do instantly as the *suta* ordered. The elephant
hesitated, as if uncertain whether or not to resume her
charge. Adi-Kavi fixed his eyes on her and seemed to hold
her with his gaze. The big animal drew back, panting and
snuffling. As Tamar watched in astonishment, she gradually
sank to her hindquarters. Adi-Kavi continued his murmuring. At last, the elephant lowered her head. The *suta* nodded
and turned away.

"She's terrified," Adi-Kavi said. "Let her rest. She's more afraid of us than we of her."

"I'm sure she is," Mirri said, going to the elephant's side and gently stroking her trunk. "Poor thing, we don't mean to harm you."

The elephant heaved a huge sigh and fanned herself with her ears. "I'm sorry," she said. "Whatever came over me— forgive me; it's never happened before."

"You can speak?" Tamar stared at her.

"Not usually," said the elephant. "Never, in fact, since I've been in captivity. If Nahusha knew I could talk, who knows what more he'd make me do."

"He won't do anything to you now," Mirri said.

"I hope not." The elephant snuffled. "My name is Arvati," she added. "Nahusha brought me with him so I could show off the tricks I'd learned."

"We're not fond of Nahusha," Mirri said. "I hope you trampled him a little before you ran off."

"Oh, no, I'd never do anything like that," Arvati replied. "I've been well trained. As for running off, I don't know what possessed me. I suppose I lost my head for a moment. It just seemed to happen. I didn't mean to." Arvati's whole bulk shuddered. "They'll punish me, of course, once they get me back."

"Get you back?" Mirri exclaimed. "How? You're a grown elephant; you're more than a match for them. You've made a good start. Keep going. Find your herd."

"If only I could." Arvati sighed. "This forest has been my ancestors' home since the Golden Age. Naturally, I inherited their power to speak—if I choose to.

"I've always dreamed of being with my herd again," she

went on. "But it's too late. I don't know how to make my way in the wilds anymore. I'm sure to be recaptured."

"Yes, if you sit and wait," Tamar said. "Do as Mirri tells you."

"No," said Arvati. "Now I've calmed down and can think more clearly, I'll go back on my own. That way, they'll see I was simply confused and they won't punish me too badly."

"Don't count on it," said Mirri. "You're better off in the forest. Here's your chance to be free of them."

"You don't understand. I'm afraid to do anything else. Nahusha's hunters captured me when I was a calf. I had a gentle nature; so, instead of training me to be a war elephant, they taught me to do tricks. I'm used to that now."

"You see what they've done," Mirri said to Tamar. "She's been so beaten and cowed, she hardly knows anything else."

"Nahusha won't get his hands on her again," Tamar said. "We can't leave her. We'll keep her with us until she can look after herself. But Nahusha won't let her get away that easily. My guess is he's already sent his people to track her down."

"Then," said Mirri, "we can't stand around waiting for them."

"That's just what we're going to do," Tamar said. "We have to deal with them. If we don't, they'll stay on her trail—which means they'll be on our trail as well."

"Right," said Hashkat, judging Arvati safe enough to approach. "She'll leave a path even a blind man could follow."

"Take her deeper into the forest," Tamar told Mirri. "I'll wait behind with Hashkat. We'll take the hunters by surprise, and that's the end of them."

"The warrior's way again," said Mirri.

"The only way I know. But—yes, I should have listened to you before. I'd be glad to listen to you now, if you have a better plan."

"Let me suggest what should settle the matter," put in Adi-Kavi. "I, for one, would relish it—it's the sort of thing that suits me more than bloodshed."

"Nor am I eager for bloodshed," Tamar said after the *suta* explained his scheme. "But—can you make the trackers believe you?"

Adi-Kavi chuckled. "Don't forget I was a royal crier. If I can make a dimwitted lummox think himself a wise and noble king, I don't see any difficulty."

Following the *suta*'s instructions, they tethered the horses out of sight and led Arvati into the screen of underbrush a little way down the forest track. In a small clearing, they set about their other preparations while Adi-Kavi turned back and, staying within eyeshot of them, hunkered down on the ground.

From his perch in the fork of a tree, Tamar watched uneasily as the hunting party made its way through the bushes: the elephant master himself, carrying a long pole with a sharp iron point and hook at the end; three of his fellows bearing coils of rope; a packhorse laden with a net, shackles, and chains.

At sight of them, Adi-Kavi leaped up and ran toward the elephant master, wringing his hands and begging for help.

"Be off, whoever you are." The elephant master roughly pushed Adi-Kavi aside. "We've no help to give, you scruffy lout. There's serious work at hand. Our king's elephant ran away. She's not long gone; her tracks are fresh."

That moment, at a signal from Tamar, Arvati trumpeted loudly enough to rattle the leaves.

"Out of my way," ordered the elephant master. "She's here under our noses."

"Wait! Wait!" cried Adi-Kavi. "Stay back. It's worth your life. She's dangerous."

"She won't be, not when she has a look at this." The elephant master grinned and held up the pole. "She knows what it means. A little taste of the hook, she'll be gentle as a lamb."

With Adi-Kavi tugging at their garments and stammering out warnings, the hunters pressed on to the clearing. The elephant master stopped short:

"What the devil is this?"

At the farther edge of the clearing—one end of the rope tied to the wooden stake set in the ground, the other knotted around his ankle—stood Hashkat.

17. The Rakshasa

Hashkat's face and body were striped with yellow clay. His hair bushed out to make him look nearly twice his size. Leaves and vines twined around his head and waist. He slapped his chest, shrieked, hooted, and flung himself about at the end of the rope.

"Devil, indeed," wailed Adi-Kavi. "A *rakshasa!* A demon! Keep away. That fiend can tear you apart," he warned, as Hashkat dropped to all fours, gnashing his teeth while he bounced up and down, sticking out his tongue and wagging it horribly.

"I confess," blurted Adi-Kavi, as the elephant master gaped. "I found your elephant wandering in the forest. I meant to steal her. I knew she'd be worth a fortune.

"No sooner do I tie her down than she turns into a *rakshasa.* I was lucky to get away with my life."

"You're out of your wits." The elephant master nevertheless drew back uneasily. "Arvati changed into a demon? What lunacy are you telling me?"

"I've heard tales like that." One of the trackers exchanged frightened glances with his fellows. "No question, it happens."

"It's this forest," Adi-Kavi whispered fearfully. "It's always been full of demons. One of them pounced out and

took possession of her. Well, you deal with her. I'm not
risking life and limb. I won't even ask a reward for finding
her.

"Best do your work quickly," he urged. "The longer
that demon stays there, the bigger it'll grow. Then you'll
have no chance at all."

"You seem to know a lot about demons," the elephant
master began.

"More than I like. I've seen a few in my day and lived
to regret it. At least I lived—which is better than some can
say."

"What do you think?" the elephant master said, with
mounting discomfort. "Will she ever change back again?"

"Oh, yes. Once you've got that demon tied hand and
foot. If it sees it can't move, it'll be gone in a flash—poof!
—and there's your elephant again."

"Here's your dear little Arvati," Hashkat called out in a
hoarse growl. He rolled his eyes and snapped his teeth.
"Come closer. I missed breakfast; I've been hungry all morning." He beckoned to the elephant master. "You first, Sala."

"She speaks?" gasped the elephant master. "Before, she
never said a word."

"She wasn't a *rakshasa* then." Adi-Kavi turned to leave.
"Well, good-bye, all. I wish you the best of luck. By that,
I mean I hope you won't be too badly chewed up."

"Hold on." Sala seized Adi-Kavi by the tail of his vest.
"You're not going anywhere. You know the ways of these
demons. You give us a hand."

"Oh, no, I'm too fond of being alive," Adi-Kavi protested. "Ah—if you insist," he added, as the elephant master
shook the goad at him. "All right, unload the packhorse.

Get those shackles ready. Is that a net I see? Excellent. We'll use it for a start."

The trackers, by this time, were trembling so violently they could hardly follow the *suta*'s directions. When at last they unrolled the net, Adi-Kavi nodded approval.

"Stay close together, shoulder to shoulder," he ordered. "Hold up that net as high as you can. Wait, I'll take one end. Easy, now. No sudden moves. Walk toward her. Get ready to throw it."

As the trackers approached, Hashkat strained menacingly at his tether. They shrank back, but Adi-Kavi urged them on.

"Never fear, you'll soon have your elephant again. Oh —one thing I forgot to mention. Don't look. Turn your heads away. Keep watching and that demon could change you all into *rakshasa*s. Better yet, close your eyes. I'll tell you the moment to open them."

The trackers, ever more frightened, squeezed their eyes shut. Adi-Kavi guided them toward Hashkat; but, as they stumbled closer, the *suta* led them past him to the edge of the clearing. Hashkat, at the same time, untied himself, pulled up the stake, and sprang silently behind them, taking hold of one end of the net. Glancing at him, Adi-Kavi nodded and suddenly shouted:

"Help! Help! The *rakshasa*'s loose!"

Tamar and Mirri, meanwhile, sped to help Adi-Kavi and Hashkat. By the time the trackers realized they were being set upon—not by demons, but by human beings and an oversized monkey—it was too late; the net was wrapped around them. Tamar ran to fetch the chains and bound Arvati's pursuers all the more securely. The packhorse had already bolted in alarm. Rajaswami trotted from his hiding place to lend a hand hauling Sala and his fellows into the brush.

Certain that Arvati's would-be captors were well tangled in their own chains and net, Tamar signaled Mirri and the others to retrieve the horses. Arvati, with Akka crouched on her head and Garuda on her haunches, plunged through the forest. The trackers' cries of rage had long since faded in the distance when Arvati's rescuers halted.

Tears of joy rolled from the elephant's eyes. "Am I really free? No more hooks and goads? It feels so strange; I don't quite know what to do."

"You'll stay with us as long as you want," Tamar said. "Hashkat, you made a fine demon. You almost frightened me. And you, *suta,* I'm ready to believe you can convince anybody of anything."

"I'm the one who scared the wits out of them," crowed Hashkat. "They won't come after us now. If they get loose, what will they do? Slink back to Nahusha? They lost his elephant; he'll have their heads for it. If they're wise, they'll quietly make themselves scarce."

"No bloodshed, in any case," Tamar said to Mirri, as Hashkat went to scrub off the streaks of clay.

"I found it entirely satisfactory," said Rajaswami. "Indeed, rather stimulating. Goodness me, I was tempted to give those ruffians a good whacking with my umbrella."

"Is this my old *acharya* speaking?" Tamar grinned at him. "Talking about whacking people?"

"An impulse is one thing; doing it is something else," Rajaswami said. "Fortunately, I resisted.

"Sooner or later, someone's bound to find them," he assured Tamar. "They may be uncomfortable for a time; but, looking on the bright side, it will be beneficial and instructive for them to reflect, while they're waiting:

> *Let patience ever be your goal.*
> *It helps to fortify the soul.*

———◆———

So as to stay well away from Nahusha and his warriors, Tamar had chosen to avoid the river road and keep to the forest, in spite of the heavy undergrowth and dense woodlands. He could not have asked for better help from Arvati.

Lumbering ahead, the elephant was able to clear a good path, trampling down thick brush and flinging aside dead branches. For all her bulk and strength, she was a gentle, sweet-natured creature. She willingly let Akka perch on her brow, where he chattered with delight at this new means of transportation. When Rajaswami grew saddle-weary, he ventured to ride on her back, holding his umbrella over his head and beaming happily. Arvati's kindly disposition even had a calming effect on Garuda, who moaned and wailed somewhat less than usual.

"I never reckoned on an elephant for a traveling companion," Tamar said with a bemused laugh, when they halted at nightfall. "Even so, I'm glad we have one." Mirri had come to sit close beside him, while Hashkat and Akka curled by the small fire and Rajaswami nodded drowsily.

The big *suta* stretched out his legs and clasped his hands behind his head. "A good deed, King of Sundari, which gains merit for all of you."

"Merit gained by accident?" Tamar said. "We hadn't planned on rescuing an elephant."

"Does it matter?" Adi-Kavi shrugged his burly shoulders.

"Merit is merit, however it's gained. Intention? That's one thing. What you end up doing? That's another. As happened with the thief and the spider. Let me tell you:

"Late one night, a thief crept into a wealthy merchant's house. Oh—first, you should know he was a young thief, without experience. He had fallen on lean times and decided that burglary was a more straightforward career than law or politics, and an occupation immediately at hand. In fact, this was his first professional appearance.

"And so he had planned everything carefully. He closely observed the merchant's house and the merchant's habits: what time he went to bed; which doors or windows would be most easily opened. Once inside the house, while the merchant was safely snoring away, the thief calculated he could search the place at his leisure and find where the valuables were hidden.

"All went marvelously well at first. He found, as he expected, an unlatched window and wriggled easily and silently through it into the merchant's storeroom. From the bedchamber, he could hear the merchant snorting and snuffling happily in dreamland. But, groping his way through the dark room, he stubbed his bare toe against a table leg.

"Choking back a yelp of pain, terrified of waking the merchant, he smacked himself on the forehead and cursed himself for a fool. He was, as I told you, a mere beginner; and, for all his planning, he had neglected to bring a light.

"In the dimness, however, he was able to make out an oil lamp on the table. He fumbled in his garments, pulled out flint and steel, and struck a spark. The wick flared brightly, and he gave a sigh of relief. As he picked up the lamp, a small spider scuttled out from under its base.

" 'Thank you for saving my life,' said the spider. 'Before

he went to bed, the merchant set this lamp down on top of me so I couldn't escape. If you hadn't come along, I wouldn't have lasted the night; indeed, I'd have perished miserably, far from my web and my brood of little ones.

" 'You have saved a life and shown compassion,' the spider went on, although the impatient thief protested he had no such intention. 'Better yet, you have done so without the least thought or hope of reward. You have gained more merit than you could possibly imagine.'

" 'But you're only a spider,' said the thief.

" 'And you're only a man,' said the spider. 'My dear thief, when you understand that life is life, whether on eight legs or two, you will have understood much. Your deed, in any case, has cleansed all evil from your heart. Go from here with a fresh spirit. And good luck to you.'

"The thief did so," Adi-Kavi concluded, "and never thought to steal again. There, King of Sundari, you have a case of doing good accidentally, even though the intention was evil to begin with. In short, you never know how things may turn out.

"The tale is true, by the way," the *suta* added. "You see, I was that thief."

"You've clearly mended your ways, which is most commendable and meritorious," said Rajaswami. "Nevertheless, let me remind you:

> *Wrong is wrong, right is right,*
> *Clear as the difference between day and night.*

"Between day and night, yes, clear enough," put in Mirri. "But, O wise *brahmana,* what if it's twilight?"

— ◆ —

Adi-Kavi's tale and Mirri's comment lingered in Tamar's mind and niggled at him for the next several days, until finally, while the others pressed on, Tamar hung back a little and beckoned for Mirri to stay with him.

"Something troubles me," he began, as they dismounted and walked their horses. "If an evil intention can turn to good, can a good intention turn to evil?"

"I'm sure it happens all the time," said Mirri.

"And can doing right lead to something wrong?" Tamar went on. "I did right, leaving Sundari. I had given my word—"

"Or so you imagined," Mirri said. "You still don't know for sure if it was only a dream."

Tamar nodded. "That makes it all the worse. If it was only a dream—I've done a terrible wrong in following it. Darshan warned me of that, but I paid no mind. I've abandoned my people for the sake of it. Who knows what that may lead to? I've put Rajaswami's life in danger, more than he ever bargained for. And you. I even tried to send you away."

"You didn't succeed," replied Mirri, with a loving smile. "Of course, I had something to say about that."

"But suppose the dream was real?" Tamar turned his gaze to the iron ring on his finger. "It's not clear to me anymore. The twilight, you said. In between right and wrong. Is everything twilight? What if Jaya cheated when we played at dice? Does my word still bind me? And Jaya himself? Garuda loves him; he'd have given his life for him. That's not the same king of Mahapura who came to me. He was brutal, heartless. Could he have tricked me with some kind of illusion? Or is everything illusion?"

"I'm not. As you'll find out—" Mirri broke off as Adi-Kavi cantered up.

"We're moving well ahead," the *suta* called out. "Arvati's cleared a new path. We can cover a good bit of ground before sunset."

"Yes, of course," Tamar said absently, remounting Gayatri. "Even so, no need to hurry."

Arvati, indeed, had trampled a good path; nearly half the day still lay ahead. Tamar nevertheless ordered a halt for the night. Hashkat gave a curious glance, but did not question him. Tamar stayed apart for the rest of the afternoon.

Next day, Rajaswami vanished.

18. Soma-Nandi

Tamar, throughout that morning, had set a leisurely pace, ordering all to walk their horses even when the forest was clear enough to let them ride swiftly. He had not shaken off an uncomfortable reluctance to reach Mahapura; a reluctance that slowed his stride and dragged at his feet. Nahusha, by now, would be well ahead. Tamar calculated no risk of running afoul of him and his warriors; so, by rights, he should have turned and followed the quicker way along the riverside. Instead, he kept to the slower paths of the forest. Caught up in his own confused thoughts, he did not notice that Rajaswami had lagged behind. Suddenly, he heard the *acharya* cry out.

Rajaswami had vanished from sight but not from sound. The old teacher, invisible, was yelling at the top of his voice. His white umbrella lay on the ground. Jagati was tossing her head and fearfully whinnying. Tamar ran to the spot, Mirri, Hashkat, and Adi-Kavi at his heels. Akka streaked ahead, chattering and beckoning. Tamar dropped to his knees at the edge of a deep pit. Below, out of reach, the *brahmana* was clinging by his finger ends to the rough earthen wall.

At the bottom of the pit crouched a huge she-tiger. Growling, teeth bared, the great striped animal leaped up, clawing at Rajaswami's feet dangling just beyond her clutches.

At sight of Tamar, Rajaswami left off his shouting. "I'm perfectly fine—as long as she can't get at me. Now, if you'd oblige me by hauling me out."

"Tiger trap," muttered Adi-Kavi. "Leave it to the *brahmana* to fall into it."

"Quite unintentionally, I assure you," said Rajaswami. "I was contemplating a difficult philosophical proposition; next thing I knew, there I was with a tiger nipping at me. The bright side is, I nearly had it solved. The question was—"

"Never mind what the question was," Hashkat burst out. "Stay quiet or you'll fall down and end up a tiger's breakfast. Then where's your philosophical proposition?"

Tamar, meantime, had thrown himself flat on the ground at the rim of the pit and was trying to stretch his arms far enough to reach the *acharya.*

Arvati had lumbered up, with Garuda fluttering beside her. "Here, allow me," the elephant said, seeing Tamar vainly trying to get hold of Rajaswami's hands.

With that, Arvati lowered her trunk, wrapped it around the *acharya,* and lifted him out in an effortless instant. From the bottom of the pit, the tiger glowered up with feverish yellow eyes.

"Help me," said the tiger, in a broken voice. "Hunters set this trap for me. They will return when they know I shall be too weak from hunger and thirst to defend myself. Help me out. Let me go my way. I promise no harm will come to any of you."

"She's hardly more than skin and bones already," Mirri said to Tamar. "She's starving to death. We can't leave her there."

"You promised not to harm us," Tamar said, while the

tiger sank back on her haunches and watched him intently. "How do I know you'll keep your word?"

"You do not know. Nor can you know until you find out for yourself."

"Then so I must," replied Tamar. "Leaving any creature to suffer would be against dharma." He glanced at Mirri, who nodded agreement, as did Adi-Kavi.

"That's correct, my boy," said Rajaswami. "You can't do otherwise—except hope for the best."

"Yes," put in Hashkat, "and we'll be ready to run for our lives."

Tamar, at first, had thought to have Arvati lower her trunk and lift out the tiger as she had done with Rajaswami. Willing though she was, the elephant could not stretch far enough; nor could the tiger spring up to grasp the trunk with her paws.

Finally, Tamar ordered the *suta* to fetch a rope from the saddle packs. With Arvati holding one end, Tamar threw the other into the trap and started to climb down.

"No, no!" Garuda wailed. "You'll be torn to bits, eaten alive, your bones crunched up. Waa! Horrible! Don't go. Send the monkey."

Tamar, meantime, had slid down the rope. The bottom of the pit was narrower than the top, and he found himself barely an arm's length from the crouching animal; close enough to see that the tiger's eyes were sunken in their sockets, her striped coat matted and spiky. Her parched tongue lolled from between her fangs as she swung her head toward him. He drew back and flattened himself against the wall of the trap.

"My name is Soma-Nandi," said the tiger. "*Namaste,*

King of Sundari. Yes, I know of you. Word has been spread by the Naga-loka, the Bandar-loka, by watchers and listeners in the forest.

"It is told that you journey to the mountains of the north, seeking your death," Soma-Nandi went on. "Do you fear that you have already found it in this pit with me?"

"You made a promise," replied Tamar. "I wish to believe you will keep it."

"Why should I? Why should any forest-dweller keep faith with your human kind?" said Soma-Nandi. "Come closer. Look into my eyes."

Tamar could not turn away as Soma-Nandi's eyes widened until they seemed to fill the pit. His mouth went dry, as the tiger's must have been, and he could barely swallow. His lips felt cracked and swollen; pangs of starvation stabbed at him as if he himself had been trapped for endless days.

"Tell me what you see," said Soma-Nandi.

Tamar peered deeper. "I see horsemen riding to the hunt. Trackers and fowlers. I see myself fleeing from them." As he watched, his heart pounded to bursting with terror. The death-cries of all forest creatures burst from his throat, as they fell pierced by arrows or struggled in nets and snares.

"This is *maya;* this is illusion," Tamar murmured.

"No," said Soma-Nandi. "It is truth. My world's truth. I wished to show you, for a moment, lives different from your own. You have seen into me, and I have seen into you. Your heart is good, King of Sundari. Remember what you have been shown.

"Now loop the rope around me," the tiger said. "My word is my law. I will not harm you."

Still trembling, Tamar fashioned a harness for Soma-

Nandi, then called to Arvati, who easily hoisted up the tiger and Tamar along with her.

One glimpse of the tiger's head rising above the edge of the pit sent Garuda squawking into the high branches. Hashkat and Akka kept a wary distance. Soma-Nandi, however, rested calmly on her haunches while Tamar undid the harness and Mirri hurried to set food and water in front of her.

"You have my gratitude and the protection of all the Tiger Clan," Soma-Nandi said, after eating and drinking her fill. "You did more than save my life."

"That's for certain, old girl." Hashkat, reassured by her words, made bold to swagger up and cock an eye at her. "I've seen stray cats in happier shape. The king of Sundari kept you from being a rug on somebody's floor."

"He did far better," said Soma-Nandi. "We can be worth more alive than dead. Had the trappers taken me, they might well have broken my teeth, torn out my claws, and sold me for the amusement of some king or other. I fear this may have happened to my mate. He has disappeared and I have been seeking him."

"Seek on! Seek on!" Garuda called from his branch. "Don't delay another moment. Monkeys! Elephants! Now this! Shmaa! My nerves won't stand it."

"She'll stay until she has her strength back," Mirri said. She put a comforting arm around the tiger's neck. "Akka was lost, then found. You might find your mate again."

"So I must always hope," said Soma-Nandi.

Tamar, meantime, went to speak with Rajaswami and Adi-Kavi, telling them of the illusion that had come over him in the pit. "How could this have happened? How could she have worked *maya* on me?"

"Ah, that I can't say," replied the *suta,* while Rajaswami, admittedly puzzled, shook his head. "*Maya* or whatever, you seem to have understood something you never much thought about before. I'll put it this way: I had my spider; you had your tiger."

19. The Hermit

He had never imagined an elephant could be light-hearted, let alone light-footed. Yet, in the days that followed, Tamar noticed how Arvati's eyes had brightened since her rescue from the trackers. Even when trampling a path, she seemed to dance more than plod. From time to time, she would flap her ears, lift up her trunk, and trumpet exuberantly.

"No more hooks, no more chains," said Mirri, who had also observed Arvati's high spirits. "I think she finally got used to the idea that she's free of Nahusha for good and all."

As Tamar learned, however, Arvati had an added reason. The heavy undergrowth and oppressive shadows of the forest had given way to sunny stretches of rolling grassland. Early one morning, as Tamar saddled Gayatri, Arvati lumbered up to him.

"I've suspected it for a little while," she said. "Now I'm sure. What I'd always dreamed—" Arvati snuffled through her trunk. "I can smell it. I can feel it. My herd isn't far from here."

"That's wonderful." Mirri laid a hand on Arvati's flank. "We'll miss you, but I know how much you want to join them."

"I can't." Arvati sadly shook her head. "For one thing,

I'm in your debt. You gave me my freedom. I have yet to repay you."

"You owe us nothing," Tamar said. "Your freedom belongs to you. We only returned what was yours to begin with."

"There's another thing." Arvati heaved an enormous sigh. "You see, I'm—I'm afraid to go. I haven't the courage—I've been so long in captivity, I don't know how to manage on my own. To make my way alone? No. I'd be too frightened."

"Allow me to help." Soma-Nandi had padded up to listen. "I, too, owe a debt to the king of Sundari. But, with his permission, I shall stay with you until you are safe among your folk. You have nothing to fear, not while there is a tiger at your side to protect you."

"Go together, both of you," said Tamar. "It saddens me to part from you, but you have your own paths to follow."

"So I must," Arvati said at last, with tears brimming in her eyes. She gently touched the tip of her trunk to Tamar's forehead, to Mirri's and the others, even giving Garuda a fond tap on his beak. "*Namaste,* befriender of elephants. We have long memories, and you shall always be in mine."

"*Namaste,* befriender of tigers," said Soma-Nandi, stretching her forelegs and lowering her head in a graceful bow. "Speak my name to any of the Tiger Clan you should encounter. They will do as well for you as you did for me."

"Find your mate soon." Mirri put her arms around the tiger's neck and pressed her lips to Soma-Nandi's brow. "That's our best wish for you."

As Tamar urged them to start without delay, Arvati and Soma-Nandi set off across the meadow, heading for the distant woodlands. They went slowly at first, pausing for many

backward glances. Their pace quickened after a time, until
the elephant was galloping at top speed, the tiger bounding
along beside her. At the line of trees, they halted a moment
while Arvati raised her trunk in farewell, then vanished into
the woods.

◆

Akka, ranging ahead of the others, had been the first to find
it, and ran back chattering of his discovery, beckoning the
journeyers to the rocky ridge. Below, nestling amid green-
gold foliage, the *ashrama* was a rambling sort of cottage. Its
flat roof of woven vines had been chinked with earth; wild-
flowers bloomed in the crevices. A wide veranda ran along
the front; at the rear, a vegetable garden, with melons rip-
ening between the cultivated rows; a little orchard just beyond. Nearby, a wide stream flowed around islands of tall
ferns and outcroppings of boulders. Tamar looked down on
the hermitage with a measure of wistfulness, uncertain if
they should intrude on its occupant. For Rajaswami, there
was no question. He was in rapture.

"My boy, you can't imagine how I've longed to find
such a resting place. I've been hoping ever since we left
Sundari." The *acharya*'s hands so trembled with joyous excitement he could scarcely hold his umbrella. "The resident
sage will be delighted to welcome us. What a comfort it will
be! Quickly, my boy. Goodness me, I can hardly wait."

"At this point," remarked Mirri, "I think I could stand
a little comfort. I won't object to eating at a table and sleeping on a bed."

"Oh, dear girl, I meant far more comfort than that," said
Rajaswami, his face alight. "I'm eager for the opportunity
to share philosophical speculations and stimulating discus-

sions with the sage, no doubt a wise and learned *rishi* who has spent years in thought and study."

"I'd be interested in meeting the old fellow," said Adi-Kavi. "A matter of simple curiosity. As for comfort, once you've lived in an anthill, you can be comfortable anywhere."

Rajaswami was bouncing up and down like an impatient child. Tamar smiled and nodded, and they picked their way down the slope to the dooryard of hard-packed, neatly swept clay. Garuda flapped to the roof while Hashkat and the *suta* led the horses to water at the stream.

Rajaswami clambered onto the veranda and poked his head through the open door. "I had hoped for someone to greet us. If not the sage himself, perhaps one of his students. No matter, we shall wait quietly and respectfully for him.

"On the other hand," he went on, "we should make our presence known." He stepped across the threshold. Mirri and Tamar followed him into a pleasant, airy room, sparsely furnished with a plank table and a few stools. Shelves of earthen pots and cookware stretched along one wall. Beaded strands hung across the doorway to a rear chamber.

Rajaswami pushed aside the beads with his umbrella and peered in, then put a finger to his lips.

"There he is," he whispered. "Deep in contemplation, as I might have expected."

In white robes, a scarf draped over his head, a broad-backed figure sat motionless on a straw mat. Rajaswami was about to turn and tiptoe away when Akka, chirping inquisitively, scampered between his feet.

At the sound, the figure roused, sprang up, and whirled around, eyes blazing. Head and shoulders taller than Tamar, stouter and heavier than the *suta*, what Rajaswami had taken for a meditating sage was a huge black bear.

Akka, jabbering in terror, streaked from the chamber. Rajaswami stumbled backward, brandishing his umbrella. Tamar and Mirri seized the bewildered *acharya* between them and hauled him through the door, out of the *ashrama* and into the yard, the bear snarling and roaring at their heels.

The commotion had brought Adi-Kavi and Hashkat racing from the stream. Sending Rajaswami and Mirri pitching into their arms, Tamar faced the furious animal, who shook his paws like clawed fists at the intruders.

Instead of pursuing the attack, however, the bear halted on the veranda, choked back his growls, and swung his head from side to side, blinking at the journeyers in the dooryard. On the roof, Garuda squawked and beat his wings.

"Shmaa! Fools!" screeched the bird. "Don't stand there. Run for it!"

The bear, meantime, set his robes in better order and, with great courtesy, bowed his head and pressed his big paws together:

"Revered *brahmana*, accept my humblest apologies. I was startled and quite forgot myself. It happens from time to time when things unsettle me. I urge you to overlook this failing and forgive my regrettable outburst."

"Ah—why, yes, of course," said Rajaswami, regaining his composure, pleased at being so respectfully addressed. "Now, be so good as to inform us: Where is the hermit?"

"I know where he is," muttered Hashkat. "That shaggy-haired, slew-footed monster ate him."

"Most assuredly, I did not," retorted the bear, with a reproachful glance at Hashkat. "It would be a physical impossibility as well as a logical fallacy. I am the hermit."

20. The Ashrama

My name is Jamba-Van." The bear motioned toward the door of the *ashrama*. "Come, all, and be welcome. Allow me to offer whatever rest and refreshment you desire."

So saying, Jamba-Van led his visitors into the main room of the hermitage, where he bustled about, finding more stools and benches, setting out bowls of fruit and pitchers of cool juices, as eagerly attentive as any human host to the comfort of his guests. When Tamar identified himself and his companions, the bear politely nodded to each in turn.

"Few travelers seek shelter here," Jamba-Van said. "More precisely, none at all. I am thus especially honored that my first guests include not only a king but, as well, a learned *brahmana*."

"Your hermitage is lovely," said Mirri. "Are you the one who built it?"

"No," said Jamba-Van, modestly shaking his head, "merely small improvements here and there. Nor is the *ashrama* mine. I am only its custodian. Naturally, I profit from the opportunity to read, study, and reflect on cosmic matters."

"Most remarkable!" Rajaswami exclaimed. "To think that a savage creature of the forest should devote himself to such noble endeavors. Most remarkable, indeed."

The bear's muzzle twitched. "*Brahmana,* are you imply-
ing that what you call a savage creature lacks the intelligence
and sensitivity to pursue those subjects? Would you find it
more appropriate"—a low growl began rising in his throat
—"for one to pass his days lurking in the woods? Benighted,
uninstructed, unaware of the finer things in life?"

"Not at all," Rajaswami protested. "I only observed that
it was extraordinary."

"Extraordinary?" Jamba-Van burst out. "Why so? Is a
bear less capable than a *brahmana?* Unfit for subtle reason-
ing?"

Jamba-Van reared up to his full height, gnashing his
teeth, roaring at the top of his voice. Rajaswami nearly tumbled off the stool while the bear stamped his feet and flailed
his arms; then, before Tamar could decide what to do,
Jamba-Van went lurching toward the shelves, where he
seized half a dozen pots and dashed them one after the other
to the ground.

"Ah. That's better." Jamba-Van blew out his breath. "I
beg your pardon. These moments do come upon me. Pay
no heed."

"That's the trouble with bears," Adi-Kavi whispered to
Mirri and Tamar. "They're moody folk, but you never
know what mood they'll be in from one moment to the
next."

"I find it beneficial and soothing, when I'm unsettled,
to break a few pieces of crockery," Jamba-Van went on. "It
never fails to have a calming effect."

"Glad to hear that, old boy," said Hashkat, while the
bear fetched a broom and swept up the shattered pots, "but
you must run through a lot of kitchenware."

"I fashion more," replied Jamba-Van, seating himself at

the table. "I find that pot making, like tending my garden, frees the mind for philosophical speculation." The bear, now altogether composed, turned a benign glance on Rajaswami. "Before I was—ah, carried away, I was about to agree. My circumstances are somewhat unusual, yet quite logical and plausible. Would you be pleased to hear an illuminating anecdote?"

"Of course, honored colleague, if I may call you that," said Rajaswami. "We shall find it most instructive."

The bear folded his paws and relaxed on the stool. "Unfathomable are the ways of karma," he began. "Consider this example:

"Once, in the forest, a wild bear caught sight of a wandering *brahmana:* long-bearded, wrinkle-browed, with an air of such wisdom that he must surely be a sage or great *rishi.*

"Instead of letting him go by in peace, the bear sprang from the bushes, snarling and rattling his claws. The *rishi,* in no way alarmed, pressed his palms together and bowed courteously.

" '*Namaste,* O worthy bear,' said the *rishi.* 'You appear disturbed in spirit. How may I be of service to you?'

" 'You can start,' growled the bear, 'by providing my dinner.'

" 'I travel lightly, as you see,' answered the *rishi,* 'and carry no edibles with me. However, I'm sure I can find something to satisfy you.'

" 'I've already found something,' retorted the bear. 'You. I intend to eat you up.'

" 'All creatures must have nourishment,' said the *rishi,* unperturbed, 'you as well as I. All right, then, go ahead and eat me up. Where do you wish to begin? Since I'm mostly skin and bones, you must be hungry indeed.'

" 'Eh?' The bear scowled at him. 'I'm not at all hungry.'

" 'In that case,' said the *rishi,* 'why do you want to eat me?'

"The bear hesitated a moment, frowning. 'Because— because I'm a bear. It's my profession. That's what I do.'

" 'Have you never contemplated doing something else?' the sage inquired. 'Perhaps you wish to become a *rishi?'*

" 'Certainly not,' snapped the bear. 'Bear I am, bear I'll be.'

" 'If you devour me, you'll surely be a *rishi,'* the sage replied. 'Once you gobble me up and digest me, will I not turn into your flesh and blood? There I'll be, in your muscles and sinews, heart, brain, and nerves, and you'll never get rid of me.

" 'Consider this logically,' the sage continued. 'You're not hungry. You don't want to be a *rishi.* I haven't offended you. Therefore, why do you choose to harm me? Further- more, you didn't get up this morning expecting to find me; and just think, suppose you'd taken another path, or I'd taken another path, we'd never have met in the first place.'

" 'Stop! Stop!' roared the bear, who was not in the habit of thinking about anything at all. 'You're making my head hurt. My brain feels like it caught rheumatism: It smarts and twinges; it's going to explode at any moment.'

" 'Yes, thinking is a bit uncomfortable,' said the *rishi,* 'but you'll get used to it. A matter of time and practice.'

" 'I'm sorry I ever laid eyes on you!' howled the bear. 'Go away, let me be.'

" 'No, I won't,' the *rishi* answered. 'You started this business, you'll have to finish it. Calm yourself. Come, walk along with me awhile.'

"The bewildered bear finally agreed. For many days, as

they strolled through the forest, the *rishi* discoursed on stars and planets, suns and moons beyond the sight of the sharpest-eyed eagle; of creatures so tiny their universe fit on the head of a pin; of paradoxes, riddles, anomalies, speculations. The bear, in time, began feeling that a bearish existence was an extremely small and boring one; and, at last, he begged the *rishi* to instruct him.

"I was that bear," said Jamba-Van. "The *rishi* became my teacher and led me to this, his *ashrama,* where he taught me to read and write. He allowed me to remain and study while he continued his wanderings, promising one day to return. Here I have waited ever since. I regret that my bearish disposition gets the better of me on occasion; but, when it does, I can always smash a few pots."

Tamar had never seen his *acharya* so happy. Rajaswami seemed to have taken root there, spending hours in philosophical discussions with the bear. When Rajaswami declared that infinity was a straight line, the bear maintained it was a circle—and grew so unsettled that he nearly ran out of cookware to break. Hashkat, during these sunny days, drowsed under the fruit trees. Garuda, in the balmy air of the hermitage, complained less than usual. The bird had lost none of his adoration for Mirri, but had, in turn, gained his own admirer: Akka, who constantly stayed close to him, groomed his feathers, and wheedled Garuda into carrying him aloft for short flights.

Each night, Tamar made up his mind that they would leave the next day. Each morning, he had no heart to order a departure. He told himself he was delaying for the sake of Rajaswami, to let the *acharya* enjoy a few more hours of pleasure, then admitted this was his own reluctance, so strong he could not overcome it. After a while, he understood. Simply, he was happy here.

Mirri—he had never felt closer to her. They were seldom apart, except for her lessons from Adi-Kavi. As promised, the *suta* taught her some of his skills.

"I try to see the world as it is," he began, "but you can see it in different ways. Our learned *brahmana* looks at it with his logic; but it's not always a tidy place, the world. It's full of odd cracks and crevices, and spaces in between; and more's possible than you might imagine. First thing is to have an open heart and a peaceful mind."

To Adi-Kavi's delight, Mirri soon caught the knack of putting herself into deepest slumber, scarcely breathing; to turn her body fiery hot or icy cold; to stay motionless, without the least twitch of a finger or blink of an eye.

When Tamar asked to learn, Adi-Kavi sighed. "If I read your heart aright, it's divided every which way; and too many things rattling around in your head, all arguing with each other. Later, perhaps, when you sort them out."

Regretfully, he knew the *suta* was right. While Mirri kept on with her lessons, he went off to find the bear, who was tidying up the kitchen.

"My learned colleague and I have paused in our discussions," Jamba-Van said cordially. "We are reconsidering our positions on the nature of infinity."

"A vast subject." Tamar smiled. "Between you two sages, you'll get to the truth of it."

"Surely not," said the bear. "Behind one truth, there is always yet another. As you may find when you reach Mahapura. Yes, your *acharya* told me of your journey and how it might end."

"If it ends," Tamar said. "Tell me, O learned bear: Suppose travelers wished to stop and live here. Would it be permitted?"

"Contemplating the hypothetical situation you propose, the answer is: yes. Of course. What is the reason for your inquiry?"

"Merely to know," Tamar said.

———◆———

During the next several days, Tamar and Mirri rambled through the woods or picked fruit in the orchard. Exploring upstream, they found a waterfall and waded, soaking wet in the spray and foaming current. As if by silent agreement, neither spoke of Mahapura and when Tamar planned to leave the *ashrama*.

One evening, they swam to the biggest of the islands. In a circle of tall ferns, Mirri paced light, dancing steps, moving from one graceful attitude to another.

Beckoning to Tamar, she murmured:

> *Once, long ago, we danced like this*
> *In a forest, by old stones of*
> *Ruined temples. Do you remember?*

Tamar answered:

> *That night, we heard a flute play.*
> *The notes were trembling and shy.*
> *Who was the player? Who were we?*

Mirri continued the verse:

> King and queen, or god and goddess,
> As we had been forever.
> What interrupted our eternity?

Tamar replied:

> Time stopped and held its breath,
> Waiting for us to rejoin each other.
> Now it begins anew.
> Forever then,
> Forever
> Once again.

In the *ashrama* that night, he dreamed of trees turning to gold. A death.

He said nothing of this omen to Mirri; nor had he the heart to tell Rajaswami, who woke bubbling with good spirits, eager to expound a new theory to the bear. Instead, he sought out Adi-Kavi and found him eating a melon in the garden. It was a pleasant, sunny morning. They talked awhile. Tamar later asked Mirri to walk in the orchard.

"I asked Adi-Kavi to carry the ruby," he began. "He said he would. I trust him. I haven't given it to him yet, but I soon will. That much is settled."

"And something else is unsettled. Why are you doing this?"

"He promised," Tamar went on, "whatever else happens, he'll find his way to Jaya."

Mirri took him by the shoulders. "You're going at this sideways. Tell me straight out. What's wrong?"

"Nothing's wrong. Everything's right." He looked squarely at her. "Have you been happy here?"

"You know I have."

"Will you stay with me?"

"Yes."

"I mean, in the hermitage. Jamba-Van will let us live here. He told me so.

"I'm not going to Mahapura," he said abruptly. "I must have known that when we first met. I kept pushing it out of my mind. I was ashamed even to think of breaking the warrior's code. Live by it. Die for it. I can't. Not now. Are love's arrows made of flowers, as poets say? No, they're stronger than that, and they've grown stronger every day.

"Keep my word to give up my life? To someone who may not exist? Once, I'd have accepted that. Promise made, promise kept. A king's dharma. No, that's over with."

He was speaking defiantly, as if to Jaya himself as much as to Mirri. "Was it real? Was it a dream? It makes no difference. I won't lose you for the sake of it. My promise to Jaya? I break it."

He pulled off the ring and threw it away.

PART III

RANAPURA

21. Garuda Does a Service

"Come. That's a burden lifted." Tamar smiled and held out his hands to her. For a king and *kshatriya* who had broken his sworn word, his code of honor, and his dharma all within the moment, he felt, on the whole, pleased with himself, unexpectedly lighthearted. He motioned toward the hermitage:

"Let's go and tell them. Hashkat should be glad. He'll go back to ruling his Bandar-loka. As for Rajaswami—that's going to be hard. My dear old *acharya*. I'm afraid he'll be shocked. At first. But he'll see the bright side: He can stay here, philosophizing with Jamba-Van. I think that's what he secretly wishes."

Instead of smiling back at him, Mirri stood staring, her dark features frozen, her eyes wide.

"What have you done?" she said in a fearful whisper.

"Done?" Tamar was puzzled. "I did what you saw. I set myself free. I put an end to a fool's journey."

"You believe so?" she cried. "You broke dharma—"

"Yes. For you. It's what you wanted, isn't it? From the start—"

"Not like this."

"How, then?" he burst out. "What more? I'm rid of Jaya. I'm not bound to him. I'm bound to no one. Only to you."

"That's not true."

"Why? Because I broke one promise, you think I'll break another?"

"No. You don't understand—"

"I understand I've thrown everything away and now you tell me it was wrong."

Without hearing her answer, he turned on his heel and strode from the orchard.

He did not go to the *ashrama*. He went, rather, to the stream. He sat on the grassy bank and looked across at the island where they had danced. He put his head in his hands. Half his heart rejoiced at what he had done; the other half was horrified. Beyond that, he was shocked, bitterly disappointed by Mirri's words.

Her hand touched his arm.

He looked up. "You say I don't understand. There's something you don't understand. I didn't tell you."

"Tell me now." She sat next to him.

"It's been in my mind for us to stay here. I couldn't decide. Then, last night, after we came back, I dreamed the trees turned to gold. Twice now I've had that dream. This time, it tipped the balance. Do you know what it means? It foretells a death. Yours? Mine? If we keep on with this journey? I can't let that happen. It won't, now I'm free of Jaya."

"You're not free of him," Mirri said quietly. "You're truly a fool if you think so."

"I put down that burden. I'd be a bigger fool to pick it up again. You, of all people, want me to do it? No. I won't."

"If you don't, you'll carry a worse burden. Your broken dharma, for one thing. For another: You'll never be sure of the truth. You'll always wonder and question, and chew it over and over: Was it a dream? Or wasn't it? You'll never be rid of Jaya until you know for certain. I've understood that since the night I offered you the garland."

"What does it matter whether I'm sure or not?"

"Because he'll always be a shadow between us. Unless you find out one way or the other, he'll haunt you every day of your life. He'll poison you. In time, it will kill you as if he used a sword. Do you call that being free?"

"If that's my karma, so be it. I can't take back what I've done."

He stood and walked up the path to the hermitage, Mirri silent beside him.

Rajaswami and the bear were at the table in the common room. Adi-Kavi sat cross-legged by the hearth.

"Revered *acharya.*" Tamar formally pressed his hands together and bowed his head. "I have something important I must say to you."

"Indeed, my boy? What a coincidence! I have something important to say to you. My learned colleague and I have engaged in many discussions on the shape of infinity. Is it straight? Is it a circle?"

"Please, *acharya*—"

"It is neither," Rajaswami continued. "It is, in effect, rather like a figure eight. A remarkable conception—"

"*Acharya*—"

"Eh? Oh. Yes. What was it, dear boy, that you wished to tell me?"

"The journey to Mahapura—"

"Ah. That. Of course." Rajaswami's face fell. "I understand. The impatience of youth. Yes, well, it has been most pleasant here."

"We aren't leaving." Tamar glanced at Mirri, who was watching him with a look half anguished, half fearful. "You see—"

"Shmaa! Shmaa! Incompetent nitwit!"

Garuda tumbled through an open window to land in a heap on the floor. He picked himself up and strutted back and forth in front of Tamar.

"You'll owe me plenty for this," Garuda crowed. "I won't forget. Don't you forget, either. I'll remind you from time to time. I've done you yet another service. A big one. Careless idiot, you must have lost this in the orchard. Lucky I found it."

Garuda opened his talons and dropped the ring at Tamar's feet.

"Good heavens, my boy, that was careless indeed," Rajaswami exclaimed. "How did you do that? And never notice? But, the bright side is: You have it back, thanks to our sharp-eyed eagle."

Tamar stared at the ring as if it had been a viper coiled to strike. Mirri's words beside the stream rang in his ears, all the more tormenting because, he admitted, they were true.

As though Mirri alone could hear, he said:

> Not for the warrior's code,
> Not for honor's sake,
> But for your heart and mine,
> Though at the end they break.

Mirri answered:

> Though at the end they break,
> Death will not keep them apart.

> *No ring can bind us closer*
> *Than your heart that holds my heart.*

He bent and picked up the ring, which seemed so heavy he could barely lift it. He forced the cold iron circlet on his finger.

"I wish to be gone from here," he said. "*Suta,* fetch the horses."

"But, my boy, what were you saying?" asked Rajaswami. "Not going to Mahapura?"

"Not going—not until I found the ring." Tamar faltered. "No. I haven't lost so much honor that I can lie to my *acharya.* I threw it away."

"Goodness me!" cried Rajaswami. "Why ever would you do a thing like that?"

Before Tamar could explain, the bear pricked up his ears. There was the sound of hoofbeats. By instinct, Tamar reached for his sword. It was not at his side; he had borne no weapon since he had been at the hermitage.

"Still more travelers? How curious to have so many all at once." Jamba-Van lumbered out to the veranda. Tamar, uneasy, stepped after him. Hashkat and Akka came running from behind the stable.

Two men had dismounted in the dooryard. Their horses had been hard-ridden, legs and flanks streaked with mud. The riders were dressed much alike in stained cloaks, long-skirted tunics, and leather leggings. They carried swords at their sides and curved knives in their belts. One seemed Tamar's age; the other, a few years older. Both were fair-haired, fine-featured, with gray-blue eyes. Their faces were as weather-beaten as huntsmen's; but, by their bearing, they were clearly *kshatriya*s despite their coarse garments.

The elder, with a short, reddish-yellow beard, moved in confident strides to Tamar. "*Namaste,* King of Sundari. I am Kirin. This is my brother, Skanda. Your trail led us to this *ashrama.*"

"Lucky to find you still here," added Skanda. "We expected you'd have left by now. This shortens our search."

"Why seek me?" Tamar demanded. "Who are you? Speak quickly. I make ready to leave without delay."

"Allow us to delay your journey a little longer," replied Kirin. "You are a friend to our eldest brother, and so we are friends to you. You know his name: Ashwara."

Tamar brightened, surprised that he had not seen the family resemblance immediately. "Is he well? Safe?"

"He is well." Kirin gave a hard smile. "Safe? Ashwara is never safe. He sends all of you his greetings; and, to you, a message."

"Rest yourselves and your horses. I'm sure that Jamba-Van"—Tamar nodded to the bear—"will gladly offer you hospitality while I gladly hear Ashwara's words."

Kirin shook his head. "Time presses on us, as it presses on you. Ashwara says only this: 'Come to me in Chandra-gar.'"

22. Kirin and Skanda

Ashwara spoke to us of your journey," Skanda said. "You'll not be much off your path. Chandragar is by the Sabla River, the course you should follow in any case."

"Did he say no more?" Tamar asked. "Why does he wish me to go there?"

"He told us little," replied Kirin. "His thoughts are his own, and it is best that he himself explain them."

"Ashwara is my friend," Tamar said. "For the sake of friendship, I will do as he bids me."

Mirri glanced uneasily at Tamar, but said nothing against his decision and set about packing her saddlebags. For Hashkat and Adi-Kavi, there was no question. They would ride to Chandragar, and Akka insisted on doing likewise. Rajaswami accepted the plan with resignation. Garuda took no pains to hide his own opinion:

"I thought we'd seen the last of that lion-headed, big-toothed forest-lurker. Now he's pounced on us again! Just when I was getting a little of my strength back. Shmaa! Some people have no consideration."

Tamar again urged the brothers to come inside, whispering that Jamba-Van was more learned than most *brahmanas* but not one to be lightly crossed. So, in spite of the delay, Skanda and Kirin accepted the refreshments the bear set out for them.

When they could stay no longer, Jamba-Van ransacked his larder for provisions enough to fill all their saddle packs. He embraced his parting visitors and waved a paw at Garuda.

"Your *ashrama* suits me better than my palace," Tamar said. "I'll remember it dearly—and its hermit."

"Remember, as well," said Jamba-Van, "to look for truth behind truth."

"I hope I know it if I see it," Tamar said.

"Honored colleague," said Rajaswami, as the bear hugged him enough to make the *acharya*'s bones crack, "I am confident that karma, one day, will lead our paths to cross. We still have an infinity of theories to discuss."

"Whatever shape infinity may be," replied the bear, "it offers not enough time for your edifying discourses."

"Nor for your own." Rajaswami dabbed an eye with his scarf. Regaining his usual cheeriness, he added, "We must, however, look on the bright side:

> *Friends who part in deepest sadness*
> *Meet again in greatest gladness.*

Tamar rode out from the *ashrama* as if leaving home for the second time.

They adored their brother. Tamar understood that from the moment they set off for Chandragar. As they made their way toward the Sabla, Kirin and Skanda talked of little else. Skanda's boyish features lit up whenever he spoke of Ashwara. Of the two, he was the more eager: bright-faced and high-spirited, laughing easily, shrugging off the dangers and hardships they had suffered as hunted fugitives; Kirin, the more intense, with lightning flashes in his eyes when he recalled Nahusha's treachery and the blazing trap set for them. Skanda told happily of his boyhood, of Ashwara teaching him swordplay and archery; Kirin, of Ashwara's nobility and wisdom as king of Ranapura. Yet, for all their differences in temperament, they worshiped him equally.

"He saved our lives twice," Skanda said, when Tamar asked to know more of their escape from the pleasure-cottage where Nahusha was sure they would burn to death. "First, when Kana set the torch to the oil-soaked timbers. We had been warned by a loyal retainer, but almost too late, for the doors had been bolted from the outside. Ashwara, even with flames bursting all around us, made us wait calmly until one of the walls had nearly burned away. Then, by sheer strength, he broke a passage through it. Kirin and I were choking and blinded by the smoke. Ashwara dragged both of us to open air and hid us amid the foliage."

"The second time," Kirin added, "was when we sought a way of eluding Nahusha's warriors. Knowing we still lived, Nahusha set his men on watch, to slay us before we could escape into the forest."

"Had they caught us, they'd have killed us out of hand," put in Skanda. "But Ashwara struck on a bold plan. He disguised the three of us as holy beggars. Not difficult. We were already half naked. We streaked our faces with ashes and covered our heads in rags, and trudged barefoot from Ranapura. None hindered us; such saintly wanderers were a common sight. They deserved reverence and their persons were inviolate."

"And so we made our way quietly, almost to the edge

of the forest," Kirin said. "But there, in our path, stood a handful of warriors on the alert, casting hard eyes on all who passed.

"We could not turn aside, for they had already seen us. To flee—that surely would have betrayed us. To fight—we were weaponless and outnumbered. And so Ashwara whispered to us to keep on our way and be silent. Indeed, as we came up to the warriors, they looked at us not with suspicion but with scorn. To their discredit, they showed neither respect nor reverence, and had only mocking laughter and coarse words for our tattered garments and humble bearing."

"Ashwara made no reply to their taunting," Skanda said, "but I can tell you my blood was boiling. Ashwara had warned us not to speak, but I could scarcely hold my tongue. It was all I could do to keep from cursing them and throwing myself at their throats. Because, you see, we knew these men and had trusted them. Now they were among the ones Nahusha had corrupted to turn against us. Standing there was a warrior named Rasha, who had been one of Ashwara's own troop captains.

"Instead of trying to pass by, Ashwara went up to them. Head bowed, eyes to the ground, he held out his hands and silently begged for alms.

"What must it have cost his warrior's pride?" Skanda shook his head. "Abasing himself to those traitors? I couldn't have forced myself to do it."

"He had to," Kirin explained. "Otherwise—a beggar who doesn't beg? It would surely have roused their suspicions. This was our most dangerous moment. No man has ever judged me coward, but I confess my heart was in my mouth. It raced through my mind that, if recognized, we could only sell our lives dearly.

"Rasha barely gave us a glance, but reproached his comrades for mocking us. Then he reached into his purse and took out a coin.

"One of his fellows burst out laughing. 'The smallest coin of the realm! Are you sure you can spare it?'

"Rasha only shrugged, and threw it to the ground. Ashwara, ever silent, bent and picked it up from the dust, and bowed his gratitude. The warriors motioned for us to be gone. And we passed by.

"As we did, Ashwara said under his breath:

" 'O Rasha, you betrayed me. Even so, for the sake of the coin you flung me, when I come again into my kingdom I vow to spare your life.' "

23. At the Gates of Ranapura

A few days later, they reached the woodlands at the out-skirts of Chandragar. Gayatri suddenly reared. As if out of thin air, two warriors sprang across their path, bows drawn. Recognizing the brothers, who spoke briefly to them, the sentries saluted Tamar and waved him on, with Mirri and the others trotting after. Only little by little, as he glanced around, did Tamar notice chariots hidden by foliage, stacks of weapons and gear set amid the brush so as to be nearly invisible. Warriors sat in the shadows along the forest track, sharpening swords and knives, waxing bowstrings, trimming the feathers of arrows.

When Tamar spoke admiringly of how cleverly the camp had been disposed, and how Darshan himself would have been impressed, Adi-Kavi nodded agreement, then sniffed the air and grimaced.

"Better than any I've seen," remarked the *suta*. "It's the smell I don't like: trouble. Something bloody's in the wind."

A little farther on, Ashwara awaited them. No tent had been pitched, only a sort of lean-to covered with branches. Ashwara went to embrace them as they dismounted. His lion eyes brightened with pleasure. "I see you have gained an-other companion." He nodded his tawny head at Akka. "I wish to hear how you rescued him. First, I thank you for turning from your journey. You will not be long delayed. To speak straight out:

"My brothers and I have done well, but not quite as well as I hoped," Ashwara said, beckoning all to sit around him in the shelter. "The king of Chandragar supports my cause with troops and equipment. Skanda and Kirin have convinced other smaller kings to join us. Since Bala chose to take neither side, as you remember, my forces nearly equal Nahusha's. Some you see here." He gestured toward the warriors scattered throughout the woods. "Still more are gathering closer to Ranapura."

"Then you have enough strength to challenge Nahusha and defeat him," Tamar said. "I could not wish better news."

"I said my forces were nearly equal," Ashwara replied, "which means they are not sufficient. Until they are, it would be rash to challenge him. My strength here is at its limit. I must seek more elsewhere. With added troops, my plan will be set, the last gap filled. Without them, if I am forced to give battle, I risk losing all. In either case, this is my only chance. This is my karma. Opportunity will not be given again.

"I do not speak to you now as friend to friend," Ashwara continued, "but as king to king. I ask you one question: Will Sundari join me and give the troops I need?"

"And I, no king, speak to you as friend to friend," Tamar answered. "Before Bala's durbar, I told you my commander, Darshan, would put Sundari's army at your orders if I wished him to do so. That was my pledge then, and my pledge now."

"My question is answered," said Ashwara. As Tamar listened closely, Ashwara detailed his need for light cavalry, foot soldiers, archers, spearmen, and warriors skilled in fighting from chariots. They would, he explained, be his strong reserves, joining his own people only out of necessity. "If all goes as I intend, they will not be ordered into the fray; but I must have them armed and ready. In the heat of battle, even the best-laid plans go adrift. Sundari's warriors will be my firm anchor. Without them, the tide may turn either way.

"Let them come in all haste," Ashwara went on. "They should follow the Rana River. The valley lands are gentle. Your troops can move swiftly through them, and join Skanda in the plains east of Ranapura. He will see to their deployment, and report their arrival to me."

"I will write that order in my own hand to Darshan. He will recognize that it comes from me," Tamar replied. "Choose your fastest galloper to carry it."

"The time it takes a horseman to reach Sundari is empty time," put in Mirri. "Days spent in his travel added to days for the army to reach you."

"You calculate as shrewdly as a moneylender or a general," Ashwara said fondly, "but, clever *gopi,* you tell me nothing I do not know. I am a miser of time; I hoard it and begrudge every wasted moment; yet, I spend it as I must."

"If you're a miser," Mirri replied, "you'd rather save it, wouldn't you? You can send your message a dozen days faster."

Ashwara laughed. "What do you propose? Have you some magical chariot, as the old tales tell?"

"No," Mirri said. "We have an eagle."

All eyes turned on Garuda, who had come to roost in

the lean-to. The bird gaped in horrified disbelief, then burst out:

"Waa! Don't look at me. I have my own troubles. Me? Go sailing across the country? I'm surely not such a fool."

"You're an eagle nonetheless," Mirri said. "You're stronger now than when you were nesting in that thornbush. Your tail feathers are growing back beautifully."

"You really think so?" Garuda said, with a melting glance at Mirri, then hurriedly added, "No, no. Stronger's got nothing to do with it. My nerves are unraveled; my head's addled as a year-old egg. Shmaa! You're all quick at finding ways to unsettle me."

"You did bravely at Nahusha's camp," Mirri reminded him.

"A mistake," Garuda snapped. "I've regretted it ever since."

"No, you didn't," Mirri said. "You were proud of yourself. I was proud of you, too."

"That was different. From here to Sundari and back? Alone? The empty sky? The cold? The wind? The silence? Not a word of cheer? You've no idea how that can tie knots in a bird's mind." Garuda rolled his eyes. "No. Oh, no. Wheedle, wheedle, wheedle. I'm not up to it."

"You won't be by yourself," Akka suddenly broke in. "I'll go with you."

"Eh?" Garuda blinked. "You would?"

"You'll carry me on your back," Akka pressed, "the way we flew around the *ashrama*. We had grand times, didn't we?"

"We might have." Garuda hunched his wings. "So, all right, there was the odd moment of enjoyment." He clacked his beak thoughtfully. "That could put a different light on the matter."

"You'll let me, won't you?" Akka turned an eager face to Hashkat. "You know it's important. Fun, besides."

"We didn't save you so you could go careening through the air on a flying dust mop," Hashkat said. "On the other hand, what I let or don't let hasn't much weight with the Bandar-loka. I won't call it a good idea, but it's not a completely bad idea. Very well. Go with the old buzzard. Have a care. You'll be looking out for him as well as yourself."

While Akka capered gleefully, Garuda flew to Mirri's lap and bent his head to be scratched. Tamar said to Ashwara:

"I'll write the order to Darshan; and, to be doubly sure, another for a horseman to carry. Garuda can leave as soon as I've done."

"It's nearly sundown," squawked Garuda. "I'm an eagle. Shmaa! You think I'm an owl?"

Mirri urged him to make the most of what light remained. Garuda finally muttered agreement. Tamar, finishing his message, rolled up the page and tied it securely to Garuda's leg. Rajaswami came to beam his blessings while Mirri, for a last time, stroked the bird's wings.

"If I were smaller and lighter," said Adi-Kavi, clapping a hand on Akka's shoulder, "I'd be curious to take an air voyage. That's one of the few things I haven't done."

"Something I want to tell you," Garuda said to Tamar, as the monkey climbed astride the bird's back. "You keep this in mind—"

"I know." Tamar grinned at him. "I owe you."

All watched as Garuda and his passenger took flight, soaring above the treetops into the crimson streaks of sunset.

That night, there was no sound of Garuda singing himself to sleep.

Ashwara, next morning, ordered his warriors to break camp and take up positions closer to Ranapura, and thus be battle-ready as soon as Tamar's troops arrived. Tamar ventured to ask the reason for Ashwara's decision.

"You're well hidden here," he said. "Will you risk letting Nahusha's scouts see your people on the march? And yourself as well?"

"Nahusha knows exactly where I am," said Ashwara. "I am safer now than I have been. He will wait until he and I come face to face. Kill me? He will prefer to take me alive.

"And you," Ashwara went on, "I thank you and wish you well. Your eagle will find you easily before you have gone far."

"Gone far? How so?" Tamar said. "I stay and await my troops. Did you think otherwise? If I order my warriors into harm's way, how can I not be with them?"

"There is no need," said Ashwara.

"There is every need," replied Tamar. "I abandoned my people once. I will not do so again when they are in danger. I start for Mahapura when your cause is won, not before."

Ashwara glanced around at Mirri and the others. "Leave us. The king of Sundari and I have hard truths to speak."

"There are no truths that cannot be spoken in front of us all." Tamar took Mirri's hand. "Say what you wish."

"Then understand this," Ashwara began. "It is agreed: I do not commit your troops to battle unless I have no other choice; but, if I must, I will not hesitate, cost what it may."

"As you have said. In any event, I lead my own men. This is as it should be."

"Is it?" returned Ashwara. "Tell me one thing: How often have you commanded warriors in battle?"

"Never." Tamar flushed. "Why ask? Do you question my courage to do so?"

"I question your knowledge. I will not have officers around me who are untried and unseasoned. The stakes are too high, the danger too great. For me. And for you."

"I question your opinion of me, but not my duty to my people. I lead them. My right. My obligation as a *kshatriya*. You will not deny me."

The two men had been standing face to face. Tamar's blood ran hot and cold. He could not believe he had dared to gainsay Ashwara as a military commander, or to show anger to him as a friend. For an instant, he half expected the lion-eyed warrior to draw sword and challenge him. His hands trembled. His gaze did not waver. Ashwara's golden features hardened. He said nothing for many moments. When he answered, his voice was icy:

"Lead your troops, King of Sundari. As you demand. Only hear me well. You will command them, but you will obey my orders. Precisely. To the letter. No question. No complaint. You have spoken. I have spoken. So be it."

Ashwara turned on his heel and strode to the horse lines, calling for Kirin and Skanda.

"What have you done?" Mirri rounded on Tamar. "You made him go against his better judgment—"

"And what of my own judgment? This is a matter between warriors. It's settled now."

———◆———

He saw little of Ashwara in the following days. As the columns of foot troops and chariots moved closer to Ranapura, Ashwara was busy with a hundred things and seemed to be in a hundred places at once. When they did meet, Tamar was not sure if he sensed a deep sadness, or a cold formality, or if Ashwara was simply preoccupied.

Mirri said nothing more on the subject, which made it worse. He could not understand why it gnawed at him. He had acted properly, according to dharma. His right, his obligation, as he had told Ashwara. If he had done right, why did it feel wrong? He finally reasoned it out: If Ashwara mistrusted his skill, the tawny-haired warrior might hold back Sundari's troops even when most needed. A fatal error that might well cost Ashwara the battle.

After another sleepless night, Tamar sought him out. With Kirin beside him, Ashwara was tracing lines in the ground, marking positions his army would take up.

Tamar began by talking about something else. "When Akka was in Nahusha's chambers, he heard there was a plan of some sort. That's all he knows, but Nahusha must be sure of the scheme, so he wasn't troubled when Bala wouldn't join him. Yet Mirri thinks he doesn't have that many troops if he asked Bala's help in the first place."

"She may be right," Ashwara said. "I must try to learn more of Nahusha's plan. Is that all you came to tell me?"

"No. My troops . . ." Tamar hesitated; his words were sticking in his throat.

"What about them?"

"When they're here . . ." Tamar began again. He looked away for a moment. Ashwara waited in silence.

"It's for the best," Tamar went on painfully, "if—if I don't command them. Darshan will."

"As you choose," Ashwara said quietly. He nodded. "A wise decision."

Later, Tamar went back to the shelter. Mirri was relieved when he told her what he had done. He did not tell her his shame at judging himself unworthy. He did not tell her that he had just given up his pride as a king and his honor as a *kshatriya,* and he had nothing left.

◆

Ashwara had attached Tamar to his personal staff, giving him a chariot and a promise that he might command a small detachment. Tamar made himself satisfied with that. But there was no sign of Garuda and Akka. Ashwara's columns had by now reached the edge of the woodlands, halting at the open ground before Ranapura. The eight-sided fortress, with massive walls of golden-brown stone, overlooked a rolling plain dotted with copses of slender trees and, here and there, a rocky knoll. Tall watchtowers rose at each angle of the fortress; Tamar could clearly see the lookouts in the turrets. Beyond Ranapura, jagged white peaks of the Snow Mountains soared into the clouds. Tamar constantly scanned the sweep of sky for a glimpse of a winged shape. None. Even by generous reckoning, Garuda should have found the camp days ago.

Neither the bird nor Akka could have failed to notice the massing of warriors, ranks of chariots, horse lines, and stacks of provisions. Ashwara made no attempt at concealment. He allowed tents to be pitched, cook fires lit. Nahusha had chosen to set his battle lines well in front of the fortress. Warriors moved, unhurried, among the pavilions. Tamar did not see Nahusha, but once caught sight of Kana strolling with a group of officers. It all seemed very leisurely.

At dusk, Tamar went to the tent Ashwara had assigned them. Rajaswami sat cross-legged, deep in contemplation. By the light of an oil lamp, Hashkat sorted out harness leathers, for the monkey had insisted on being Tamar's chariot driver.

Adi-Kavi and Mirri were setting out food. Seeing Tamar's worried frown, the *suta* laid a hand on his arm:

"Put your mind at rest. They'll be here, and your troops soon after. Nothing will happen meantime. Ashwara won't issue his challenge until your people are well in position. Nahusha won't fight until he's formally challenged. You're a king, you know how these things are done."

"I don't," said Mirri. "Ashwara's here, armed to the teeth. Nahusha sees him. What more challenge?"

"Formalities," Adi-Kavi said. "Above all, the formalities must be properly observed. What will happen, when Ashwara's ready, is that he and his brothers will ride up to Nahusha's lines with a flag of truce. Ashwara will declare his grievances and why he intends to fight. He'll demand Nahusha's surrender. Nahusha won't do it, of course. They'll trade some elegantly polished insults; each will declare right and justice on their side. Ashwara will ride back. And so it begins.

"Every game has its rules," Adi-Kavi continued. "This is a game for *kshatriya*s. There are rules about surrendering, carrying away the wounded, breaking off a combat— Oh, it's all neatly planned out.

"Naturally, there's always some hotheaded, battle-mad fool who goes rampaging. It's contagious. His comrades join in, rules to the wind. Then it's butchery, plain and simple: Kill, kill, no matter how. They call it *sankula*." Adi-Kavi grimaced. "*Sankula?* Bloody lunacy, as I see it."

"How do you know all this?" Mirri asked. "You're a *suta;* you're forbidden to fight."

"True," Adi-Kavi said. *"Suta*s don't bear arms, but I still had to learn. As a royal crier, my duty was to be with my king; and, when the battle ended, make a show of praising his great valor and dauntless courage. I can tell you, though, when you see a king in full regalia leaning over his chariot to puke out his poor terrified guts—praising his valor takes a certain amount of inventiveness.

"At sundown, they leave off slaughtering each other. The warriors go back to their tents, eat, drink, and tell dazzling lies about their heroic deeds. No one fights at night, you see. That's one rule never broken. Unthinkable. Simply not done. At dawn, they go at it again.

"Rules, sweet *gopi,"* said Adi-Kavi. "Absolutely necessary when disemboweling your enemies. Otherwise, we'd be no better than barbarians."

Late morning of the next day, Nahusha attacked.

24. "Sankula! Sankula!"

Skanda, flushed and furious, was shouting for him. Tamar stepped out of the tent; he could not believe what he was hearing. He told Skanda it was not possible.

"Not possible?" Skanda retorted. "You think not? Yes, well, Nahusha's done it. No challenge. No warning. Ashwara just found out. All officers report to him."

Kirin and other commanders were already there when Tamar, still disbelieving, hurried into the headquarters tent. The *kshatriyas* were muttering angrily among themselves. Ashwara silenced them with a gesture. He motioned with his head toward a warrior, begrimed with sweat and dust, standing, arms folded and face tight-set.

"A rider from the king of Chandragar," Ashwara said quickly to Tamar. "King Rudra. First to support my cause. A strong warrior, my firm ally from the beginning. His army holds my left flank, close by the Rana." He turned to the message bearer. "Speak further."

"I have spoken all I know," the rider said, "and all that Rudra himself can tell you. A little before midday, Nahusha's warriors attacked us in force. They took us by surprise. No challenge had been given—against honor and the rules of war. How could Rudra have foreseen such a deed?

"They fell on us as if out of nowhere: spearmen, bowmen, hurlers of *chakras*. We took heavy losses, many slain before Rudra could rally his people and strike back. But when he struck," the man added with grim satisfaction, "he shattered them. They fled, leaving their dead behind. Rudra holds his position. One thing more." The warrior grinned. "Rudra sends these words: 'Say this to Ashwara: If Nahusha thinks to defeat me, he must swallow me whole. If he tries to bite me, he will break his teeth.' "

"Rudra has done nobly," Ashwara said. "Tell him we shall strive to match his courage."

Ashwara ordered his commanders to reinforce all battle lines and stand ready to answer any action by Nahusha. Skanda and Kirin hurried to assemble their troops. Tamar held back a moment, to ask Ashwara:

"How did Nahusha send warriors against Rudra without our knowing? We've watched his camp every day. There was no sign of movement. Even if his columns left by the rear gates, we'd have seen them on the march."

"One answer," Ashwara said. "They did not march from Ranapura. They were already in position, lying in ambush, long before now."

"That's what I'd have guessed." Mirri had been standing unnoticed in a corner of the pavilion. She stepped closer to Ashwara. "I have another idea about it too."

"Speak your mind," Ashwara said. "By rule, women have no part in warriors' concerns." His face softened. "Even so, no rule forbids me hearing a *gopi*'s thoughts."

"Nahusha never intended waiting to be challenged," Mirri said. As Ashwara nodded, she went on, "And you? Did you believe he would?"

Ashwara's golden eyes darkened. "No. I suspected he would not wait; yet, I could not bring myself to strike first and break my dharma. In my heart, I still hoped that he might redeem his own dharma and meet my terms. I had to allow him that chance. King Rudra has paid dearly for my hope. His warriors' blood is on my hands, as surely as if I myself had slain them.

"Now there is no turning back. I do what I must. At Bala's court, I vowed I would fight for justice, not revenge. The moment is upon me, but I question: Can I fight without rage? Without pride in battle? Without joy in victory? Can any man kill and keep his heart pure? If not, then is all slaughter alike, good cause or bad, and the same death for all at the end? Once, I believed that death is the warrior's final truth. Is it only his last illusion?

"Until I understand this," Ashwara continued, "I will not raise my own hand in battle. I will take no part in mortal combat—except against Nahusha himself; he and I, face to face. The path of my karma will cross his for one last time.

"Stay awhile," he said to Mirri. "A *gopi*'s thoughts may be clearer than a *kshatriya*'s. You, King of Sundari, go to Skanda. Put yourself at his orders."

Word of the treacherous attack on Rudra had blazed through the camp. Trumpet calls rang out along the lanes of tents. Warriors ran to assemble, still buckling leather breastplates. Field officers shouted for their companies to form ranks. Without waiting to be told, Hashkat had hitched Gayatri and Jagati to Tamar's light, four-wheeled chariot. At its high, shieldlike prow, the monkey had filled the weapons rack with Tamar's sword, bow, a full quiver of arrows, and set long, slender lances within hand's reach.

Even before Hashkat could rein up, Tamar vaulted over the side rails to gain his footing on the flat bed of planks that served as a fighting platform. He sighted Skanda's own chariot and motioned for Hashkat to catch up to it.

"Nahusha's warriors are in line of battle," Skanda called out as Hashkat drew alongside. His face was flushed; his blue-gray eyes danced and sparkled. He looked like a happy boy. "Kirin's people are going to engage them. I'm in support. We'll have to go at them smartly. Too bad there's not much daylight left.

"Orders?" he said, when Tamar repeated Ashwara's command. "I really don't have any for you. Later, perhaps. Meantime, you'll want friend Hashkat to keep your chariot in a little better trim."

With a wave of his hand, he sped off.

◆

It teetered on the fine edge of insult. Ashwara's army was in high spirits; they had won almost every engagement; Tamar had not been in so much as a skirmish. He had handed over the ruby to Adi-Kavi. Risk of losing it in battle? He could as well have kept it. Ashwara had not given him a company. When Tamar questioned this, Ashwara, too busy to discuss it, urged patience. He wondered if the lion-eyed warrior was deliberately shielding him and if Mirri had anything to do with it.

He did not face her with his suspicion. They saw little of each other. He awoke each dawn, armed quickly, tumbled out Hashkat, and rode to the warriors' assembly. He waited. Neither Kirin nor Skanda had need of him. He was fuming. Also, he was relieved.

His shameful secret: fear. It was like some kind of small, pale worm hiding unnoticed until now. It had raised its head the first day he had seen the dead and wounded carted off the field. The dead, at least, were quiet; he could turn his eyes away. Some of the wounded were very loud. Worse, they were still alive. The worm thrived and fattened, feeding on him. Tamar understood: Before it grew bigger, he would have to kill the worm.

He calculated how to do it. One morning, leaving Hashkat asleep, he rode Gayatri to the assembly. He knew Ashwara's battle plan was to hold Nahusha's troops in check with foot soldiers and chariots while King Rudra swung his lines across the open side of the plain to cramp Nahusha's movement. Skanda's light cavalry harassed Nahusha's flank whenever and wherever least expected. That afternoon, when Skanda's horsemen took the field, Tamar galloped after them.

They skirted the main body of clashing warriors and wheeling chariots, the knots of foot soldiers striking out with spears and heavy clubs, then veered toward the fortress. Skanda was heading behind Nahusha's battle line, attacking the supply tents and stores of weapons.

Except for the first moments, when Tamar thought his heart would leap into his throat, it was marvelous. Everything was suddenly bright and sharp, sparkling clear. He was light-headed, swept up in a wave of wild freedom. He could do anything he wanted. Sword out, he slashed tent ropes, trampling any warriors trapped inside. Everyone was shouting enough to burst their lungs. Skanda's horsemen were torching the provisions and smashing the stacks of arms. Tamar jumped Gayatri over a flaming heap, and pressed on. The worm was definitely dead.

Nahusha's troops fought back as best they could; but they were rear area foot soldiers, not *kshatriya*s. Skanda's riders cut most of them down with least expense of effort and wasted motion; the rest fled—slowly, for it seemed that time had become sticky and sluggish, barely moving. A man stumbled and flopped awkwardly across Tamar's path, got to his knees and raised his hands. Tamar could have taken the soldier's head off in one easy, looping stroke. The man stared, openmouthed; he was gray-faced, with bad teeth, and did not want to die. Tamar stared back. As once he had looked into a tiger's eyes and felt the fear and pain of a trapped animal, he felt his blade cutting flesh and bone of his own neck. He pondered this for a seemingly long while. He turned Gayatri aside. The man got up and went away.

Skanda was whistling for the riders to withdraw. The raid had wrought satisfactory havoc. Tamar thought it had lasted all afternoon. It had only been a few minutes. The sun was still high when Tamar, trailing the horsemen, galloped to Ashwara's lines.

After sundown, Ashwara's field officers gathered in one of the pavilions. Tamar joined them. Kirin and Skanda were there amid a crowd of cavalrymen, laughing and tossing rough jokes back and forth. Skanda caught sight of him:

"Why, here's the king of Sundari." He grinned at Tamar. "Don't think I didn't see you tagging along with us. Against orders?" Skanda winked. "Never mind. I know you're keen to be in the thick of it. I like that in an officer. Oh—by the way, did you kill your man?"

"Yes. Of course."

Skanda clapped him on the shoulder. "Good fellow. Good fellow."

Tamar left the tent and did not go back.

They were killing the horses.

For a moment, Tamar thought he was having a nightmare. He came full awake. Horses were shrieking in agony at the far edge of the camp. He flung on whatever garments lay at hand, snatched his sword, and plunged out of the tent. The sky was as pink as dawn. It took him another instant to understand it was still night. Flames billowed from the pavilions. A fist of hot wind struck him in the face.

He turned back. Mirri and Adi-Kavi were on their feet. Hashkat, blade in hand, started off to hitch up Gayatri and Jagati.

"Let be," Tamar ordered. "Mirri. Adi-Kavi. Take the horses and chariot. Get Rajaswami away. Ride into the woods. Stay there."

Rajaswami rubbed his bleary eyes. "What's the commotion? Good heavens, don't they realize people are trying to sleep?"

Tamar shook him. "Go with Mirri. We're attacked."

"Oh, I shouldn't think so." Rajaswami yawned. "It can't be morning—"

Tamar hauled up the *acharya* and sent him stumbling into Adi-Kavi's arms.

"How will I find you?" Mirri called.

"I don't know. Hashkat—with me." He ran from the tent, the monkey humping along beside him. Rajaswami, fussing and fretting like a child, was demanding his umbrella.

Nahusha's horsemen, brandishing torches, were galloping through the camp, behind them spearmen and sword fighters. When Tamar finally grasped that Nahusha had done the unthinkable and launched a night attack, he also realized it was even worse. Not a sudden raid, a quick and savage foray. Nahusha was throwing most of his forces against them all along the line. Tamar headed toward Ashwara's pavilion. The camp had turned rosy red and orange, bright as day.

The little worm of fear stirred. It was still alive. It had only been sleeping. Tamar shuddered so violently he could scarcely grip his blade. Ashwara's warriors were grappling hand to hand with their attackers. There were no ranks, no formations, only swarms of figures that broke apart and clashed together again. Someone had begun shouting *"Sankula! Sankula!"* The cry spread: one voice, then another. The whole camp seemed to heave like a single, convulsing body.

"Sankula!" Roaring, cursing, warriors flung aside broken weapons or ripped at opponents' faces with jagged ends of shattered blades, clawing, kicking, gouging—it was all *sankula*. Tamar ran blindly on. Hashkat at his heels, he lunged through a thicket of flailing arms and legs, struggling to reach Ashwara's tent. Free from the press of warriors, he sped across a patch of empty ground, lost his footing in a slick of mud, and pitched headlong. When he realized it was not mud, he promptly threw up and continued doing so until his stomach turned inside out. Hashkat crouched beside him.

"A royal sight you are, King of Sundari." The monkey grinned all over his face. "We'll get Adi-Kavi to spout some heroic praises for you."

They both began laughing like a pair of fools.

A yellow-bearded *kshatriya* ran past. Kirin. Tamar scrambled to catch up with him. "Where's Ashwara?"

Kirin had to squint a moment before recognizing him. "In the field." He gestured toward Ranapura. "He's ordered a counterattack."

Tamar looked at him dumbly.

"Are you deaf? Or stupid?" Kirin snapped. "Nahusha's got nearly all his troops here. Who's left? A rear guard with no support. We strike them now. Ashwara thinks we could even take the fortress. So do I."

Kirin ran on. Beckoning to Hashkat, Tamar headed from the blazing camp toward the plain. The *sankula* still raged. Nahusha's troops showed no sign of breaking off their attack. There were no orderly formations, no commands given, only shapeless clumps of men killing each other. From one moment to the next, Tamar could not even be certain which direction he was going. He flung himself into a thicket of struggling warriors. Pulling Hashkat along, he fought clear only to find himself caught up in a stream of carts and supply wagons, the rear area cooks and quartermasters fleeing for their lives into the fringe of woods.

To keep from being borne away by this tide, Tamar wrestled his way free. All around him, the ground was littered with discarded pieces of gear and clothing cast aside in panic, forlorn and ownerless. Hashkat, panting, dropped to one knee. Someone—it might have been Kirin—was shouting for the warriors to disengage and regroup in the field.

Chariots had begun rolling out of the devastated camp, with some foot soldiers running beside them. Hoisting the monkey to his feet, Tamar was about to follow. He stopped abruptly. He stared more closely at one of the chariots. Mirri was driving, Adi-Kavi beside her. Rajaswami, a glazed look in his eyes, was sitting at the rear of the platform, holding his umbrella over his head.

Tamar was furious. He ran to the chariot. "I told you to keep away. Are you out of your mind? What are you doing here?"

"Looking for you." Mirri hauled on the reins. "Get in."

"You should have stayed in the forest—"

"It's full of troops."

"Darshan!" Tamar cried. "He's here at last!"

"No. Bala. He broke his word. He's joined Nahusha."

25. "See the Trees Turn Gold . . ."

Bala's army—they're spread all through the woods," Mirri hurried on, as Tamar sprang over the railing. "And moving this way, fast."

"What's it cost to buy a king?" Adi-Kavi put in. "Nahusha must have sweetened his offer, enough to make Bala change his mind."

Hashkat had vaulted onto the platform. Mirri threw the reins to Tamar, who sent the chariot rolling into the field. Rajaswami blinked and brightened:

"Is that you, dear boy?" the *acharya* called out in a small voice. "I'm so glad to see you. But, good heavens, you look dreadful. Whatever have you been doing? Are you taking us home now?"

Adi-Kavi glanced at Tamar. "He's got no idea what's happening. He's somewhere else. A blessing for him."

Tamar tightened his grip on the reins. Gayatri and Jagati plunged over the rutted ground. The chariot lurched and nearly overturned. Rajaswami sat smiling calmly.

Tamar urged more speed from the straining horses. "I'll find Ashwara," he shouted to Mirri over the rattle of the wheels. "He doesn't know Bala's attacking."

The sky had turned a delicate pink. Rags of smoke drifted over the plain. Tamar thought, first, that flames were streaking from the camp; then realized it was morning.

Ahead, he could make out lines of racing spearmen. He had
no idea whose people they were. Chariots sped crazily
among the ranks. Tamar drove faster, hoping for a glimpse
of Ashwara. The sun was up, the sky a deep blue. For the
first time, he could see bodies sprawled on the field.

The gates of Ranapura had flung open. Chariots poured
out of the fortress. Nahusha's reserves were greater than
anyone had calculated. The din had become earsplitting.
Tamar feared his head would burst from the endless yelling
and screaming, war cries, roars of rage and pain.

"There!" Mirri seized his arm. "There he is."

Tamar turned where she pointed. Ashwara was on foot
with half a dozen of his kshatriyas about him. Some of Nahusha's warriors had set upon them. Ashwara, however, had
not drawn his sword. Tamar, in dismay, remembered the
lion-eyed man had sworn to fight only Nahusha.

With a shout of fury, Tamar sent the horses galloping
into the knot of struggling kshatriyas. Nahusha's soldiers scattered, the kshatriyas in pursuit. Before Tamar could halt the
chariot, Ashwara strode alongside and swung himself over
the railing.

"Go there." Ashwara gestured toward a rocky knoll.
When Tamar blurted that Bala had broken his vow and was
attacking in strength, the tall man only nodded curtly.

"The camp will be overrun by now." Ashwara's face
was as grim as his voice. "Rudra's lines are adrift, too."

"We disengage, then," Tamar said.

"No," Ashwara said between clenched teeth. "Too late
for that. We still have some chance. Withdraw, we have
none at all. Leave me by the knoll. Find my brothers and
bring them to me."

As Tamar hurried to obey, one of Nahusha's chariots

wheeled to head straight for Tamar's car. The warrior, sword raised, was leaning over the railing. Tamar flung the reins to Hashkat and snatched his blade from the weapons rack.

Mirri seized one of the lances. She braced to fend off the onrushing chariot. At the last moment, Hashkat veered. The attacking car raked Tamar's vehicle along its length, breaking one of the shafts, shearing away the railing, then galloped on. The shock set Tamar back on his heels. The chariot shuddered to a halt. A wheel had shattered. The disabled car listed sharply to one side, its axle furrowing the ground. Gayatri and Jagati sank to their haunches.

"Unhitch!" Tamar threw aside his blade. With Hashkat and Mirri, he ran to free the horses from the tangled harness.

He did not notice until he heard Adi-Kavi call out. He turned to see Rajaswami, jolted into sudden awareness, staring openmouthed at the scene around him. Another moment and the *acharya* jumped to his feet, scrambled from the chariot, and went off at a determined trot, indignantly brandishing his umbrella.

"A *brahmana* commands you!" he burst out in his sternest voice. "Cease and desist immediately, all of you. Disobey at your soul's peril!"

Tamar started after him. The *acharya* was hobbling resolutely into the fray. Taken aback at the sight of him and his umbrella, a few of the fighters halted. Then the press of warriors swirled around the old man. Tamar, with a cry of anguish, tried to force his way through. Rajaswami had vanished in the crowd. Tamar had only a glimpse of the white umbrella before that too disappeared.

Mirri and Ashwara had come to join him. Tamar had no idea where Hashkat was. A handful of Nahusha's warriors raced across their path. The officer, sighting Tamar, broke stride and, brandishing a bloody sword, made straight for him.

Then the officer halted and stared, only now realizing he had come face to face with Ashwara. Even as Tamar sought to grapple with him, in one powerful sweep of his arm he threw Tamar to the ground.

"Ashwara! To me!" The *kshatriya* swung up his blade.

Tamar staggered to his feet. Ashwara stood motionless, his gaze fixed on his attacker. It was Adi-Kavi who sprang forward. Tamar had never seen him move so quickly. Suddenly the *kshatriya*'s blade was in the *suta*'s hand, the man's arm wrenched behind him, legs kicked from under him. Adi-Kavi's boot was on his chest and sword point at his throat.

"Stand away!" Ashwara's voice rooted Adi-Kavi to the spot. "Do as I order you, *suta*. Put down the sword. Weapons are forbidden to you."

Adi-Kavi, bewildered, threw aside the blade and peered uncomprehending at Ashwara, who had come to stand, arms folded, looking down at the *kshatriya*.

"Rasha. So. It is you," Ashwara said.

The warrior bared his teeth. His face was bloody and smoke-blackened. He sat up. Cold lights flickered in his eyes.

"So it is." Rasha blew a short, hissing breath. "Strike, then, Ashwara."

"You threw a coin to a beggar, once." Ashwara raised outspread hands. "For the sake of it, I vowed to spare your life. Go."

"I remember no beggar. I remember no coin," Rasha said. "You vowed to spare my life? I made no vow to spare yours."

It was so quick, faster than Tamar's eyes could follow. Ashwara had started to turn away. Rasha was on his feet. Tamar barely saw the flash of the knife that Rasha seized from his belt. In the instant, he plunged it to the hilt in Ashwara's breast, ripped it free, and made to stab again.

Ashwara put out a hand as if to steady himself, then sank to one knee. Tamar sprang at Rasha. Adi-Kavi had already leaped ahead. Roaring with fury, the *suta* gripped Rasha in his burly arms and heaved him off his feet. Rasha's men were running to him. Adi-Kavi lifted the struggling *kshatriya* above his head. With all his strength he flung Rasha into the midst of the oncoming attackers.

The warriors staggered back. Rasha lay motionless, crumpled on the ground. Adi-Kavi picked up the sword. Whirling it around his head, he started toward them. At sight of the *suta* and his whistling blade, they turned and fled.

Tamar and Mirri had taken Ashwara between them and were carrying him to the shelter of the mound. Adi-Kavi dropped the sword, waved them aside, and picked up the silent form in his arms. Just behind the rocks, he set Ashwara at length on the ground. Mirri cradled the tawny head in her arms while Tamar undid the leather breastplate.

"Get him off the field," Tamar said, still disbelieving what he had seen. "Find a chariot—"

Adi-Kavi had torn open Ashwara's shirt front. He glanced at Tamar. "No use trying to move him. Let him rest. He has his death on him."

"He is right." Ashwara raised his head. "Leave me to it." He turned his eyes on Adi-Kavi. *"Suta,* you did what was forbidden you."

"And would do so again," Adi-Kavi said. "Does it matter, at the end?"

Ashwara smiled. "I think not." He put out a hand to Tamar. "Go on your journey. I follow my own. Mirri? Where is the *gopi?*"

"Here." Mirri bent toward him. "Are you in pain?"

"No. It comes easily enough." Ashwara's lion eyes widened. He looked around at the bare rocks. His face was suddenly shining. "The trees," he said in a voice hushed with wonder. "See the trees turn gold. All the leaves, the branches. How beautiful they are."

"Yes, they are very beautiful," Mirri said.

Ashwara did not speak again. He died soon after.

"I dreamed of golden trees," Tamar said in a torn whisper. "Omen of death. But it was his. Why not mine?"

Drums had begun a frantic pounding. Trumpet calls rang over the plain; warriors were shouting. Tamar sprang to his feet. Rage burned away his grief. Red mist blurred his eyes. He did not hear Mirri cry out to him as he ran beyond the knoll.

A troop of Nahusha's horsemen galloped past, bellowing at the top of their voices. Tamar heard no sound. He snatched up the sword Adi-Kavi had thrown aside. He raced to them eagerly, as if he had something extremely interesting to tell them, and began striking blindly. Arm upraised, one of the riders leaned from the saddle. The last thing Tamar saw was warrior's iron mace sweeping down on him.

26. The Burning Ground

It was all very puzzling. He was in a tent, but he had the dim recollection of leaving the camp in flames. Also, he was lying on his back and could not move. The war drums were still beating in frenzy. It took him a little while to grasp that the pounding was inside his head. Everything was swimming. Splinters of memory floated by. When, bit by bit, they finally came together, he gave a terrible cry. Then his stomach began churning violently. People seemed to be talking among themselves, making comments about this.

"Stand him up," somebody said.

His legs buckled a little when he was hauled upright. He discovered why he could not move his arms. They were tied behind him. A circle of officers watched with idle interest. One of them was Nahusha.

"It's over, you know." Nahusha had taken off his breastplate and helmet; his sword, as well. They lay in a pile nearby. He was wrapped in a handsome white silk robe, the sash loosely knotted around his waist. "Do you understand? Over. Done with."

Tamar said nothing. Nahusha fluttered his fingers. "Flown off. Scattered to the wind. Gone to lick their wounds or whatever one does when thrashed. Ah, my unfortunate cousins. I should make some effort to feel sorry for them. One must always pity fools.

"But do set your mind at ease. It's all been taken care of," Nahusha went on smoothly. "The noble Ashwara—by the way, is it true, as I've heard? He vowed to fight no one but me? I regret the lost opportunity. In any case, he's been properly dealt with—as a piece of carrion. Your friends will no doubt turn up when we clear away the bodies.

"Oh—the *brahmana*. He's quite well. He's in the palace now. Someone found him wandering around the field and kindly took him in. I commend that. It would be immoral to harm a *brahmana*.

"Forgive me, I almost forgot the most delicious news of all. My beautiful *gopi*. A charming, delightful little thing, and so energetic. Have no fear. She's safe and comfortable, lodging in the women's quarters for the moment, until I can make other arrangements, so to speak. I think, in the long run, she'll do nicely."

Tamar spat in his face.

Nahusha started. His cheeks went dead white. He sucked in a long breath and snapped his fingers. A servant quickly brought a handkerchief. Nahusha carefully wiped his lips.

"That was discourteous of you," he said. "You really should not have done that. You've spoiled things for yourself."

Nahusha looked with distaste at the cloth and threw it away. As an afterthought, he drove a fist into Tamar's face.

Tamar felt something crack. Blood began pouring out of his nose. He would have lunged at Nahusha, but the men on either side of him held fast. He kicked and bucked, trying to wrestle free. Nahusha calmly observed his efforts.

"Little king," he said, "I warned you to keep out of my way."

"Fight me!" Tamar shouted, raging. "Fight, Nahusha! I

challenge you. In front of your officers. They hear me. Accept! You must. Dare refuse? Let them see you shamed."

"What challenge?" Nahusha said. "How can there be a challenge from a dead man? As you are, for all practical purposes. It is merely a question of technical detail. You understand that, surely.

"Only, now, what to do with you?" Nahusha frowned thoughtfully. "You've made me change my plans. I intended killing you, of course. That goes without saying. But, you see, you behaved so badly. You were crude and insulting: conduct unbefitting even your own rustic dignity. In view of that, have you the arrogance, or stupidity, to expect an honorable death? There are limits even to my indulgence."

Nahusha stepped away and called his officers around him. Tamar caught nothing of their conversation, only murmurs back and forth; and someone gave a sour laugh. Then, with barely a glance at him, Nahusha strode from the tent; his *kshatriya*s followed.

Tamar stood waiting. In a little while, when no one came back, he sat down. His shirt was damp and sticky. The two guards, bored, shifted from one foot to the other. They finally sat down too. Tamar's head throbbed; his face had swollen, his eyes puffed. All in all, he did not feel very well. When he asked the guards how long he would be kept there, they shrugged.

Eventually, two foot soldiers came into the tent. He was almost glad to see them. They got him up and took him outside. The bright sun hurt his eyes. It was hot, probably only afternoon, but the morning seemed long ago in some different world.

Nahusha's warriors were striking the last of the tents, loading gear, trundling carts through the open gates. A char-

iot and driver waited. When Tamar was unable to climb
aboard, the soldiers hoisted him onto the platform and clambered in beside him. The charioteer set off at an easy pace,
heading from the encampment and skirting the western walls
of the city. Tamar saw a wide river sparkling in the sun. He
assumed it was the Rana. He wondered, with only passing,
objective interest where they were taking him; he did not
wish to speculate much on the meaning of Nahusha's parting
words. Whatever Nahusha had in mind for him, past a certain point it would not matter.

Closer to the Rana, with the city some way behind, he
began to notice a rank odor. Faint at first, it soon grew
stronger. The chariot halted at the edge of a barren field.
Wisps of smoke rose from nondescript heaps here and there.
The stench had become intense. It filled his nose and throat.
He could taste it. He gagged uncontrollably. He had, by
now, fully understood what it was. He could not hold back
a cry of horror. He stumbled to his feet and tried to pitch
out of the chariot.

It was the paupers' burning ground. The *shmashana.*

They were expecting him. A few more soldiers and a
nayka, a low-grade officer, stood in front of a ramshackle
hut. They looked impatient, uncomfortable, not at all happy
to be there.

The *nayka* beckoned. "Bring him. Get this over with."

Tamar had a flash of memory: of Rajaswami, before
Muktara, shuddering at even a passing glimpse of the *shmashana.* He turned and twisted, scuffed his feet on the stony
ground. They finally had to drag him.

The *nayka* had something in his hands. Tamar could not
see what it was. It was of no great interest. His immediate
concern was to be away from this place. He counted his life

lost. Worse, his caste was threatened. Whatever else, he was a *kshatriya*. Let them kill him on the road, the riverbank, anywhere but this polluted ground. He had been terrified during the night attack; that already had been shame enough. But now he was on the brink of panic.

He tried to run. They kicked his legs. He stumbled to his knees. The *nayka* stepped behind him, took him by the hair, and pulled his head back. He assumed the man was going to cut his throat.

Instead, something like a thick leather dog collar was quickly set around his neck. He heard the snap of a lock. The *nayka* attached the collar to a heavy length of chain, paid it out, and bolted the end into an iron ring set on a wooden stake. The *nayka* hastily moved away. Tamar lunged to the full length of the chain. The force of his effort jerked him back. He fell down.

The *nayka* paid no further attention. He was talking with his men. "Where's he gone?" he asked the soldiers. "Curse him, he was here just before the chariot came."

"Who knows?" one of the soldiers said. "Doing whatever he does. He'll be back."

"Damned if I wait for him. He's been told. He understands."

The soldiers, relieved to be on their way, trotted toward the road. A figure had come shambling from somewhere behind the hut. Without breaking stride, the *nayka* hurriedly called over his shoulder:

"That's him. Get on with your business."

Tamar could barely keep from screaming. He had never seen one before; but he had been well bred, carefully and thoroughly instructed. He knew instantly what the creature was; and the mere sight was an offense to his eyes. The lowest of the low, as Rajaswami told him. Even too low to have any caste at all.

A *chandala*.

Tamar flung himself as far as the chain allowed. The *chandala* stood looking at him. He was short and stocky, bandy-legged, with long, muscular arms, naked except for the dirty rags roped about his waist. His dark skin was further blackened by streaks and smudges. The tangled, greasy hair fell below his shoulders. The *chandala* studied him a few moments, then said:

"So, you're here. Did they tell you why?"

Tamar did not answer. He was choking on his bile. The *chandala* was actually approaching him. Tamar heaved at the stake, trying to uproot it. Failing, he scuttled crablike out of reach. The chain limited the distance.

The man moved quickly upon him. Tamar glimpsed the knife in his hand.

The *chandala*, with remarkable strength, easily threw him facedown and set a foot on the small of his back. He bent and gripped Tamar's arms. The man had a ferocious stench about him.

"Lie still or I'll cut you."

Tamar realized the *chandala* was slicing through the ropes tying his hands. As soon as he felt the bonds part, he began clawing at the dog collar.

"Leave off," the man ordered. "A waste of time. It's a good strong lock. I know. I have the key."

Tamar stopped short. "Set me loose. They've gone. Who'll know? What difference can it make to—someone like you?"

"A big difference."

"You're going to kill me. Have done with it."

The *chandala* laughed. It was a wheezing, rattling sound. "Do you take me for a fool?"

"What, then?"

The *chandala* squatted down beside Tamar, who shrank back as the man thrust his face closer. "You don't know?" He peered at Tamar with bloodshot eyes. "They didn't tell you?"

Tamar shook his head.

"Why, you've been given to me. Here you are, here you stay. You're mine. My property." The man gave a broken-toothed grin. "See the joke? A *chandala* owning a slave."

Tamar saw the joke. It was too horrible not to be seen. The ground lurched under him. He finally realized what Nahusha intended. He had to be reasonable or go mad. "No, no, this can't be. I'm a *kshatriya*. King of Sundari—"

"You're in my kingdom now," the *chandala* said.

"There's been a terrible misunderstanding," Tamar pressed on. "I'm supposed to be killed. Please. I ask you. I beg you." Tamar could not believe his own words. A *kshatriya* was begging a *chandala*. "For the sake of mercy."

"I'll keep you alive. That's all the mercy I can afford. You'll work for me. Once you're settled in and see how things go, you'll have plenty to do. It's always busy, days after a battle."

The *chandala* stood up. The sun was beginning to set. Wisps of smoke from the burning ground merged with the gathering dusk. "The chain's long enough. You can sleep inside the doorway."

When Tamar said nothing, the man shrugged. "Suit yourself." He started toward the hut. "Oh—watch out for the pye-dogs. They come scavenging around this time. They don't much care if their pickings are alive or dead. Change your mind, the door's open."

He disappeared inside. Tamar sat, face in his hands. He had been touched by a *chandala*. Caste broken. Himself a *chandala*. This was not acceptable. Therefore, the immediate thing was to convince himself the *chandala* had not really touched him.

Given this urgent task, he set about rearranging his memory. He had not even been near the *chandala*. It had worked out in some other way. His caste was unbroken. That was a lie. He knew it. Even so, he had to bury the fact—if he could not erase it—somewhere deep inside his head and let it shrivel there, forgotten. He did not succeed.

The *chandala* came out of the hut. He set an earthen bowl in front of Tamar, who stared at the broken bits of food as if they were scorpions. The man waited a moment or two. Seeing Tamar had no intention of eating, he shrugged and went back inside, leaving the bowl on the ground.

The moon was up, stars clotted around it. Tamar sat motionless, telling himself over and over that he was not a *chandala*. From the tail of his eye, he glimpsed vague shapes, like smears of ashes, darting furtively.

A pye-dog, scenting the food, slunk up, tail between its legs. It was more a skeleton of a dog, ribs jutting from sunken flanks, fur spiky, with bald spots and open sores. It crept forward, belly scraping the ground.

The pye-dog stopped in front of Tamar. Its hackles went up. The creature bared its teeth: half snarling, half whimpering. Tamar still did not move. The pye-dog inched ahead, then halted again. When, at last, it understood there would be no quarrel over the food, it stuck its muzzle in the bowl and gulped down the contents, then drifted off like a puff of smoke.

From across the burning ground, they began to howl: first one pye-dog, then another, until the whole pack was in full cry, baying and wailing. Tamar clamped his hands to his ears. When the pye-dogs finally stopped, he still heard the howling.

27. The Chandala

O nce, long ago, there was a tiger named Soma-Nandi; and there was a young king who climbed down into the pit where she had been trapped. Soma-Nandi was a big, powerful animal. With her sharp teeth and claws, she could have torn apart any hunter who came near. However, as she explained, the hunters knew this. So, they would merely stay away until she grew too weak to defend herself.

Also, somewhere in all this, there was a *gopi* called Mirri; but that was another, different story. He preferred concentrating his thoughts on the tiger. There was a point to be understood. After a couple of days, chained outside the hut, refusing to enter, Tamar at first believed he had grasped it.

Originally, the man had said he would put Tamar to work. He had not done so. Tamar was disappointed. He had reckoned otherwise. If the *chandala* made him work, he would have to unlock the collar; or, at least, the end of the chain attached to the stake and hold him like a dog on a leash. When that moment came, Tamar would rip the chain from the man's hands—always being careful not to touch him—possibly hit him with it, or whatever was needed to make him give up the key, and be gone.

Nothing simpler—until Tamar realized the *chandala*'s cunning. Like the hunters with the tiger, the man was patiently waiting for Tamar to be broken by starvation.

One thing puzzled him: Why did the man keep putting out bowls of food? The man must know that everything he touched was polluted and Tamar would never eat it. He would have to change his plan a little.

Next time the man brought food, Tamar kicked the bowl away and upset it. The man picked up the morsels, dirt and all, and put them back in the bowl.

"I'm not wasting good victuals," the *chandala* told him. "You want; you ask."

After that, he brought no more.

Tamar was pleased. He gleefully calculated how he would cheat his captor, and Nahusha as well, by starving to death as soon as possible. He failed. Hunger did not defeat him. It was thirst.

The *chandala* left the hut each morning and came back late in the afternoon. That day, Tamar was stretched on the ground. His tongue felt as if it had been roasted, and his mouth full of sand. He would have been screaming in agony if his throat had not been parched shut.

As usual, the *chandala* stopped in passing to have a quick, appraising look at him. Tamar could barely raise his head. His tongue, which felt much too big for his mouth, lolled out between split and blackened lips.

"Drink?" said the *chandala*.

Had there been any moisture in his eyes, Tamar would have wept with rage at his weakness. He gave a small nod.

The man had a flask slung over his shoulder. He unstoppered it, knelt, lifted Tamar's head, and carefully poured the tepid water into Tamar's mouth. Tamar drank every drop.

His caste was broken.

There was no way he could lie to himself or pretend

otherwise. He had drunk a *chandala*'s water from a *chandala*'s hands. He had become a *chandala*. However, once his disgust and horror damped down a little, he realized there was an advantage. He had nothing more to lose.

His mind was still working. From then on, he ate every scrap and asked for more. His strength came back; he was actually feeling quite well. This was as it should be; because the next time the *chandala* brought his meal, Tamar set his new plan in motion.

He jumped up, seized the *chandala* by the neck, and began throttling him.

The man stared at him with bulging eyes, his face turning blacker than it was. He made no attempt to break away.

"Key," Tamar said, between clenched teeth.

The *chandala* made gurgling noises. He fumbled in his garment and brought out the key.

"Unlock." Tamar loosened his grip enough to let the man breathe. "Then stand clear."

The *chandala* obeyed. Collar and chain fell to the ground. He stepped away, rubbing his neck.

"Why didn't you just ask?"

"And you'd have given it?" retorted Tamar. "Of course. I'm sure you would. Out of my way."

"You'd have figured some trick, sooner or later," the man said. "You might even have killed me. So, avoid inconvenience. You've killed me anyway.

"You really don't understand, do you?" he went on, as Tamar hesitated. "Nahusha put you on a chain. He put me on one, as well. That's something else they didn't explain to you.

"If you, my lad, escape—they'll kill *me*. They'll look in from time to time to make sure you're here. If you're not, they'll have my life for it. They were clear and detailed along the lines of torture, too. Nahusha can be imaginative when it comes to torture. I'd die, at the end; but it would take a good while."

"You're lying." Tamar knew the man was telling the truth.

"Why should I? It's not your concern, in any case. Go."

"Do you think I won't? You'll do the same, if you have any sense."

The *chandala* shook his head. "I've got my work. Has to be done. It's important."

"To you, not to me. Don't hang your life on mine."

"I don't. Nahusha did that. You stay, I live. That's all there is to it."

"I owe you nothing."

"Did I ask?"

Tamar had begun pacing, agitated. The *chandala* watched, neither pleading nor threatening, saying nothing. Tamar wished the man would attack him, try to force the chain on him again. It would give him excellent reason to fight him to the death. Whose? He knew the man's strength; it had surprised him how easily he had surrendered the key. The *chandala* could likely break him in half without too much effort. That, at least, would settle it. The *chandala* waited, arms folded. The man even looked sorry for him. Tamar hated him for that.

"What will you do?" the *chandala* said at last. "Go or stay? Make up your mind. I'm getting hungry."

It had never occurred to him that a *chandala* might be hungry. It also occurred to Tamar that he was hungry likewise. "I warn you," he said, "I make no promise. If I leave, I leave. What you do about it is up to you."

"Fair enough." The *chandala* jerked a thumb toward the hut. "Go in. Eat."

———◆———

The pye-dogs' howling kept him awake. Worse, after he stretched out on the thin mat the *chandala* gave him, he was terrified of closing his eyes. The nightmare came to him: The man would put the collar on him while he slept. He thought of getting up and running as fast as he could—wherever, anywhere. Let the *chandala* look after himself. Tamar had warned him. The howling of the pye-dogs turned into the screams of someone being tortured.

Tamar sat bolt upright, sweating. The *chandala* was snoring peacefully in a corner of the hut. Tamar's thoughts went around in circles. Nahusha had put him on a chain. The *chandala* had put him on a heavier one. He told himself this was not true. He could escape whenever he pleased.

He sank back on the mat as exhaustion washed over him. Tomorrow. He would go tomorrow, while the *chandala* was out of the hut. For some reason, he could not bear the idea of leaving while the man watched him do it.

He did not leave the next day. The *chandala* had plans:

"Get moving. There's work to do. I told you I could use some help."

Tamar had not expected to be quite so horrified; or, at least, to show it.

"What, afraid?" The *chandala* cocked an eye at him. "You were a *kshatriya*. Killing's a *kshatriya*'s trade, isn't it? A potter makes pots, a warrior makes corpses. Who should fear their own handiwork?"

"I'm not afraid."

"No?" The *chandala* snorted. "I can see it in your face. You're sick with it, enough to drive you mad. Well, that's what Nahusha wants. He counted on that. You couldn't stand it. He was right. You'd best get out of here."

"He was wrong. I'll go with you."

Behind the hut was a stack of kindling wood. He and the *chandala* loaded a cart with it. The man tossed in some buckets, then, like a horse, set himself between the shafts. He motioned for Tamar to join him. Together, they hauled the cart across the barren ground toward the river. The bandy-legged man plodded on, back bent against the burden.

It was all Tamar could do to pull his share of the weight. He had begun breathing hard. He was gasping by the time they came in sight of the river. It was not the effort of heaving at the shaft. The reek of the place was choking him.

The *chandala* halted. There were some shapes lying on the ground. They looked like bundles of sticks wrapped in rags. The *chandala* unloaded the kindling.

"They bring them in wagons from the city," he said. "It was busy days after the battle. I've taken care of all that. These are just your ordinary paupers, starvelings, beggars. The usual.

"Set up a pile of kindling. Careful how you do it. Don't waste wood. I'll show you how. Fetch water. They have to be washed."

Tamar turned away. He put his hands to his mouth. He could carry water; he could manage to deal with building a fire. The rest—his stomach heaved. "Not touch them," he whispered. "I can't."

"That's right. You can't. Because I won't let you." The

chandala rounded on him. "How dare you think I would? They've had no kindness, no respect: nothing, nothing, all their lives. I'll give that to them now, at least. You? Even lay a finger on them? They disgust you. They sicken you. You loathe them—as much as they were loathed when they were still alive. You're filled with horror; you can't bear to face them. Ah, my lad, they deserve better than you. Get away from them. Let me do my work."

Despite himself, Tamar shrank back. He had never supposed the truth could shame him.

The *chandala*'s anger passed. The man was looking at him with an infinite pity such as Tamar had never seen. "Empty your heart," the *chandala* said quietly. "No disgust. No fear. Only love for them. Do that, you might earn the privilege."

For the next few mornings, he went with the *chandala* to the burning ground. He had not noticed, until now, the small bunches of faded flowers or sticks of incense that had been left there.

"Why not?" the man answered, when Tamar questioned him. "Do you think a beggar is mourned any less than a *kshatriya*? What caste is grief? Here, my lad, these folk are equal to a maharajah. All end the same."

"If the same at the end," Tamar said, "why should there be caste at the beginning? What does it matter?"

"You tell me," said the *chandala*.

The man still kept him at a distance and gave him only small tasks: fetching water, unloading wood. To Tamar's surprise, the reek that hung over the *shmashana* had vanished as well as the horror that first overwhelmed him. Watching the *chandala*'s gentleness and humility at his work, he remembered the man telling him, "They deserve better than you." He wondered, now, if he better deserved them. Finally, he asked the *chandala* if he might help. The man looked him up and down. Tamar waited.

"Since you ask," the *chandala* said. He nodded briefly and pointed to a small figure. "Try."

As it was only a newborn child, it was easily done and took hardly any time at all. Even so, he felt greatly blessed.

That evening, as they sat in the darkening hut, for the first time Tamar could bring himself to speak his heart. In one burst, he told of his dream and journey, his love for Mirri, his dear *acharya,* his companions lost. For the first time, as well, he could grieve for Ashwara and dare to remember his look of joy at the end.

"He was the best of kings, a king as I'd have wished to be," Tamar said. "Dead. Slain by a traitor. An evil man still lives. Adi-Kavi would have told me that's the way of the world."

"One of its ways." The *chandala* set down his bowl of food. "There are others."

"Not for me. My way leads to Nahusha. I want his death."

"How will that serve you? Ashwara fought for justice, not revenge. Will you be less than he was?"

"I'm already less. A *chandala*. Do you say I should even give up vengeance? No. I eat it. It keeps me strong. Better than meat and drink."

"Beware how much you eat, then. It will poison you."

"Let it."

"If that suits your taste." The *chandala* shrugged. "Only tell me: How are you different from Nahusha?"

Tamar did not answer. He stretched out on the mat and went to sleep. The pye-dogs had started baying. He did not hear them.

Next morning, at the edge of the *shmashana,* Tamar sighted a figure stumbling over the barren ground. He dropped his load of kindling.

Rajaswami, arms outstretched, was hobbling as fast as his spindly legs would carry him.

"*Acharya!*" Heart leaping, Tamar ran toward him, then stopped short. He stepped back and raised his hands. "*Acharya*—no, no, keep away. You'll break your caste. I'm a *chandala*—"

"My dear boy. Oh, my dear boy." Rajaswami did not halt but, against all warnings, flung his arms around Tamar. He looked aged even beyond his years, his face gray and haggard. "It doesn't matter. Let it break." Tears streamed down the *acharya*'s cheeks. "It makes no difference. I'm with you again."

Two soldiers were trundling a handcart behind the *acharya.* They drew up and, between them, hauled out a shrouded figure. They roughly threw it to the ground, turned, and left the *shmashana* in all haste. The *chandala* went to see what they had brought.

"Stay calm, dear boy," pleaded Rajaswami. "Listen to me—"

Tamar broke from his embrace. The figure's wrappings had fallen away.

It was Mirri.

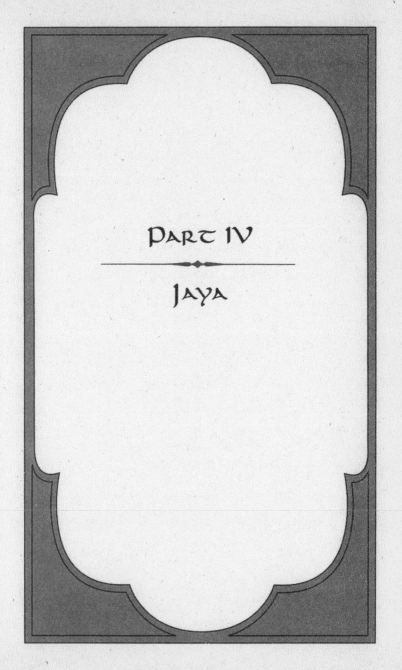

PART IV

JAYA

28. A Life Thread Broken

The soldiers had halted by the roadside at the far edge of the burning ground. They stood idly watching. The *chandala* had started toward the shrouded figure. Tamar seized him by the shoulders and pitched him aside so violently, the man lost his footing. Rajaswami was plucking at Tamar's sleeve, stammering something. Tamar struck away the *acharya*'s hand.

"Leave me," he said. "Both of you."

He knelt beside her. Mirri's long, black hair was unbound and draped around her. She had not been in pain. There were no marks on her features. Her eyes were closed, her face peaceful. She was very beautiful. Rajaswami was still babbling.

"I told you. Go away from me," Tamar said. "Do so."

Life had suddenly become quite simple for him. It was so clear and elementary. The first thing he would do was kill the soldiers who were still lounging around. He had no ill feelings toward them, nothing against them personally. He merely wanted their weapons.

Once he got them, he would go and kill Nahusha. No more to it than that.

He stood up and began walking briskly to the roadside. As if reading his thoughts, the *chandala* grappled and held him.

"Dear boy!" Rajaswami was flapping at him. "Dear boy, I beg you. Listen. The bright side, always the bright side—"

"*Acharya,*" Tamar said in a tone like a brutal blow, "you are a fool."

Rajaswami bowed his head. "Yes. I have been foolish in many ways. I taught you my own foolishness. Caste, honor, dharma—it all breaks. Only hear me—"

The *chandala* had been keeping an eye on the road. "I don't like those fellows there."

"Nahusha ordered them," said Rajaswami, "to witness —the burning."

"They won't live to see it. Nor will you," Tamar flung at the *chandala,* "unless you take your hands off me."

"They must," Rajaswami insisted. "They must report to Nahusha. If not, all goes awry. Start the fire."

Tamar, at this, began roaring and struggling with the *chandala.*

"Stop!" commanded Rajaswami. "Be silent!"

The *acharya*'s voice had a snap to it, a teacher to an unruly student, and it set echoes ringing in Tamar's memory; a child at the old man's feet—Tamar obeyed. The *chandala* loosened his grasp.

"It must seem to be done properly." Rajaswami spoke quietly once more. "How, I don't know. A most dangerous business, but all hangs on it. Because—dear boy, the bright side: Mirri is alive."

Tamar stood, mute. Rajaswami was making no sense. The *chandala* moved quickly to bend over the motionless form. He glanced up at Tamar.

"Yes, she lives. Barely."

"How else could we get away from Nahusha?" Raja-swami pressed on. "A desperate measure——"

Tamar heard no more. He dropped to his knees beside Mirri. Even as he stared dumbstruck, her breast began slowly to rise and fall. Her eyes opened. She smiled at him; then grinned broadly; then winked. She was Mirri, with him again.

"Keep your wits about you," she said, making no attempt to get up. "You'll need them. Do as Rajaswami says. If I'm to be burned to a cinder, you'd best be careful about it."

The *chandala* had understood the matter faster than Tamar, still speechless. "Stay there. I see how to deal with this."

"I started planning it out as soon as Nahusha hauled me to the palace," Mirri went on, as the *chandala* hurried away. "I couldn't have done it sooner. It would have looked suspicious. Too convenient. So I waited a little while.

"Nahusha had me locked up in the women's quarters. Once I was there, I pretended to be sick. Horribly, disgustingly sick. I heard Rajaswami was in the palace too; so I insisted on having him come and treat me. When I told him my scheme, he agreed to make a great show of being alarmed. He swore to Nahusha that my life was in danger."

"My *acharya* told a lie? Not Rajaswami."

"Yes. He's not quite the same *brahmana* he used to be. It must have torn the dear old fellow apart, breaking his dharma by lying. But he did it. For your sake and mine.

"The rest—you can thank Adi-Kavi. When we were in the *ashrama,* you remember, he taught me to breathe so little it didn't seem I was breathing at all. He showed me how to make my heart beat so faintly and slowly no one could tell it hadn't stopped altogether. I never thought the knack would come in handy someday.

"From then on, I made believe I was getting worse and worse. Rajaswami played at being more and more in despair. When I knew the time was right—I died.

"Rajaswami claimed I was dead from camp fever or some such fatal illness. Nahusha was in a rage. I'd slipped out of his clutches, so he thought. He raved and cursed, and ordered me carted to the *shmashana*—as I'd counted on.

"He was vicious beyond that. He made Rajaswami go there with me—which I'd also counted on. He expected Rajaswami to be horrified to have his caste threatened, to beg and plead to be let off.

"Rajaswami was very convincing. He wept and wailed, tore his hair. Pretending, yes. But I knew he was in real torment, too. Even so, he went to the last place in the world he wanted to be.

"Your *acharya* loves you, dearest Tamar, and he turned out to be a very brave man. Nahusha didn't care if he came back or not. Caste broken, Rajaswami was good as dead himself.

"And you—Nahusha gloated about having you chained up here. You'd be a *chandala,* a living death. You'd see me on the burning ground, a cruelty on top of cruelty—"

Mirri broke off. The *chandala* was back. Following his instructions, Tamar took the girl in his arms and carried her to a pile of kindling.

"Set her down." The *chandala* pointed to a spot behind the pyre, out of the soldiers' line of sight. He unwound Mirri's shroud and wrapped it around some of the larger branches of wood.

Between them, making sure their watchers could see, Tamar and the *chandala* lifted what they hoped looked like a body and set it amid the kindling. The *chandala* struck a light. The fire blazed.

The soldiers observed the flames awhile. Satisfied, they hurried away. Mirri jumped to her feet. Even after she had thoroughly embraced him, Tamar had some difficulty convincing himself that any of this was happening. It took a few more embraces for him to believe it.

Mirri was urging him to leave the burning ground. He held back. Rajaswami, head lowered, stood apart.

"*Acharya*—" Tamar went to him and put his hands on the old man's shoulders. "I called you a fool. Forgive me. I didn't know what I was saying."

"You spoke out of grief," Rajaswami answered, "but you spoke truth. Indeed, I have been very much a fool. I thought it better to be cut in pieces than lose caste, and I taught you likewise. Now it's gone, I hardly miss it. In fact, I can't tell the difference."

Rajaswami fumbled in his robe. He took hold of the knotted string he wore across his bony chest. "The sacred emblem of my caste. I treasured it. This was my pride—no, my secret arrogance. I give it up. It means nothing now." He hesitated a moment, then, with a little sigh, snapped the string and tossed it into the embers. "But—there's a bright side. I suddenly feel much lighter."

"Come quickly," Mirri said to Tamar. "There's a lot to do. I thought you'd still be chained up, but you're free."

"Am I?" Tamar turned to the *chandala*. "You knew I'd leave. I must. But I won't put your life in danger. Come with us. I'll make sure you'll be safe."

"I can take care of myself."

"When Nahusha finds out you let me escape, you know what he'll do to you. I can't let that happen."

"It won't," said the *chandala*. "Go. Now."

"If that's what you wish," Tamar said reluctantly. He pressed his palms together. "You taught me much. I thank you."

"Did I teach? Did you learn?" the *chandala* said. "That remains to be seen."

"I never asked your name," Tamar went on. "Forgive me. Tell me now so I may remember it and be grateful."

"Does gratitude need a name? Your chain's gone. That's all you need to know."

"More than a chain binds us," Tamar said. "*Namaste*. I honor you."

"*Namaste*," the *chandala* said. "I honor what you might become."

Tamar, still unwilling, turned away. Mirri led him across the burning ground, with Rajaswami hobbling after.

"I told you I decided to die when the time was right," Mirri said, as they hurried to the road. "I waited for what I hoped would happen. When it did, I knew the moment had come for me to get away."

"Moment for what?"

"Garuda's back," Mirri said. "He brought your army with him."

29. Garuda's Journey

Darshan comes in time to see us broken," Tamar said bitterly. "A little sooner— Now, what use? I trusted Garuda. I never believed he'd fail us."

"He didn't. Not at the end," Mirri said. "You'll see him soon. Akka, too."

The girl was heading toward a wagon that stood a little farther down the road. Tamar would have asked for more news, but something about the horses, befouled and mud-coated, caught his eye. He quickened his steps, then broke into a run. The animals whinnied and tossed their heads.

"Gayatri! Jagati! Poor creatures, what have they done to you?" he cried, as Gayatri nuzzled him and Jagati stamped the ground. "This is shameful."

"No, it's cautious. They look like cart horses instead of warhorses." The driver, a heavy man wrapped in a dirty cloak and headcloth, jumped down and grinned at him. It was Adi-Kavi.

"Better that none of us look like who we are," the *suta* explained, giving Tamar a burly bear hug. Mirri and Raja-swami had reached the wagon. Adi-Kavi motioned for them to climb quickly aboard. "Your message reached me safely," he said to Mirri. "Passed yourself off as dead, eh? I'm glad I taught you that trick."

Adi-Kavi slapped the reins and set off following the river.

As much as Tamar rejoiced to see the *suta* alive, there was one question he feared to ask. He asked it:

"What of Hashkat?"

"Mending," said Adi-Kavi. "He managed to crawl off the battlefield. I found him at the edge of the woods. I'd lain quiet among the bodies until dark, you see, and made my way clear of the mess. He'd been badly cut up. I did what I could for him, though I didn't think he'd last the night. He'll be fine. Your horses were wandering loose, no doubt looking for you. Luckily, they came to me."

"Skanda? Kirin?"

"Alive. Heavily wounded, both. They'd fallen back into the Rana valley with what was left of their people. I joined them there.

"King Rudra's dead," Adi-Kavi grimly went on. "His army was pretty well mauled, but Skanda rallied them. The rest of the butcher bill: Nahusha didn't get off free of charge. He lost a lot of troops and half his best officers. Kana: dead. Bala: dead. So, that's how the account stands."

Tamar found no great joy or much satisfaction in Kana's fate or Bala's. His thoughts circled like a hawk around Nahusha, and none other. To no purpose, for he saw no clear way to face him. He had even half forgotten his journey. The iron ring still was on his finger, but it only reminded him vaguely of something that happened long ago or never happened at all. Mirri was talking to him, but his attention kept drifting.

"I learned Nahusha's plan," she was saying. "He told me. He boasted that Ashwara's cause was lost from the start. He'd already decided to attack without warning. The night he stormed the camp—he and Bala agreed on that after we left Muktara. They'd worked it all out ahead of time."

"None of that matters. It's over."

"Is it?" Mirri said. "I might have some ideas of my own. Nahusha had me locked up, but he didn't keep me from knowing what was happening. I had news every day.

"Monkeys," she went on. "Some of the Bandar-loka had been trailing Hashkat. He had a few slip into the city. They found me, and told me how things were going. We sent word back and forth. That's how Adi-Kavi got my message. Then, Akka himself sneaked in. As for Nahusha—"

Mirri broke off as Adi-Kavi turned the wagon off the road. "Some of Hashkat's folk," she said, pointing to shadows scurrying among the trees. "They're always close by him, keeping watch. Hashkat never thought much of himself as a king, but his Bandar-loka are really devoted to him. They're good scouts and sentinels, too. He'll know we're on the way long before we get there."

The light had begun to fade while Adi-Kavi drove deeper into the cover of the woodlands. By the time he rolled to a halt at the edge of the encampment, Hashkat was waiting for them—grinning, waving his arms, overjoyed to see Tamar and Mirri.

Tamar jumped down from the wagon, ran to embrace him, then gasped in dismay. Hashkat's luxuriant tail was gone.

"Not half as bad as what Nahusha did to you," Hashkat said, when Tamar tried to console him. "I lost my tail but kept my life, and that's a good bargain. I miss it; I won't deny that. Still, I'm getting used to being without it."

Little Akka had scurried up, chattering with delight. At the same time, Garuda fluttered awkwardly from a branch and made straight for Mirri. The bird had lost most of his feathers, one wing dragged on the ground, and he looked more than ever like a half-plucked chicken. Still, he chuck-led and croaked happily while Mirri stroked what was left of his plumage. Deciding he had enough pampering for the moment, he turned a beady eye on Tamar.

"Irresponsible dimwit! Careless incompetent! Where's my ruby?"

Tamar had almost forgotten the gem. He paused to col-lect his thoughts. "I—I gave it to Adi-Kavi before the battle. For safekeeping—"

"That's right," the *suta* agreed, digging into his garments and bringing out the stone. "I have it. Here, look. I held on to it for you. I told you that before."

"I just wanted to bring it to this imbecile's attention," retorted Garuda. "Giving it to you showed a glimmer of intelligence. You weren't supposed to fight, eh? You did anyway. That was stupid. Shmaa! No consideration for others!"

Garuda turned back to Tamar. "You should have taken better care of my property," he rattled on, as Adi-Kavi now passed the ruby to Tamar. "While I was risking my life, you were playing fast and loose with a precious gem. You're a careless lot, all of you."

Tamar took the bird's reproaches in good spirit, only too glad to see Garuda alive. "The ruby's safe," he said. "But you? What happened? Your feathers—"

"You noticed? How kind of you to ask," Garuda snapped. "Well, it's luck Akka and I are here at all. You sent a horseman with your message, too. Oh, that was clever—he never got a mile through the valley."

"One of Nahusha's bowmen shot him," Akka put in. "We flew down to see if we could help the poor fellow. Nothing to be done—"

"The disgusting ruffian sent an arrow at me, then," Garuda said indignantly. "Out of pure spite and malice. He didn't know me; it was plain, common nastiness. Yes, and he hit me, the villain. I tried to stay aloft as long as I could. Did you ever try to fly with an arrow sticking in you? It's not easy."

"We went crashing to the ground, finally," said Akka. "I didn't remember much for a while after that. Garuda's wing was broken; he'd lost a lot of blood—along with his feathers. My leg was broken, too. We weren't well off, I can tell you."

"My poor friends!" exclaimed Tamar. "Couldn't you find any help? Were none of the Bandar-loka nearby?"

"Monkeys? Shmaa!" Garuda quacked. "There's never a monkey around when you want one. No—nothing, nobody. We holed up for a few days. Akka had gone feverish—and I had my own troubles, too, I'll have you know. I thought if I could rest I'd get my strength back. I still couldn't fly, and we were a long way from Sundari."

"But then," Tamar asked, "what did you do?"

"Shmaa! Idiot! What do you think we did?" retorted Garuda. "Walked."

"That's right," said Akka. "With my bad leg and Garuda's bad wing, we managed to lean on each other. We couldn't go very fast, and it got harder and harder. I thought we were goners for sure. Especially when the hunter saw us."

"And a mean-looking, scruffy fellow he was," Garuda continued. "We tried to get away from him. He grabbed us. I fought him off as best I could. No use. Waa! There, I think, there's the end of poor Garuda."

"It wasn't," said Akka. "Can you imagine? He didn't

harm us. No, he took care of us. Nursed us night and day. We'd never have lasted if it hadn't been for him. He fixed my leg and Garuda's wing, good as new. When Garuda could fly again, the hunter wandered off into the forest. We never saw him after that—never knew his name."

"And so we got to Sundari," Garuda concluded. "A long time. No fault of mine. Oh, now you really owe me plenty. Don't you forget it."

"I owe you more than I can repay," Tamar said fondly. "You can be sure I won't forget."

"Nor will I," said an old familiar voice. "The bird has a braver heart than any warrior. The monkey, too."

Darshan was there. The warrior's eyes brightened and he held out his arms. "Majesty, if only I'd come sooner—"

Tamar drew back. "My caste is broken. Touch me and you risk your own."

"Do you think I care a rap?" Darshan snorted. "I never put stock in that sort of nonsense. I'm a soldier; being alive is the only caste that means anything. And you—I should have disobeyed and never let you leave Sundari without me."

"You're here now, and we need you more than ever," Tamar said. "How many troops with you? What weapons? How soon can they take the field?"

"Hold on, hold on." Darshan raised a hand. "I've been talking with your comrades, Kirin and Skanda. Fine commanders, both. They've regrouped, pulled their people together, and that's a wonder in itself. What chance they have against Nahusha—that's another question."

"I have to talk with them. Where are they?"

Darshan motioned for Tamar and the others to follow

him into the woods. The encampment, Tamar saw, was smaller than Ashwara's had been. The warriors, scattered among the trees, still showed the ravages of battle. Cooking food or mending gear, they were grim and silent. Darshan pointed to a pavilion and Tamar stepped inside.

He barely recognized them. Ashwara's brothers were sitting on the ground, maps spread in front of them. Skanda had lost all of his boyish air; the lamplight deepened the circles under his eyes. Kirin's features were somber and heavily lined. Seeing Tamar, the two got quickly to their feet. As with Darshan, Tamar warned them away; but neither hesitated to embrace and gladly welcome him.

"Doing as he did, Nahusha shamed himself, not you," Kirin said. "Caste brings no honor to a man; a man's worth is what brings honor to his caste."

"So Ashwara would have said," added Skanda, "and I say the same. He was your friend, as we are still."

"I offered Ashwara my help in a just cause," Tamar said. "I offer it again to set his death aright. Now, counting my army and yours, what strength do we have?"

"Strength alone may not be enough." Kirin pointed to the maps, showing Tamar how their troops had been deployed. Skanda, he explained, now commanded Rudra's warriors; Kirin himself, the rest. After their king's death, Bala's troops had withdrawn to Muktara and no longer threatened.

"With your own people," Skanda said, "our numbers match close to Nahusha's."

"What question, then?" Tamar said. "You'll attack, surely. Do as he did to us," he hurried on, his blood rising. "No warning, no challenge. Rules of war? He broke them.

So shall we. *Sankula* from the very start. Give him his fill of *sankula* until he chokes on it. He owes Ashwara a death. I'll see him pay—"

He fell abruptly silent. The rage that swept over him had brought, as well, the nightmare memories: the camp in flames, his terror, Ashwara bleeding his life away. The *chandala* had asked: Who should fear his own handiwork? He feared it. And hated it. Was he still a warrior? Had he ever been? Or had he become simply a washer of corpses?

"Listen to an old campaigner," Darshan said quietly. "Will you let your anger cloud your common sense? Attack Nahusha? Inside the city, he's in a stronger position than any of us outside. He has no need to meet you in battle. Why should he? He'll only wait. What then? Lay siege? How long? We'd wear ourselves out to no purpose."

Tamar nodded. "My words were empty, foolish ones. Yes, I see that."

"Darshan is right," Kirin said. "Nahusha will do nothing but sit behind his walls and let us break our heads on them. If we could take the city by storm—"

"No," Mirri said. "You can't get close enough. There's something you don't know. The front gate's clear, but he's dug trenches all around the walls. Set with spikes and spearheads. Too wide to bridge, too deep to fill. They're death traps."

"He holds us at arm's length," put in Skanda, "with no effort, no cost to himself."

"That's right," Mirri said. "But only as long as he stays inside Ranapura. So, make him come out. There's a way."

30. Mirri's Plan

Is this a *gopi?*" Darshan laughed good-heartedly and clapped his hands. "Here she sits, cool as you please, ready to tell *kshatriya*s how to go about their business. From the look of her, she knows more than milking cows. Say on, little *gopi*. What makes you think you'll get Nahusha to send out his troops and give us our chance against them?"

"I might do even better than that," said Mirri.

As Kirin and Skanda turned their full attention on her, she quickly told them the shape of her idea, warning it would take some days to set in motion. When she finished, the brothers spoke between themselves, asked her many questions, and, finally, agreed to the attempt.

"I know tactics and order of battle," Darshan declared, "attacks and counterattacks, but never such a plan as this." He rubbed his chin thoughtfully. "And yet, as the *gopi* lays it out, it might well serve. Yes, let her try. Come what may, I'm with her."

Adi-Kavi and Hashkat were both willing. Even though Tamar agreed, he was still troubled. "Too much can go wrong. Too much risk."

"Kirin and Skanda are willing," Mirri reminded him. "Your own commander, as well."

"It's their trade to take risks," Tamar said. "I didn't mean them. I meant *you*. I lost you once. I won't lose you again."

"You never lost me in the first place," Mirri said.

"When it comes to the sort of mischief you have in mind," said Hashkat, impatient to follow Mirri's instructions, "my Bandar-loka won't fail you. I'm only surprised they didn't think of it themselves."

Before the week was out, Akka had done all that Mirri had asked and was back in camp. Darshan, Kirin, and Skanda had already set their troops on the march toward Ranapura. They made no attempt to hide their movements. Instead, they stretched their ranks of warriors and chariots across the plain, in full sight. That alone, Tamar thought, should have been challenge enough, and an insolent dare; but he saw no sign of an answer from Nahusha.

Early that morning, Tamar and Ashwara's brothers, bearing no weapons, mounted their horses and cantered across the plain. Adi-Kavi rode ahead, holding up a flag of truce. It was cool and quiet. The walls of Ranapura were soft pink in the first rays of the sun. The trees had come into rich foliage. There were still a few traces of the ruts left by the wheels of chariots and horses' hooves; but tender blades of new grass had begun to spring up, dew-covered, silvery green. What had been a killing ground looked no more than a pleasant stretch of open countryside. He could not pick out the rocky knoll where Ashwara died. He found that monstrous.

Adi-Kavi, in his loudest royal crier's voice, began shouting for Nahusha to come and meet with them, declaring that someone wished to see him face to face. No answer came from the city. The horses pawed the turf and blew out steaming breath. Skanda glanced, questioning, at Tamar.

They waited. Adi-Kavi was about to turn back, when the gates flung open.

Nahusha stood in the prow of his chariot, flanked by a guard of bowmen. At a leisurely pace, he drew closer, until his driver reined up a few yards distant.

"I heard dogs barking at my gate." Nahusha addressed Kirin, who had trotted forward. "Have you brought your pack for another whipping? What do you seek of me?"

"Since you refuse to give battle, and fear to stand against us," replied Kirin, "I seek nothing else of you."

"I do." Tamar had turned away and hung back a little, unobserved by Nahusha. He now urged Gayatri nearer to the chariot. "I seek your life."

"It speaks?" Nahusha, taken aback for an instant, covered his surprise with a poisonous laugh. He raised an eyebrow and peered curiously at Tamar. "Remarkable. A piece of carrion, a less-than-nothing, actually ventures to say something to me. The animal seems to have slipped its leash. Its master will pay a high price for such inattention."

"You, likewise," Tamar said. "Once, I wished for your death. I yearned to kill you with my own hands. No longer. It is your life, not your death, I seek. I want you to live, Nahusha. As I did. I learned much in the burning ground. For that, I thank you. I hope you too may learn. The chain you put me on waits for you."

"What's this, what's this? Does the creature threaten me?" Nahusha replied. "Put me on a chain, indeed? Bold words. The doing is something else again. If this—this thing—were still a man, I would have it thrashed for its insolence. However, I take no notice of dunghills, let alone converse with them."

Nahusha faced Kirin and Skanda. "Take the cur away.

It offends my sensitivities and befouls my air. Take yourselves
away, as well. It pains me too much to see *kshatriyas*, pitiful
though they are, debase themselves with the company of a
chandala. What sorry times we live in. You have sunk even
lower than your brother.

"You summoned me for this?" Nahusha went on. "Had
you come begging to serve me, I might have been inclined
to listen. You disturb me for no reason, waste my time, and
try my patience. I have occupations more agreeable than the
mouthings of a corpse-washer."

"That is not our purpose," Skanda said. "You have a
right to your trophies of war. We come to give back one
you have lost."

Hashkat, meantime, had driven up in a light, two-
wheeled cart. Seeing this, Nahusha pulled away.

"What trophy?" he cried. "What treachery is this?"

Hashkat reined in Jagati. At the rear of the cart, a heap
of rags stirred. A shrouded figure rose up. The cloth wrappings fell away.

Mirri stood smiling at Nahusha.

"The *gopi!*" Nahusha burst out, his face livid with rage.
"Alive!"

"Am I?" Mirri answered. "How could I be? You saw
me die. Your warriors watched me burn."

For the first time, Nahusha's arrogant bearing was
shaken. He stared at her in fear and revulsion as she held
out her hands, beckoning to him.

"Come," urged Mirri, "I've been impatient for you to
journey with me. You'll see many strange things along the
way."

"Trickery!" Nahusha shouted, horrified nonetheless.
"Illusion!"

"Are you sure?" Mirri said. "If I'm an illusion, why fear me? If I'm alive, claim your prize again. Come, find out for yourself—if you dare."

"Keep away! Don't touch me!" cried Nahusha, recoiling as Mirri made to climb from the cart. "You reek of the *shmashana.*"

"You used to find me attractive," said Mirri. "I'm disappointed in you, Nahusha."

"Ghost or *gopi,* I stomach none of your mockery. Flesh and blood? I'll see that." He motioned to the bowman closest to his chariot. "Shoot!"

The warrior drew his bow and sped the arrow plunging into Mirri's breast.

31. The Bandar-Loka

Mirri looked down calmly at the arrow. She gave a little shrug of unconcern as she pulled out the shaft and threw it aside.

"I thought you'd be glad to see me." Mirri shook her head regretfully. "I'd hardly call this a fond welcome. Come, Nahusha. I'm waiting for you."

"Shoot again!" Nahusha's face twisted in fear and fury. "Dead or living, kill her! Kill them all!"

Mirri made no attempt to move. The bewildered warrior notched another arrow to the string. No sooner did he draw the bow than the stave snapped in his hand.

"Enough of that," said Mirri. "You could hurt someone. Have a care. I might take you with me, too."

The warrior gaped at her, then at his shattered bow. He backed away. His terrified comrades dashed for the gates and he fled after them.

Raging and cursing, Nahusha snatched the reins from his driver, wheeled the chariot, and sent it racing toward the city. Adi-Kavi sought to bar the way, but Nahusha plunged past as if Mirri's vengeful ghost were at his heels. Darshan's horsemen and charioteers had broken from cover to charge across the plain. Troops poured from the city gates. Nahusha's commanders, seeing their king in peril and Ranapura

coming under attack, had taken their own decision to meet
the oncoming assault.

"That brought them out faster than I hoped," said Mirri.
"Hashkat, it's time to leave. We have other things to do."

Tamar's worst moment of fear for Mirri had passed. The
breastplate of tough leather, padded with rags hidden beneath her robes, had shielded her. Now all depended on the
Bandar-loka.

He clapped his heels against Gayatri's flanks and set off
after Nahusha. Kirin and Skanda galloped to join their troops
advancing on the city. Nahusha, Tamar saw, was forcing his
chariot through his warriors' ranks, trampling and running
them over in his haste to reach the gates. Flailing at his men
with the flat of his sword, Nahusha shouted at them to withdraw inside the city. It was too late; his commands went
unheeded; the battle had gained momentum and a will of
its own, as yet more warriors streamed out.

By now, the leading ranks of Darshan's horsemen had
clashed with Nahusha's troops. Tamar had only one thought:
Nahusha. He galloped clear of the press of foot soldiers and
riders. He strained his eyes for a glimpse of him through the
rising clouds of dust.

At the same time, one of Nahusha's chariots burst
through the ranks of warriors. The driver lashed the horses
to greater speed. The *kshatriya* on the fighting platform bran-
dished a spear. Before he could hurl it, the chariot jolted to
the ground. A wheel had spun loose from its axle. Kicking
and bucking, the horses broke free of the shafts. Trailing
their harness, they bolted from the wreckage. Warrior and
driver ran for safety within their ranks.

Tamar cried out in triumph. The Bandar-loka! Night

after night, following Mirri's plan, a secret army of monkeys had scaled the front wall of the city. Like silent, long-tailed shadows, they slipped into guard rooms and stores of weapons. They loosened chariot wheels, frayed bowstrings, weakened bowstaves with unseen cuts from thin blades; the bow that shattered in the archer's hand had been the work of their deft fingers. The Bandar-loka had done all they could to cause as much hidden damage as possible.

Akka himself had brazenly stolen into Ranapura a dozen times or more in broad daylight. He perched impudently on rooftops, scuttled among the fruit sellers in the marketplace until he became a familiar sight and harmless amusement. Yet he kept shrewd eyes and ears open, bringing back whatever news he gleaned.

Tamar galloped to snatch up the *kshatriya*'s discarded spear. The Bandar-loka's work had begun taking a heavier toll. Several more of Nahusha's chariots raced into combat, only to overturn as linchpins broke, wheels fell off, and harness leathers parted. For each arrow that flew straight, another was likely to miss its mark or fall from the archer's hand as the bowstring snapped.

Still seeking Nahusha, Tamar urged Gayatri into the fray. Rage swept away fear as he forced his way through the press of warriors. Some thrust at him with their swords or tried to pull him from the saddle. He struck them aside with the spear shaft; their lives were not worth taking. If he was to have blood on his hands it would be Nahusha's alone, as Ashwara himself had vowed.

At first, when so many of their weapons failed them, Nahusha's troops had fallen into disarray. Now, they rallied and fought with the strength of despair. The wreckage of chariots had been turned into barricades; from behind them, warriors hurled *chakras*, the deadly, sharp-edged iron disks. The lines of battle surged back and forth.

Darshan had galloped up to him. "Fall back! Fall back!"

Tamar could barely hear his shouts over the clash of arms. When he heard, he could not understand. When he understood, his heart sank. Darshan was pointing toward the gates.

Nahusha had sent out his war elephants.

One after another, the immense animals lumbered onto the battlefield. The elephant masters goaded them onward as the *kshatriyas* mounted on their backs flung spears and *chakras*. Kirin's foot troops, running to support Darshan, wheeled away to escape being trampled under the elephants' feet or gored by their iron-capped tusks. Nahusha's warriors took heart, cheering as the gigantic beasts plowed ahead, scattering all in their path.

Tamar sighted Hashkat astride Jagati and urged Gayatri to his side. "The plan's gone wrong. What happened?"

Hashkat only grinned from ear to ear. That same instant, from the woodlands at the edge of the plain, came a rumbling like the beating of great drums. The ground shook as the pounding grew louder, a rolling thunder over the din of battle.

A huge bull elephant charged onto the field, trunk upraised, trumpeting at the top of his voice. Arvati followed, with Akka perched on her shoulders. Behind her, a herd of elephants bellowed and tossed their heads as the ranks of Darshan's warriors parted to let them pass.

Nahusha's elephants halted in their tracks. First one, then another, then all flapped their ears, waved their trunks, and trumpeted in joyful recognition. The mahouts goaded them mercilessly to attack, but they reared up to shrug off their riders and send them headlong to the ground.

Arvati and her kindred moved steadily across the field. Nahusha's elephants paid no heed to the threats and commands of their masters, but eagerly joined Arvati and their long-lost relatives. Free of their tormentors, they swept away the barricades of wrecked chariots. The warriors scrambled to escape, only to find themselves beset by other foes.

Through the gates rushed wild boars, slashing with curved tusks; wolves, snarling and snapping, followed them; a half-starved tiger and a ragged-maned lion sprang roaring into the midst of the terrified troops.

"More monkey's work!" Hashkat bounced up and down on the saddle. "They've unbolted Nahusha's animal cages!"

Seeing their foe in such confusion, Kirin and Skanda joined forces with Darshan to press a renewed attack. Some of Nahusha's troops had thrown down their weapons and raced in panic from the field. Others tried to make a stand as best they could. The folk of Ranapura had flung shut the gates, leaving the embattled warriors no choice but to fight or fly.

From the tail of his eye, Tamar glimpsed a burly, white-robed figure heaving his way into the midst of Nahusha's ranks. He thought, first, it was a *brahmana* gone mad, then saw the powerful arms and shaggy head.

"Jamba-Van!" Tamar cried, as the bear charged on, dashing to the ground all who stood in his way, as if they were no more than pieces of crockery in his *ashrama*. He turned and saw Mirri.

"Keep back!" Mirri had changed her shroud for hunter's buckskins; and, long hair flying, she sat astride Soma-Nandi.

The tiger, teeth bared and tail lashing, bounded abreast of Tamar. "Stay clear. Leave the rest to Arvati."

As she spoke, Tamar saw the herd of elephants break off their rampage. Arvati was beckoning with her trunk. All her kindred hurried to join her; and, shoulder to shoulder, the elephants formed a massive gray wall to surround the remnants of Nahusha's defeated army.

At the same time, Tamar caught sight of Nahusha's chariot. The driver had jumped out to run for his life. Nahusha, gripping the reins, lashed savagely at the horses. The chariot careened along the wall.

Tamar kicked his heels against Gayatri's flanks. Nahusha had slewed the chariot around the angle of the wall, but Tamar galloped after him through the ranks of retreating warriors. Nahusha was rapidly outdistancing him.

At full stretch, Gayatri checked and nearly stumbled. Ahead, Nahusha's chariot skidded to a halt and tipped sideways. The horses foundered, broke free of the shafts. Gayatri swerved, almost plunging into the wreckage. It took Tamar a moment to understand: Nahusha had driven too close to the edge of the pits encircling the city.

Tamar halted and swung down from Gayatri. Nahusha had clambered out of the disabled chariot.

"Well, well, here's the corpse-washer." Nahusha set his hands on his hips as Tamar leveled the spear. "It seems to have found a pointed stick. Does the creature play at being a warrior?"

Tamar took a pace toward him. "As I told you, Nahusha, I want your life, not your death. Surrender. Face justice honorably and I vow to let you live."

"You bargain with me?" Nahusha glanced scornfully at Tamar. "You want my life? Then come and get it. Throw

your little stick at me. I have no weapon. I broke my sword
on one of the rabble you sent against me. Are you afraid to
kill an unarmed man? You were so eager, once, to challenge
me. Now it is I who challenge you. In even combat, hand
to hand, by the warrior's code of honor. Have you the stomach to face a real *kshatriya* on equal terms? As I warned you,
corpse-washer, I bite very hard."

Tamar gripped the spear shaft and drew back his arm,
fury mounting at Nahusha's contempt. In his ears rang Ashwara's question on the eve of battle: Can any man kill and
keep his heart pure, or is all slaughter alike? And the *chandala*
asking: How are you different from Nahusha?

With an anguished cry, he flung away the spear and
sprang to grapple with him.

"No sword, corpse-washer," hissed Nahusha, one hand
seizing him by the throat with a strength Tamar had not
imagined. "No sword—but this."

Nahusha snatched a dagger from beneath his breastplate.
Tamar fought to twist away from the glinting blade. With
all his might, he wrestled free of Nahusha's grasp and stumbled back. Before he regained his balance, his legs were suddenly knocked from under him. He fell to the ground as
blurred shapes hurtled past. He heard Nahusha cry out, and
he flung up his arms against the dagger thrust.

32. To the Snow Mountains

It was too late. Tamar could do nothing to stop them. The once-caged animals attacked their tormentor from every side. The wolves flung themselves on Nahusha, one at his throat, the other sinking fangs into his upraised arm. The boar, whose onrush had knocked Tamar to the ground, charged ahead, savaging Nahusha with his tusks. The lion and tiger clawed Nahusha to his knees, while the wolves snarled and set their jaws tighter. The creatures, Tamar saw, all bore marks of the lash or branding iron; half starved though they were, their fury had given them strength to take revenge on their captor.

Nahusha screamed in rage and pain as the animals swarmed over him. For an instant, he kicked free; but, as he tried to stand, he stumbled over the brink of the pit, clutched at empty air, and plummeted onto the piercing spikes at the bottom.

Tamar jumped to his feet. The animals scattered to freedom. The tiger wheeled, fixed glowing eyes a moment on Tamar, then sprang.

The striped body vaulted past him. Mirri had ridden up on Soma-Nandi, and the tiger made straight for them. The girl barely had time to slide off Soma-Nandi's back as the pair of tigers rushed together, rubbing heads, licking each other's ears, rolling on the ground as playfully as kittens, and rumbling out loving purrs.

"This is Sunda, my mate." Soma-Nandi paused a moment from the joyful reunion. "I kept searching for him after I left you. When the Bandar-loka spread word that you needed help, I came as quickly as I could." She turned melting eyes on Sunda. "I never lost hope of finding you."

"Nor did I," said Sunda. "Even so, without the Bandar-loka I'd still be in Nahusha's cage."

Mirri had gone to the edge of the pit. She glanced down, then turned abruptly away. "He'll keep no more prisoners —animals or anyone else."

Kirin and Skanda had entered Ranapura when Tamar, Mirri, and the tigers galloped back. The cheering townsfolk had flung open the gates in welcome. Nahusha's shattered forces had fled or begged to surrender. Broken chariots and weapons still littered the field; stragglers wandered where the battle lines once stretched. Darshan was shouting for his troops to form orderly ranks. Arvati and her relatives had already gone in a triumphant procession through the city, but Tamar sighted Hashkat in the midst of the commotion. The monkey had tossed aside his warrior's gear and was cavorting gleefully. Tamar jumped down from Gayatri and made his way to embrace him. Adi-Kavi elbowed through the crowd, with Rajaswami and Jamba-Van behind him.

"It was all I could do to hold him back." Adi-Kavi chuckled. "*Brahmana* or not, he'd have run into the thick of it."

"I was quite carried away." Rajaswami tried his best to

sound apologetic. "My goodness, I don't know what came over me. And you, dear boy, you're undamaged? Excellent. All went as our dear *gopi* planned. And look who's come to join us," he added, as Jamba-Van laid an affectionate paw on the *acharya*'s shoulder. "What a pleasure to meet again, even in these disruptive circumstances."

"I never foresaw a day when I'd leave my *ashrama*," the bear said, "but when I heard my dear collague was in danger, I had to come here myself. Now that I've learned what happened to all of you"—Jamba-Van bristled and growled at the recollection—"I only wish I'd come sooner."

"Here's someone who wants to thank your Bandar-loka," Mirri said as she brought Sunda to Hashkat's side. "When they unbolted the cages—"

"What, another tiger?" broke in Garuda, who had flapped down to perch on Jagati's back. "Isn't one enough already? Two? Shmaa! You expect me to put up with both of them?"

"Skanda and Kirin were looking for you," Adi-Kavi told Tamar. "How you'll find them in all this lot, I can't imagine. The whole city's turned out to celebrate."

"I have one thing to do first." Tamar swung astride Gayatri; before Mirri could question him, he made his way over the crowded field, heading toward the river.

He went to the *shmashana*.

The burning ground was empty. The door of the hut stood open. He called out. No answer came. He dismounted and walked across the stretch of rubble. The wooden stake and the chain were gone. He stepped across the threshold and peered into the shadows of the room, bare except for a straw mat and a few pieces of earthenware.

Footsteps scraped the gravel behind him. He turned, about to speak. A bent-backed old man, tangled beard falling to his waist, stared at him with surprise and discomfort.

"The *chandala* who lived here," Tamar began. "Where has he gone? I must find him."

The old man shuffled back a few paces and put up his hands to keep Tamar at a distance. "Come no farther," he warned in a cracked voice. "You should not be in this place."

"Yes, I should. The *chandala* was my friend. Grandsire, tell me what became of him."

The man blinked his clouded eyes. "Tell?" He cupped a hand to his ear. "What?"

"All you know. Did warriors come and take him away? Did he escape? Save himself? Where is he now?"

The old man frowned and shook his head. Tamar repeated his questions. "Grandsire, do you understand me? There was a young man, as well. On a chain. Did the *chandala* speak of him?"

"Young man? No. Only me. I know nothing. I mind my own business. I do my work."

"When did you come here?" Tamar pressed. "How long ago?"

"Long?" The man was growing unhappy in Tamar's presence. "Long ago? When? Why do you ask? Go, leave me in peace. This is a place for the dead, not the living."

The old man clamped shut his toothless jaws, shuffled into the hut, and closed the door.

Tamar followed, but stopped at the threshold. He stood some while. Finally, he went back to Ranapura.

The townsfolk had begun decorating the streets with banners and garlands, in memory of Ashwara and in celebration of their freedom. Tamar understood that Kirin had been welcomed and acclaimed king. He made his way quickly to the palace. Mirri was waiting in the courtyard.

"The *chandala* said he'd take care of himself," Mirri replied, when Tamar told what had happened. "I'm sure he's all right. We'll try to find out later. Come, Kirin expects you at his durbar."

She led him, still troubled, to the great audience chamber. He had never seen a durbar such as this. Monkeys perched in every nook and cranny, under the eaves of the high ceiling or on the crossbeams. Arvati and several of her relatives towered over the *kshatriyas* thronging the hall. Beside her crouched Soma-Nandi and Sunda. Garuda and Akka were aloft, amid the Bandar-loka. Paying not much mind to anything else, Rajaswami and the bear were deep in conversation.

Taking on the duties of royal crier, Adi-Kavi called out their names and beckoned Mirri and Tamar to join Hashkat, Skanda, and Darshan flanking Kirin's throne.

"*Namaste.*" Kirin rose and pressed his palms together as Tamar and Mirri approached. His brow was even more deeply furrowed now; his face was heavy with sorrow. "King of Sundari, you have well kept your promise to our brother, and have done far better than your word. And you," he said, turning to Mirri, "with the help of all these forest creatures, you have given us our victory. We thank and honor you.

"Even so, I do not rejoice," Kirin went on. "Ashwara

should be in my place. I take this throne in the shadow of grief for him; and I vow, for all present to witness, that I will rule as he would have done.

"King of Sundari and you, worthy *gopi,* your rewards shall be as great as your service to our cause—"

"Reward? For keeping a promise?" Tamar broke in. "I claim none."

"Neither do I," Mirri added. "We don't ask anything for what we'd have done anyway."

"I offer it nonetheless," Kirin said. "The greatest treasure one kingdom can bestow on another: friendship and peace between my realm and yours."

"I do likewise," said Skanda. "King Rudra gave his life for Ashwara's sake, and I owe a duty to his people. Rudra's *kshatriya*s want me to be king of Chandragar. That's something I never expected, but a high honor"—for a moment there was the trace of his boyish grin—"and, yes, of course, I'll accept. So, I ask that you, in turn, accept my own vow of peace."

"That, gladly," Tamar said.

"I do have one question," Rajaswami put in, when Kirin declared the durbar at an end. "I suppose it's too much to hope, but has anyone noticed an umbrella lying about? No? Ah, well, since everything else turned out so happily, one should be willing to make a small sacrifice."

◆◆

They rested, for the next several days, in the Ranapura Palace. Skanda then left for Chandragar; and, one after the other, Soma-Nandi and Sunda, Arvati and her kindred, exchanged fond farewells with Tamar and Mirri. Jamba-Van, last to take his leave, did so with reluctance.

"My dear colleague, we part once again," the bear said as Rajaswami embraced him, "but my best hope is that you will someday find your way back to my *ashrama*. I have refined my views on the shape of infinity and would be glad for your opinion."

"I have refined my views on a number of things," said Rajaswami, "and would eagerly discuss them."

❦

"Majesty, when you left Sundari," Darshan later said to Tamar, "I laid your sandals on your throne to betoken that you are still our king—"

"Am I?" Tamar broke in. He had, with Darshan, gone to the rooftop terrace. Beyond Ranapura rose the heights of the Snow Mountains. "Should a king know fear? As I did? In battle, I was terrified—"

"Lad, so was I. Who isn't, if truth be told? You faced it down; no more can be asked. A man who claims to be fearless is an idiot or a liar."

"Even a *kshatriya?* When I rode with Skanda, I spared a man's life and told Skanda I'd killed him. Nahusha—at the end, would it have been my hand that slew him? I'll never know."

"Better a king who holds back from bloodshed than one who relishes it," Darshan said. "Enough, enough, lad. Come home. You see what this dream of yours has cost you already. Give it up; only more ill can come of it."

"Once, I might have done so," Tamar said. "I even tried to throw away my ring. I couldn't." He shook his head. "Tomorrow, we'll go into the mountains. As I must."

"For the sake of a promise you made? Or didn't make?"

Darshan burst out. "That's more than even a king's honor demands."

"This is for my own sake and by my own choice," Tamar said. "You think I only dreamed? That may well be. But I'll never be at peace until I'm sure one way or the other. Mirri understood that better than I did.

"You, old friend, go back to Sundari. Rule well. Love my people; do the best for them. This is my last command to you."

33. The Traveler

Next morning, on the field at Ranapura, Tamar rode through the ranks of his *kshatriyas*, honoring them, saying his thanks and farewells. At the end, he put his arms around Gayatri's neck, taking loving leave of her and Jagati. As Adi-Kavi warned that the high passes would be too difficult and dangerous for the horses, Darshan promised to take the steeds with him.

"They'll be fondly tended," the old warrior said. "They'll wait for you, lad, as I will." With a show of gruffness, he added, "Not happily or patiently."

"You, too, wait for me," Hashkat told Akka. "If I wore sandals, you could put them on my throne—if I had a throne. In any case, you keep an eye on the Bandar-loka while I'm tramping through the mountains."

"Who's tramping?" Garuda squawked. "Shmaa! What about me?"

"Fly, you malingering bird. What else?" Hashkat retorted. "You and Akka did well enough going to Sundari."

"Oh, yes, so I did," Garuda said sourly. "If you don't count being skewered with arrows and lurking in holes in the ground. But I'm not up to flying, let alone tramping."

"Of course you're not." Mirri hid a smile. "You'll stay with me until you get your strength back."

"Faker," muttered Hashkat, while Garuda, cooing happily, flapped to Mirri's shoulder. "Next, he'll want his meals served on a platter."

—◆—

Kirin had generously outfitted them with warm cloaks and stout boots, as well as stores of food, tents of coarse canvas, and other gear. Rajaswami insisted on carrying as much as his frail bones allowed; the others divided the burdens among themselves. By the time they reached the foothills overlooking Ranapura, Tamar realized why Adi-Kavi had warned against taking the horses. There were no paths, and the rocky outcroppings were too treacherous for even the most surefooted pack animals.

"Something puzzles me," Tamar said, as they gained the first heights. "How did Jaya travel to Sundari?" He pointed toward Kumeru and Sumeru. "No sign of a road, no trail, no footpath. Yet he had elephants, chariots, horses."

"Don't ask me," Garuda said. "I don't recognize any of this. Perhaps I've forgotten; it was so long ago."

"He might have taken a different way," Mirri said. "There could be a dozen roads out of the valley, for all you know, circling around in some other direction."

"If he ever came to Sundari in the first place."

"That's why you're here, isn't it? To find out."

Adi-Kavi was calling them. The *suta* had picked a sheltered spot amid the wind-twisted trees and was lashing together the panels of the tent. Tamar glanced back a moment over the distance they had covered, the stretches of shale and gravel, the stunted vegetation. Black against the setting sun, the bare branches shuddered in the sharp breeze. He blinked and looked again. Far below, a dark shape skirted a ravine, then, within the instant, vanished amid the trees.

Tamar shaded his eyes, waiting to see if the shadow would reappear. Nothing moved. He watched a little longer. It was, he decided, a trick of the light. He went to help pitch the tent and thought no more about it.

Two days later, he saw it again.

They had been following the high ridges overlooking the Sabla. Tamar, at first, hoped to find easier ground along the river itself but, as Adi-Kavi pointed out, the walls of the gorge were too sheer, the iron-dark cliffs falling straight to the water's edge. The *suta* was confident they would soon reach the slopes leading into the valley; and so they pressed on, keeping the winding blue and white current always in sight. That afternoon, Adi-Kavi had chosen to halt in a rocky cavern where wind and weather had eaten away a domed chamber; in the middle, a pool of clear, drinkable water.

They had begun hauling in their gear when Tamar again saw the dark figure appear and disappear behind a distant tumble of boulders. This time, he was sure it was no trick of the light. This time, he was sure it was a man.

He called Mirri and the others and pointed to where he had glimpsed the figure. By then, it was gone. Even the sharp-eyed Adi-Kavi could make out no sign of it.

"You're certain it wasn't a mountain creature of some sort?" Mirri said. "A stray animal? Too bad you didn't have a better look."

"What creature would be fool enough to roam around in this desolation?" said Hashkat. "Not one of the Bandar-loka, I can tell you."

"As long as whoever or whatever it is keeps a polite distance," put in Rajaswami, "I shouldn't be too concerned. He'll go his way, we'll go ours."

Tamar was not satisfied. "If he's following us, I want to know why. Stay in the cave, all of you. I'll go and find out."

"It'll be dark before you get back," Mirri reminded him. She turned to Garuda, perched on a pile of gear. "Can you fly there and see? It's no distance—for an eagle. You'll take a quick glance around and be here again in time for your food."

Garuda grumbled and muttered; but, finally, with a toss of his beak, he flew where Tamar pointed. While Tamar and Mirri hauled gear and provisions into the cave, Rajaswami bustled about laying blankets and lighting lamps. Hashkat and Adi-Kavi had set off to find dry twigs and bits of moss for a cook fire. By the time the monkey and the *suta* were back, the shadows had deepened and pellets of snow whirled over the ridges.

Tamar paced uneasily. Garuda had been gone overlong. Mirri, too, was anxious. They were ready to throw on their cloaks and search for the bird when he swooped into the cave.

"I saw! I saw!" Garuda crowed. His feathers were crusted with sleet, an icicle hung from the tip of his beak, but he squawked jubilantly as he landed on the earthen floor. "It was marvelous!"

"I knew you'd find out." Mirri tried to calm the excited bird, who was clucking with gleeful self-satisfaction. "Tell us—"

"Shmaa! Wonderful. I flew like—like an eagle!" Garuda cackled proudly. "Soaring, diving—"

"Leave off, you puffed-up chicken," Hashkat cried. "What did you see?"

"A man? An animal?" Tamar knelt beside Garuda. "Did you have a clear look?"

"Eh? Oh, that." Garuda shrugged his wings. "No, not a trace of anything or anybody. A waste of my valuable time. I gave up searching. But then, since I was already in the air, I thought: Why not fly just a little farther, toward the valley. And there it was. Mahapura!

"Just as I remembered—or, I'm starting to remember. Beautiful! The tall towers, the eight gates—we're nearly there; I'll finish my errand after all this time. Oh, I hope King Jaya forgives me for taking so long. But I didn't fail him. I'll put the ruby in his hand—"

Garuda broke off and cast a beady eye on Tamar. "The ruby—you've got it safely put away, don't you? Yes? Well, let me see it," he went on, as Tamar took the gem from beneath his garments and held it in front of the bird. "You'll still carry it the rest of the way for me. We've come this far, I'm taking no chances on dropping it again. I just want to look and admire."

"Gloat is what you mean," said Hashkat, as Tamar set down the ruby.

"Call it what you please." Garuda squatted on top of the stone as if about to hatch an egg. "The gem's been tossed around enough. I want it to be with me a little while. I find it very comforting. Do you mind?"

"Enjoy yourself," said Mirri, while Garuda crooned and rocked back and forth. "Sit on it as long as you want. You have a right to be pleased."

"So there truly is a palace," Tamar began, "truly a King Jaya—"

A heavy-set figure was standing in the mouth of the

cave. Tamar got hastily to his feet. The man was wrapped
in a cloak of animal skins, a fur cap pressed over a hedge of
black hair. Frozen droplets glittered in his beard; snow
crusted his heavy boots.

"No harm, no harm," he called out, holding up his
hands as Tamar reached for his sword. "I only beg a little
warmth, a mouthful of food if you can spare it. My name's
Griva."

"I saw you before." Tamar looked closely at him. "In
the ravine. Then, by the mound of boulders. Why are you
following us?"

"Am I?" Griva stepped all the way into the cave. He
seemed to bring the night chill with him. "Following you?
We only happen to find ourselves on the same path."

"What path is that?"

"I might ask you likewise. But, your business is your
own and no concern of mine—unless we have an interest
in common."

"And that would be?" said Mirri.

Griva's eyes darted around the cave. His weather-
blackened face folded into a grin. "Stones," he said.

34. The Fire Flower

That's right. Stones. Bright, shiny ones. Gems, eh? You've found a few yourself, I'd not be surprised." He stamped the snow off his boots and started toward the cook fire. Tamar put out an arm to hold him back, but Griva shouldered past, skirted the pool, and hunkered down by the flames. "These mountains are full of them. They hide in all manner of nooks and crannies. Sometimes," he added, with a wink, "where you'd never think of looking. But I sniff them out and pry them loose."

"That's not our business." Tamar drew his sword. "If it's yours, go on about it."

Griva eyed the blade and gave a throaty laugh. "Now, now, no need to get the wind up. I'm no robber, if that's what you fear. Food and drink's all I ask. A little corner to sleep in. You'll not deny me that much, will you?"

"He has a point, my boy," Rajaswami whispered. "Hospitality and courtesy. You can't turn him away."

Griva, meantime, had attacked the food that Mirri handed him, grinding it in his heavy jaws and wiping his mouth on the back of a hairy hand. He squinted an eye at Tamar.

"I'll not intrude on your snug little corner here," he said, settling himself. "I'm not one to stay where I'm not welcome. Oh, yes, you're thinking you'll be glad to see the

back of me. Who could blame you? A stranger out of nowhere. You'd not expect to have dealings with a rough-
and-ready fellow like me.

"But don't be too quick to send me away," Griva added.
"There could be a tidy profit for both of us."

"We're not looking for profit," Mirri said.

"What if it jumped out at you?" Griva reached under
his cloak and pulled out a leather pouch. He untied it and
spilled the contents into his palm: a heap of gems.

"Little twinklers, eh?" Griva licked his lips. "Beauties.
You'd almost want to eat them up. I have more, besides.
Plenty for all of you."

"Why show us these?" Tamar demanded.

"Whispers. I've heard a few. A word here, a word there.
Nothing that means anything by itself. Put them together,
you have an interesting tale. How a young lad—very much
like yourself—got his hands on something. And what would
that be? A stone. A shiny little red stone. Do you follow me
so far?"

Tamar did not answer. Griva went on in an amiable
tone:

"For the sake of the tale, let's call that little stone a ruby.
Now, let's suppose there's a rich man: a gem-fancier, a col-
lector, as you might say. He wants a stone like that—not
for its value; it's half the size of the ones I've got right here.
No, it's just a curio, an odd sort of trinket. But he's made
up his mind. You know how these collectors are.

"So he sends a fellow with an eye for such things—a
fellow like me, if you will—to track it down and buy it for
him. At a good price, that's understood.

"There's a happy ending to the tale," continued Griva.
"The young lad's delighted at the chance to reap a fortune;

he trades that little ruby he's carrying for, say, a fistful of diamonds. So, everybody's overjoyed with the bargain; they go their own ways, simple as that. A pleasant story, don't you agree?"

Tamar tightened his grip on the sword. "I don't know who you are or who you serve, and I don't care. Get out."

Griva shrugged and poured the gems back into the pouch. "There's yet another ending to the story, and not such a happy one. That young man and his friends are suddenly dead."

Griva leaped to his feet. Quick as an eye-blink, he wrenched away Tamar's blade and broke it over his knee.

"No more tales, King of Sundari." He gripped Tamar by the front of the jacket and pulled him close, until their faces nearly touched. Griva hissed and bared his teeth. "Play no games with me. I know you've got the ruby. I'll have it now."

Adi-Kavi had sprung up to grapple him from behind, but Griva shook him off and sent him sprawling. "Give. I'll tear you apart, you and all the rest. Look at me. See who you're dealing with."

Griva's face blurred and shifted before Tamar's eyes. The teeth lengthened into fangs, the body swelled and burst from its garments, the fingers clutching Tamar's jacket turned to claws.

"Rakshasa!" The *suta* flung himself again on the demon's back and seized him by the hair, holding on with all his strength.

"Garuda, take the ruby!" Mirri shouted. "Fly! Fly to Jaya!"

Seeing the bird snatch the gem from under its feathers, the *rakshasa* tossed Tamar aside and lunged for Garuda.

Wings beating, the eagle streaked from the cave. Hashkat darted across the ground and wrapped his arms around the demon's legs. Mirri threw herself on the struggling *rakshasa*. Rajaswami picked up a burning branch from the cook fire and shook it at Griva with all the ferocity he could muster.

Growling, the *rakshasa* seized the branch in his jaws, snapped it into bits and spat them blazing at Rajaswami. Griva heaved himself closer to the mouth of the cave.

"Hold fast!" Tamar understood that Griva was not so much trying to escape his attackers as he was seeking a different victim. "He's after Garuda."

"Let him go," Rajaswami called. "He can't catch an eagle."

Tamar was about to follow the *acharya*'s urging. It crossed his mind that Garuda was already aloft and safely in flight to Mahapura. But, even as he watched, the *rakshasa* hunched up his shoulders. He spread out his arms: They shuddered for a moment, then turned into powerful wings. Glossy feathers like iron scales covered the demon's body. The legs, with their talons, had become those of a hideous bird of prey.

Hashkat screamed. The hooked beak now jutting from what had been the *rakshasa*'s face ripped into the monkey's arm. Bleeding, Hashkat still clung to the raging bird, but the creature flung him to the ground. Adi-Kavi, shaken loose, tumbled backward. As Mirri kicked and pummeled the *rakshasa*, Tamar sprang past the buffeting wings, leaped onto the demon's back, and locked his hands around its neck.

The *rakshasa* doubled its efforts to gain the mouth of the cave. Tamar felt his fingers slip as the huge bird twisted its neck around, trying to savage him with its beak.

That same moment, wings flapping, screeching at the top of his voice, Garuda streaked back into the chamber.

"No! Get out!" Mirri ordered. "Do as I told you. Save your ruby. Save yourself!"

The *rakshasa* whirled to fend off Garuda's attack. Tamar's grip at last gave way; he fell and skidded across the cavern floor. Garuda swooped and circled, striking out with beak and talons. Wind whistled as the *rakshasa*'s wings unfolded to their full breadth, beating Garuda to the ground. The *rakshasa* sprang into the air, ready to plummet onto the stunned eagle.

In the pool, the water roiled and churned into foam. A long shape burst up, scales glistening. The great serpent flung itself at the *rakshasa*.

"Shesha!" Tamar cried.

The Naga prince had lunged to grip the *rakshasa* in his coils. The demon bird flailed its wings, fighting to break free of Shesha's encircling body. The Naga tightened his hold and bore the creature to earth. The *rakshasa* shrieked in fury. Its feathers began glowing red-hot; a tongue of flame shot from its beak. Shesha writhed closer to the edge of the pool; then, with the *rakshasa* locked in his grasp, rolled into the water and vanished in its depths.

The surface of the pool hissed, as if a flaming torch had been quenched. Tamar ran to the edge. He could see nothing of the Naga prince. The water was calm again. Mirri and Adi-Kavi drew him away.

"We were enemies, Shesha and I," Tamar murmured. "We fought once. He would have drowned me. Yet, he came—"

"Yes, King of Sundari, so I did." Shesha's head rose from the water. "For the sake of the mercy you showed me."

The Naga prince slithered all his length from the pool. "The *rakshasa* is destroyed, as he would have destroyed you. His powers were great; only a Naga could have stood against him."

"But you—Prince Shesha, how have you come here?" Tamar pressed his palms together and bowed his head in gratitude. "We owe you our lives. You followed us. Why?"

"We feared for you," answered the Naga. "Some while after you departed our realm, we had word of a *rakshasa* seeking your trail. We could only guess that it had to do with the ruby you chose from our treasure, and that the gem was of even greater value than we had supposed.

"For a time, I lost track of you, and knew only that you wished to go to Mahapura. I could reach you no sooner. The Naga kingdom runs through all waterways and secret springs," Shesha added, "but none of us has dared to venture this far."

Mirri had gone to cradle the motionless Garuda in her arms. Shesha lifted his head, crowned by the glittering sapphire, and cast unblinking eyes around the cave.

"The thieving monkey is still with you." Shesha darted out his forked tongue. "I expected the wretch would have long since deserted you."

"He became a brave friend," Tamar said, "and a worthy king of his people."

"And badly hurt," put in Adi-Kavi, leaving Hashkat's side. "A *rakshasa*'s bite is venomous." He laid a hand on Tamar's arm. "Come to him. I fear he's dying."

35. The Palace of Illusions

ashkat slumped against the cave wall. The monkey's face was drawn, his eyes sunken. Tamar, with Shesha slithering after, knelt beside him.

"What, the overgrown angleworm?" Hashkat raised his head a little and grinned painfully. "Still after me? I've heard of bearing a grudge, but not so far as this."

"He killed the *rakshasa*," Tamar said quietly. "He came to help us."

"In that case, what took him so long? If that wiggler had a shell, he'd be a snail." Hashkat tried to regain his old impudence, but his voice faltered and he shuddered violently.

Mirri, cradling the stunned Garuda, glanced, questioning, at Adi-Kavi. Rajaswami whimpered in distress. Hashkat curled into himself, his chin sinking to his breast.

"Strong poison," Adi-Kavi said aside to Tamar. "I have no antidote. Nothing I can do for him. This is beyond my skill."

"Not beyond mine." Shesha spread his hood. "I carry the means to heal him. Take the gem I wear. Hold it to his wound. The venom of a *rakshasa* is fatal. It will take all the power of my jewel to work against it. After that, the stone will be worthless. Use it carefully; it will serve this one time only."

"You'd give up the jewel he tried to steal from you?"

Tamar said. "At the riverside, you'd have taken his life on account of it."

"Now I give him his life," replied Shesha. "My father pardoned the foolish creature. Can I do less? The Naga Raja reproached me for letting wrath drive out reason and compassion. His words have weighed on me ever since. As I wish to heal this frivolous monkey, so I wish to heal my own dharma."

Prince Shesha lowered his head. Tamar took the jewel from the Naga's brow; and, as Shesha instructed, set it on Hashkat's arm. Hashkat lay motionless. Tamar feared that the poison had spread too far and had already claimed the monkey's life. The sapphire's blue inner flame dimmed little by little, then winked out.

"It is done," Shesha said. "The stone is useless. Cast it away. If it has failed, I have no more to offer."

Hashkat stirred and opened one eye. "What's that crawler done now?" He sat up and peered at his arm, as whole as if it had never been wounded.

"Saved an impudent monkey is what he's done," Mirri said, smiling.

Hashkat popped his eyes at Shesha. "In spite of all—?" He bowed his head and pressed his palms together. "*Namaste,* Prince of the Naga-loka. I'm grateful. You're a fine fellow." He stuck out his tongue and grinned wickedly. "For a royal wiggler."

"*Namaste,* O flea-ridden tree-climber," Shesha replied, with a fond glint in his eyes. "May your life be as long as your insolence is great."

The Naga folded his hood and turned to Tamar. "King of Sundari, our quarrel is over. Go your way. Guard the ruby well. Its power may be greater than any of us know. I dare stay no longer. Without the protection of my jewel, my own life is at risk. *Namaste.*"

The Naga prince heaved his coils to the edge of the pool. Hashkat scrambled after him:

"Wait, wait! As you saved my life, at least I owe you the truth. I really did mean to give back your gem."

By then, Prince Shesha had slid into the dark waters and vanished.

Garuda, meantime, had begun coughing and wheezing in Mirri's arms. "Set me down, set me down. Shmaa! I can hardly breathe."

"You shouldn't be here in the first place," Mirri said. "I told you to fly off."

"Well, I didn't," Garuda snapped. "Leave my friends in danger? What kind of eagle would I be? I thought—what I wanted to do—" Garuda sniffed and hesitated. He gave Mirri a sidelong glance. "I was going to give that disgusting *rakshasa* the ruby. That's all he wanted; he'd have let you go."

"Oh, I very much doubt it," said Rajaswami. "You can't bargain with those fellows. They never keep their word."

"Even so," Garuda said, "I thought I'd try."

"You'd really have done that for us?" Mirri said.

Garuda ducked his head and shuffled his feet. "Well, yes," he grumbled. "No matter how much aggravation you've caused me—all right, if you must know, I—well, I'm fond of you all, even the monkey. Ruby? Shmaa! A shiny stone. Who cares?"

"You meant to save our lives," Tamar said. "We owe you."

"You can be sure—" Garuda shook his head. "You owe me nothing."

"The ruby's safe?" Mirri said. "Where?"

"There was an accident." Garuda coughed and snorted. "It's stuck in my craw. I swallowed it."

"Ate it?" Hashkat slapped his knees. "You silly rag mop! Come, open your beak. I'll fish it out."

"Get away!" Garuda squawked. "Leave it alone. At least I know where it is."

◆━◆

The world turned green, so green it dazzled him. From the time they left the cave, that next morning, until Adi-Kavi led them on to their final descent, Tamar had seen only grim black outcroppings of bare stones, glaring stretches of empty snowfields, pinnacles of ice. Once, as they inched their way downward, the *suta* had been obliged to chip footholds in what looked like a frozen waterfall. Then the valley burst around them, with sun-swept woodlands and rich meadows; and, ahead, as Garuda had told, the walls and soaring towers of Mahapura.

Hashkat's jaw dropped. Rajaswami stared, eyes full of wonder, and murmured, "Who could have imagined? Yes, this is indeed the realm of a great maharajah."

"And so, at the end, it's true." Tamar took Mirri's hand. "Not a dream, after all. I wish it had been. How Jaya means to deal with me—"

"He'll have to deal with me, too," Mirri said. "He expected a *kshatriya*. I don't think he reckoned on a *gopi*."

Garuda, impatient, had flown ahead. With Mirri beside him, Tamar walked reluctantly through the gates. Before him stretched tree-lined avenues, parks, lakes, and promenades.

"Do you see those crowds?" Hashkat frowned and scratched his head. "Astonishing!"

"I see none," Tamar said, looking where Hashkat gestured.

"That's what's astonishing," said Hashkat. "Nobody. Nowhere. Where are the people? The place is empty. The city of a maharajah? There's not even a monkey."

"Curious, but easily explained," Rajaswami suggested. "They've all gone to—ah, yes, to some local festival."

"Hush." Mirri put a finger to her lips. "I don't see anyone either, but I can hear them."

As Tamar listened, voices rose from all sides: water sellers and hucksters crying their wares, merchants haggling, the laughter of children at play, all the sounds of a busy capital.

"What is this place?" he whispered. "Where have we come?"

A many-towered palace loomed in front of him, the gates open and unguarded. More perplexed than ever, he crossed the wide courtyard, as empty as the rest of the city.

"Where are Jaya's warriors? Chariots? Elephants?" Tamar stepped past the tall portals into a corridor stretching as far as his eyes could see, glittering as if paved and walled with crystal. He took a pace forward, then shouted a warning. The ground had opened in front of him. He stared into a shimmering pool at the bottom of a steep gorge. He stumbled back. Mirri was calling to him. He turned in the direction of her voice, only to collide with a wall.

A dozen figures sprang up, roughly garbed, their faces wind-hardened and sun-blackened. He reached for his sword, forgetting the scabbard was empty. He flung up his arms. The figures did likewise. Only then did he realize he was seeing himself in the surrounding mirrors.

Another corridor opened. He plunged through. Mirri was there. He ran to her. Hashkat and Adi-Kavi had halted farther on, where the passage abruptly ended. Rajaswami, bewildered, turned first one way then another.

"The palace is a trap!" Tamar burst out. "Jaya's caught us in it." He stared around him, raised his clenched fists and shouted, "Show yourself, Jaya! Do you claim my life? Then let me see you: king to king, man to man."

"You waste your breath," said Adi-Kavi, coming to Tamar's side. "If I see the world as it is, I also see the world as it isn't. This is *maya*. Illusion. Nothing more than shadows in our minds. Our eyes are telling us lies and we're believing them."

"We're still caught," Tamar exclaimed. "We can't get out."

"Shadows, only shadows," Adi-Kavi said. "Why fear them? Do as I tell you. Pay them no heed. Don't even look. Close your eyes to them. Walk straight on, wherever it leads you."

Hashkat and Rajaswami had come to join them. With Mirri's hand in his, Tamar stepped blindly ahead, expecting at every moment to lose his footing and topple into a void. When he ventured to open his eyes, he was at the doorway of what was clearly a royal chamber. He glimpsed couches and draperies, richly ornamented silken screens on frames of polished ebony.

"Stay back," he warned Mirri and the rest. "Jaya wants my death, none other. But I mistrust him. He already tried to deceive us. All our lives could be in danger."

Before Mirri could protest, he stepped across the threshold. He glanced hastily around, and took another pace into the chamber. Near a pile of embroidered cushions, he saw a table holding dice, cup, and board for a game of *aksha*.

A figure in white robes and a shawl stood looking out one of the tall casement windows. The man turned and beckoned.

Tamar found himself face to face with the *chandala*.

36. Jaya

So. You're here, are you?" the *chandala* said. "You found your way after all."

"And you?" Tamar, hands outstretched, had started toward him. He stopped short. The *chandala* was smiling, but something in his voice and bearing puzzled him. "I looked for you at the burning ground. I was afraid you'd come to harm. You'd gone. Here? With Jaya? Where is he?"

"You see him. I am Jaya."

Tamar stared. "This is more illusion. Trickery!" he burst out. "What mockery is this? Who are you? What are you?"

"As I told you."

"Why do you lie to me?" Tamar flung back. "No. The one who came to me in Sundari was a king, a warrior. An arrogant, pitiless *kshatriya*. No man of kindness or compassion. Not you, not you."

"Call me a liar if you will; it is truth nonetheless. Do you doubt me? Shall I repeat the verses your *acharya* recited? The hawk and the sparrow. Not so? Shall I tell you the numbers we threw when we played *aksha?*"

"Tell me what you please. I saw what I saw."

"So you did. Because you yourself were a *kshatriya*. You could not have imagined me as anything else. Would you have welcomed a *chandala* to your palace then?

Would you have agreed to my little game? And given your word, as one warrior to another?"

"Rajaswami and Darshan were there. All my courtiers—"

"You thought so. They were not with you. I caused them to sleep soundly. I laid *maya* on you. There were only the two of us.

"A hunter challenged you in the forest, did he not?" Jaya went on. "And you shot an arrow that set in motion all that followed. I was the hunter, the same who tended Garuda and Akka when their need was greatest—"

Jaya broke off. During this, Mirri and the others—paying no heed to Tamar's warning—had come into the chamber and had been listening, as much taken aback as Tamar himself.

"*Namaste,* Mirri." Jaya put his palms together. "You have endured much for the sake of your love. Your spirit has only grown more beautiful. And you, *suta,* I am glad to see you safe and well. What a clumsy thief you were. Do you recall a spider whose life you saved? I can tell you now: It was I.

"An insolent youth named Hashkat mocked a wandering *rishi* who turned him into a monkey," Jaya said. "I was that *rishi*. And you, *brahmana,* as for your cherished colleague, I was the sage who offered him knowledge when he intended to eat me.

"I have been all those and many others," Jaya said. "I am as I choose to be."

"I must believe you," Tamar said, after a long moment. "Truth behind truth, as Jamba-Van told me. It wasn't a dream. It happened. We gambled, life against life. I lost.

"Darshan reproached me when I left Sundari. He told me I knew nothing of the world. I know a little more than I did. I've seen kings betray their word, noble *kshatriya*s break their warrior's code, honor meaningless, dharma forgotten. The way of the world. There are other ways—as a *chandala* told me, on the burning ground. He was right. I've seen as much goodness as evil.

"In Sundari, I told a maharajah I was not his dog. Nor am I now. But even a dog's life is as precious as a king's. Death—I've seen my fill. I fear and hate it. I look at my own and see it wears the mask of a friend. Even so, I defy you.

"Once, I'd have accepted death as the price of a game. For the sake of honor. Not now. A fool's wager. A man does not stake his life on a throw of the dice."

Tamar looked squarely at Jaya. "Do you claim my life? You won't take it easily. I'll stand against you with all my strength." Tamar held up his hand. "Your emblem. It binds me no longer. I give it back to you."

In one motion, he tore the iron ring from his finger and flung it on the gaming table. The cup overturned, the dice scattered. In a voice half amused, half pitying, Jaya said:

"Who spoke of taking your life? Is that what you understood? No, I said only that your life was mine. Destroy it? Why should I? You've done as I hoped."

"You hoped? For what?"

"Even I do not know all the paths of karma," Jaya said. "I knew only this: Had Nahusha triumphed, his lust for power would have goaded him to conquer kingdom after kingdom. Yours would not have been spared. I warned you of wild dogs on the hunt. Your *gopi*'s village would have fallen to him as well. Your people, Ashwara's people: all, all, would have been no more than Nahusha's slaves.

"I gambled," Jaya went on, "that you might prevent it. The stakes were higher than any game of *aksha.*"

"Are you telling me you foresaw this?" Tamar rounded on him furiously. "Had you no other way to stop him? Only bloodshed and destruction? You caused it? You let it happen—?"

"No." Jaya silenced him with a glance. "You have your dharma as I have mine, and I am bound by it. I set possibilities in motion. They must work themselves out in their own way."

"Why, then, choose me?"

"Choose?" Jaya raised an eyebrow. "Do you suppose you were the only king to play *aksha* with me?

"There were others I visited before you," Jaya continued. "Some declined the game and I went my way. Of those who lost, some refused to honor their pledge. Others tried to keep their word. They lost their lives in the course of their journey, or gave up before it ended. Your kingdom was the last, the least, at which I stopped.

"Take no offense," Jaya added. "You simply happened to be available."

"No more than that?"

"No more than that—at the beginning. At the end, you became a great deal more."

So many questions began jostling into his mind that Tamar was at a loss which to ask first. Meantime, an eagle had glided through the casement. The bird's feathers shone golden, glistening in the sunlight as it flew straight to Mirri's shoulder.

"I'm sorry I couldn't stay with you lot," the bird said. "Did you ever have a ruby stuck in your throat? It hurts. I needed my master's help right away."

"Garuda?" Mirri cried. "Is that you?"

"Shmaa! Who else?"

"It's him," said Hashkat. "I'd know that 'Shmaa' anywhere."

"You're beautiful," said Mirri. "You look—not like yourself at all."

"On the contrary, he looks exactly like himself," Jaya said. "As once he was, so he is again. I admit he was a pitiful sight. I took out the stone—no harm done."

Garuda bobbed his shining head. "I owe you. All of you."

"I, too," Jaya said. "His task was even more important than your own." He opened his hand. The ruby lay like a flame cupped in his palm. "The Fire Flower, as you call it, has come back to me. Had it not, King of Sundari, the consequences would have been far worse than anything Nahusha could have done.

"Even the Naga Raja did not guess its power. The *rakshasa* who stole it from me understood it very well. He had not learned how to make it serve him. In time, he would have done so. Then all would have been lost.

"The Fire Flower is a gem of death—and of life," Jaya went on. "Whoever learns to use it can, within an instant, call down death on anyone he chooses; or, if he so wishes, summon the dead to life. With it, the *rakshasa* would have held the world and all its creatures in bondage."

"And I carried such a gem," Tamar murmured, "never knowing what it was."

"Just as well you did not," Jaya said. "Even to suspect its nature would have been a temptation to use it. Such power is too great for anyone to hold."

"Now you have it again," Mirri said. "It's in safe hands."

"No, it is not," Jaya said. "When it was in my possession, even I found myself drawn to use it. Its flame whispered and beckoned; my heart hungered for it. I told myself I would make it serve only good: Yet, I knew, in time I might not be able to tell good from evil—and do evil, telling myself I was doing good.

"I sent Garuda to regain it for me." Jaya fixed his eyes on the Fire Flower. The man's face, Tamar saw, clouded with regret close to grief. "It draws me, still. I do as I must."

He set the ruby on the flagstone floor and trampled it under his heel.

The gem remained unbroken.

"How can this be?" Jaya murmured. "Have I no strength to shatter it?"

There was fear in the man's voice that Tamar had never heard before. Jaya stared down at the Fire Flower:

"Does a hidden corner of my heart yet wish to keep it? And holds me back, at the end, from destroying it?" Jaya put his palms together and pressed them to his brow. "May I do this in all purity, without misgivings. May this truly be my will, fully and completely."

Jaya drew a long breath and, again, trampled the gem with all his might. Tamar threw up his hands to shield his eyes against the sudden, blinding shaft of crimson flame. It shot upward, whirled in a blazing cloud, then burst and filled the chamber with jagged streaks of scarlet. That same instant,

Tamar felt the ground heave and shudder beneath his feet: a long, sickening tremor as if a crack had opened in the earth.

Wind shrieked in his ears. He flung himself toward Mirri and held her as the chamber seemed to tilt askew. Everything blurred, turned fluid and shapeless. His heart pounded: Each beat took forever, as if time itself had ripped apart.

Then, within the moment, the room was clear and sunlit again. Jaya was standing, head bowed. Of the Fire Flower, there remained only a little heap of red powder.

"It is done." Jaya, after some while, looked up. "I am free of it. Leave me. I wish to be alone with my meditations.

"Our dealings with each other have well ended. Return safely, all of you. I promise your journey will be quicker and gentler than the paths that brought you here.

"Take with you my love and gratitude. You, *suta,* what may I offer you in token? What is your fondest wish?"

Adi-Kavi shrugged. "I've been cursed—and blessed—with curiosity. I'd ask only that I never lose it. Apart from that—as a matter of curiosity—I'd wish to know why Mahapura, so empty of people, is filled with their voices, and your palace with illusions."

"Illusions are made to be seen through, as you did," Jaya said, "and the city is not empty. You have yet to see all that lies beyond your vision. As you will, be sure of it. You see the world as it is; someday you will see it as it might be.

"As for you, Hashkat," Jaya said, hiding a twinkle behind a stern glance, "I suspect you are as impudent now as when first we met. Even so, you have been punished long enough. Monkey, I restore you to your human shape."

"Hold on a minute," Hashkat broke in. "I appreciate

your kindness, but—no, thank you. I've seen enough of humans and their doings. I'm happy as I am. I'll stay a monkey.

"What I might ask, what I've missed more than anything," Hashkat added, "is—my tail. If you could possibly arrange—"

"Your wish is already granted."

Hashkat twisted his head around and whooped with delight to see his tail, longer and more luxuriant than it had ever been.

"And you, King of Sundari? And you, his beloved *gopi,* what are your wishes?"

"For myself?" Mirri said, with loving eyes on Tamar. "All I could wish, I have."

"I, too," said Tamar. "For my kingdom, I wish it to be happy, its people loving and merciful toward each other. I wish there to be an end of caste, a time when *chandala*s will be as honored and cherished as all others."

"I am sorry. I cannot grant that wish," Jaya said. "Only you and your *gopi* bride, and those who come after you, can make it come true.

"But you will not go empty-handed. One thing I give you." Jaya went to a side table and took up a wreath of flowers, still fragrant and unwithered.

"I wove this," Mirri murmured. "I thought it had been long lost."

"Only waiting for you," Jaya said. "Set it now around your beloved's neck. These blossoms that you picked once will never fade."

As Mirri did so, Jaya turned to Rajaswami. *"Brahmana,* what is your own heart's wish?"

"Why—I hadn't really given it much thought," Rajaswami answered. "Since everything's come out on the bright side, I'm quite satisfied. All I would hope is to visit my dear colleague, Jamba-Van, again."

"So you shall," Jaya said. "When the time comes, you will know it is the moment for you to go once more into the forest. You will find the bear's *ashrama*. He will be awaiting you, and there will you stay to your heart's content.

"And so shall you all," Jaya added. "I built the *ashrama* for travelers like yourselves. Your paths will lead you there, if you so desire.

"You, Tamar, and you, Mirri, will find the island where once you danced. You will dance there as you did, and your hearts will ever be those of young lovers. *Forever then, forever once again.*"

"You know the verses we spoke to each other?" said Mirri.

Jaya smiled. "I was the flute player in the shadows." He pressed his palms together. "Go in peace. *Namaste.*"

"Ah—one thing did occur to me," said Rajaswami. "Only a passing thought, a triviality. I wonder—no, no, never mind. It's of no importance."

"On the contrary," said Jaya. "I'd not have let you leave without it."

He went again to the table. "Things that are lost have a way of turning up here. I believe this is yours," he added, putting an object in Rajaswami's hands, as the *acharya* beamed with delight.

It was a white umbrella.

———◆———

Glossary

acharya (ah-*char*-yah): teacher, scholar, spiritual counselor

aksha (*ahk*-shah): gambling game involving dice-throwing

ashrama (ahsh-*rah*-mah): secluded forest retreat for study and meditation, hermitage

Bandar-loka (*ban*-dahr *loh*-kah): kingdom of the monkeys, monkey-folk

brahmana (brah-*mah*-nah): member of highest caste of priests, scholars, philosophers

caste: ancient system of class structure and social order. Of highest rank, the *brahmana*s—scholars, priests, philosophers. Next, the military class of warriors, *kshatriya*s. Third, *vaishya*s, merchants and farm owners. Last and lowest, the *shudra*s, peasants and unskilled laborers. Excluded from the caste structure were the shunned "untouchables," the *panchama*s or *pariah*s, who performed the most menial, undesirable, distasteful work; still lower and most degraded, even criminals, were the *chandala*s.

chakra (*chah*-krah): sharp-edged discus thrown as a weapon

chandala (*chahn*-dah-lah): lowest, most despised, and degraded outcast

dharma (*dahr*-mah): goodness, virtue, righteousness, conscience; a code of proper conduct, a deep and driving sense of obligation to do what is right

durbar (*duhr*-bahr): royal court, assembly, audience

gopi (*goh*-pee): young woman cow-tender, milkmaid, dairy-maid

karma (*kahr*-mah): series of deeds and actions with their consequences; loosely, "fate," or the actions that are the contents of one's fate

kshatriya (kuh-*shah*-tree-yah): warrior, of the high military caste

maharajah (masc.), maharani (fem.) (mah-ha-*rah*-jah, mah-ha-*rah*-nee): great king, great queen; exalted ruler

mahout (mah-*hoot*): elephant driver

maya (*mah*-yah): illusion, spell, enchantment

Naga-loka (*nah*-gah *loh*-kah): serpent kingdom, serpent-folk

namaste (nah-*mah*-stay): expression of respect, honor, reverence; shown by pressing one's palms together

nayka (*nah-ee*-kah): army corporal

pye-dog (pie dog): wild, scavenging dog

raja (masc.), rani (fem.) (*rah*-jah, *rah*-nee): king, queen; powerful ruler

rakshasa (rahk-*shah*-sah): evil demon, able to assume human or animal shape

rishi (*ree*-shee): sage, of great wisdom and spiritual powers

sankula (*sahn*-koo-lah): violent combat; vicious free-for-all fight where no rules of war are observed

shmashana (shmah-*shah*-nah): cremation area where bodies are ceremonially burned

shudra (*shoo*-drah): peasant, unskilled laborer, member of lowest caste or social standing

suta (*soo*-tah): court attendant who declaims praises for a king

Lloyd Alexander's interest in the world's mythology has provided the inspiration for many of his greatest books. The author's numerous honors include a Newbery Medal for *The High King*, a Newbery Honor for *The Black Cauldron*—both in the Prydain Chronicles—and National Book Awards for *The Marvelous Misadventures of Sebastian* and *Westmark*. His five Vesper Holly Adventures are also beloved.

Lloyd Alexander lives with his wife, Janine, and their cats in Drexel Hill, Pennsylvania.